"*Moon Over Taylor's Ridge* explores one woman's journey back to her home town after the death of her father. Janie Dempsey Watts envelops us in the big drama of small town Southern life and the impact it has on Avie Williams Cole's marriage, motherhood and beliefs. The fascinating characters that fill this seemingly sleepy locale are vividly drawn, and Watts' rich language is evocative of the place where her story unfolds. This is a beautifully written novel that tugs at your memory and your heart strings even after you're done.
—Natasha Bauman, author, *The Disorder of Longing*

"*Moon Over Taylor's Ridge* gives a chuckle with the turn of each page. The author, Janie Dempsey Watts, has produced a symphony of words to create a delightful and entertaining story that brings a group of quirky characters to life. Indulge yourself."
—Susan Noe Harmon, author, *Under the Weeping Willow*

MOON
Over
TAYLOR'S RIDGE

Janie Dempsey Watts

LITTLE CREEK BOOKS
A division of Jan-Carol Publishing, Inc.
Johnson City, TN

LITTLE CREEK BOOKS
A division of Jan-Carol Publishing, Inc.
Johnson City, TN

This is a work of fiction. Any resemblance to actual persons, either living or dead is entirely coincidental. All names, characters, and events are the product of the author's imagination.

Moon Over Taylor's Ridge
Janie Dempsey Watts

Published August 2012 by Little Creek Books.

ISBN: 978-0-9848050-8-2
Library of Congress Control Number: 2012943782

You may contact the publisher at:
Jan-Carol Publishing, Inc.
PO Box 701 Johnson City, TN 37605
E-mail: publisher@jancarolpublishing.com

Letter to the Readers

Dear Readers,

Although Taylor's Ridge is real, this novel is a work of fiction. Names, characters, businesses and incidents either are the product of the author's imagination or are used fictitiously. Any resemblance to actual events or persons, living or dead, is entirely coincidental.

Janie Dempsey Watts

Acknowledgements

I would like to thank the many people who generously offered their time along the path to publication of this novel. David Gomez, site manager of the New Echota State Historic Site, clarified Cherokee history and Nancy and Alva Crowe shared their wealth of information on Cherokee customs, history and expertise with blow guns. Alan J. Giles, information geologist with Georgia's Department of Natural Resources, provided information on silver production. Answering my many questions about the Catoosa County area were Waymond Watts and the late Harry Watts. Always offering their feedback after reading one, or more, drafts of the manuscript were Ellen Young McCashin, Dean Watts, Gail Lingerfelt Watts, Judy Watts, Ned Colby, Ernestine Dempsey Brinson, Anne Turley, Linda Ashour, Rose Davis, Barbara Sternberg, Waymond Watts, Emily Yellin, and the late Christie Watts Kelly. Thanks to Emily Card, Sue Dempsey, Polly Cloud, Loraine Despres, Donie Nelson, Mollie Gregory, Janis Helbert, Hannah Heineman, Tamlyn Collins, Kim Correll, and Marcia Kling for their encouragement. Cheering me along the way were my fellow writers of the Chattarosa writers' group. For uplifting me in prayer, I thank Frances Shortino Spataro and my friends at Woodstation United Methodist Church.

Thank you especially to Jill McCorkle for guiding me in the right direction on my manuscript and to Tammy Robinson Smith who believed in my story and gave me the opportunity to share it with readers. A special thanks to authors Natasha Bauman, Susan Gregg Gilmore, Susan Noe Harmon and Jennifer Youngblood.

I am grateful to my family, Steve, Anthony and Jack Spataro, for having faith in me and for being there during the journey.

Dedication

To the memory of Anne Dempsey Watts who paints sunsets with God And Christie Watts Kelly who lives on in the stars.

A Note from the Author

Near the southern end of the Appalachians in northwest Georgia, Taylor's Ridge is a narrow, low-slung mountain that runs north to south for almost 40 miles. The ridge is named for a Cherokee Chief, Richard Taylor, a prominent leader and businessman in the early 1800's who lived near the ridge in the small town today known as Ringgold.

Native American trails run all over the ridge and through the valleys alongside. Mound Builders, Creek, Cherokee, pioneers and Civil War soldiers have all walked its paths. Cherokee hunting parties tracked game through its forested slopes, and Sherman's troops drove teams of horses and supplies up the Nickajack Trail on their way south to burn Atlanta.

In 1838, at the time of the Cherokee removal, Chief Taylor left north Georgia on the Trail of Tears, leading a party of 897 men, women, and children. Along with those who survived the journey, he settled in Oklahoma. Taylor died there in 1853. His name lives on in the ridge.

Taylor's Ridge stands as a landmark to the area's Cherokee heritage, and connects natives and visitors alike to the past. Whether seen under a rising sun, or in the pale wash of moonlight, the ridge continues to capture a sense of adventure for those who know its rich history.

"To one who has been long in city pent,
'Tis very sweet to look into the fair
And open face of heaven."

—John Keats

CHAPTER 1

It wasn't a good time to return to Georgia, but was there ever a good time? As executrix of my father's estate, I had no choice but to go back, and quickly. My errant half-sister Jolene, one of the heirs, had called to say she was going to move into Daddy's empty house, our former childhood home.

"Avie, you're going to have to beat her down there and do an inventory before she arrives there with her gypsy fingers," said my husband, Michael, who was a lawyer and knew these types of things. He said he couldn't go with me; he had a trial coming up. He promised to fly out and join me in two weeks.

"Don't worry. The lawyer down there will guide you through it," he said. But it wasn't the estate work that frightened me. It was me.

In the twelve weeks since my father had died, my emotions had spun out of control on a daily basis. I felt like the homecoming queen on a TV program I'd seen. She was riding across a football field in a horse drawn buggy, smiling and waving. Her world was perfect—until that horse bolts away, dragging the buggy and the poor girl behind him. She spills out of the buggy and falls

1

on the ground, then quickly collects herself and stands up. And that horse plows right into her again. Since Daddy had died, I was that girl, and my emotions that crazy horse.

I was about to tell Michael that I couldn't go there without him but he spoke first.

"It might be good to get some time away," he said. I knew what he meant, but didn't say so. Except when he drew me to our bed with his chameleon eyes, I found most everything else about him irritating in the past few weeks. We had been fighting over the smallest things. None of it made sense. Maybe being apart would give me the space to grieve, and our marriage a chance to breathe. And just maybe that crazy horse would finally stop plowing into me and knocking me down. I packed up my things, and those of our son, Joseph, 13, and left as soon as we could get a flight out.

Flying into Atlanta, I noticed my big-eyed, freckled face son staring out the window at the pale amber haze.

"Is that smog?" Joseph asked. I reached under my seat for his bag of medicines.

"Yes, better take a puff or two," I said. I pulled out his inhaler, handed it to him.

"Mom, that smog's nothing compared to L.A.," he said, pushing the inhaler back to me. As I tucked it back into the bag, I remembered how we'd almost lost him to asthma the year before, how the paramedics had told us he would have been dead in another few minutes. Ever since, my days fell to the rhythms of his medication schedules and nebulizer treatments, to the cadence of his seasonal colds and allergies. Joseph and I were tied together by the umbilical cord of asthma.

After we rented a car, we drove through the city and headed north on the I-75 towards Dalton, and Chattanooga. At the Ringgold exit 348, not too far from the Tennessee state line, we got off and turned south on the Old Alabama Highway.

Taylor's Crossing was less than 10 miles from the small town of Ringgold, but as civilization started to peel away, it felt much farther. While Joseph slept, I thought about the place where my father had lived and where I had spent my childhood. I remembered how my mother, who had not grown up there, had described Taylor's Crossing in a letter she wrote to her family when she was a bride newly arrived to the Valley.

Taylor's Ridge Valley lies softly next to the long and firm Taylor's Ridge, covered with dense trees from its foot up to its crest, in many places as pristine as it was when the Cherokees lived there. On the other side of the valley, a series of light, green grassy ridges rolls away, soft and calming. Cows and horses graze these ridge lands, nurtured by the tender grass and the sleepy, opaque waters of the Little Chickamauga Creek that meanders through.

The valley itself, the community, lies between the hardness of the dark high ridge on its east and the softness of the gentle, smaller, submissive ridges on the west. The valley itself is verdant with sweet damp earth that has yielded up its crops and wildlife to feed the inhabitants for hundreds of years. Sustained by the rich land, the moderate climate, and protected on both sides, many of the people born in the valley, stay there until they are tucked into the yielding earth and become a part of the land forever.

For many years, people from the valley have been tempted to cross over it, to Dalton or Rome, points east, or south. During the Civil War, when Sherman started his march to the sea, the Yankees passed through the valley, and started up Taylor's Ridge with wagon loads of supplies. But on a treacherous curve on Nickajack Trail, now Nickajack Road, they lost everything to the ridge. Wagons careened off the steep dirt road, spilling coffee, sugar and hams down into a ravine. Sacks of flour burst open and covered the ground like snow. The people of the valley went up on the ridge side and gathered all they could, making the most of the calamity. Even today, the people of the valley laugh about the Yankee blunder.

On this fall evening, there were no sounds of laughter. As I rode down the sleek ribbon of road that cut through the valley, I saw the full moon rising in the gray-violet sky, its underside caressing the top of Taylor's Ridge. Other cars and trucks passed me as they hurried on to somewhere else. I drove slowly, listening for familiar sounds. The cicadas were silent on this fall evening, but I thought I heard the whispering wind as it brushed against the stiff, drying leaves on the ridge.

Everyone except for the animals had gone inside at dusk. The cattle were lowing, the night birds calling. The evening air was fresh and crisp, except for the occasional whiff of a skunk. I detected a scent of burning wood and I spotted smoke coming from the chimney of a cabin nestled into the side of Taylor's Ridge. Someone's fire offered up warmth against the night chill that spread down across the valley, alongside the ridge. Looking up I saw the moon, pendulous, full and heavy, just above the crest, out of reach.

I turned off the highway onto Ridgeview Road toward my father's house and land. As I made the sharp right turn, a jackknife turn as Daddy used to call it, Joseph moved and slumped towards me.

"It's alright sweetie," I told him, hoping he'd stay asleep for a few more moments. I pulled into the driveway and stopped to collect myself before entering my father's house. I sat staring through the darkness at the empty shell that once housed the man who had given me life.

It was a simple wood-framed home with two porches; one facing toward the west, the lower ridges, and my father's siblings' homes; the other facing east, with a view of Taylor's Ridge. A year before her death, my stepmother, Ruth Mae, a practical woman, had spruced up the house by painting the exterior a bright white and replacing the windows with a newer, bigger paned style. I often wondered if this was what finished her off, this last effort to bring beauty to her demanding life. Being married to my perfectionist father wasn't easy, I was certain of this. A few days after the remodel was completed, not long before their 20th anniversary, she dropped dead on their kitchen floor in the line of duty, her hands clutching the soft dough she'd been rolling out for Daddy's nightly biscuits. A year later, languishing without a woman to boss around or wait on him, forced to use a cane because of his hip, but otherwise in good health, Dad passed away unexpectedly in his sleep.

The house had been theoretically unlived in since my dad died. His brother, Uncle Earl, used his key to go in, supposedly to check the place over, but I suspected to also make a snoop of him self. At first when I was in the initial stages of shock about Dad's dying so suddenly and unexpectedly, I'd gratefully accepted his offer to keep an eye on the home place. A few weeks later, though, I received an anonymous letter informing me of Uncle Earl's questionable activities. It read, "You ought to be ashamed of yourself. Earl and his no-count wife are helping themselves to Thomas Lee Williams' wardrobe, including his Georgia Bulldogs cap, his rifle collection and silver dollar collection. They also ride up and down the road in the Lincoln. If you need proof you can check the odometer and the tire tread, or what is left of it. Missy, wake up before they rip off everything your poor old Daddy worked hard for. Do him right and come on home. Signed, A Concerned Neighbor." The words "poor" and "old" were a dead giveaway. The "concerned neighbor" had to be my Aunt Ardelia, who lived up the hill from Dad's place but always seemed to know what was going on, right down to my dad's phone conversations. Aunt Ardelia, a sharp 75, had a Masters degree in guilt infliction and never hesitated to point out what was wrong with her many nephews and nieces and their offspring. Ardelia had refused to speak to me since she'd heard Daddy had named me, not her, as executor. It would be an understatement to say I didn't miss actual contact with the abrasive and bitter Aunt Ardelia.

But I appreciated the letter cluing me in. I didn't care so much about the material things, except perhaps that Bulldogs cap, but as executor, as Michael had reminded me, I had to protect and preserve my father's assets until I could divide up the inheritance. And even though we sometimes disagreed on business matters his instincts were always right.

Immersed in my thoughts, I sat immobilized in front of the garage door feeling the chill of the September air, trying to will myself to get out and go in. I fumbled in my purse for the key, quietly climbed out, leaving Joseph asleep for the moment. First I'd go in, turn on the lights, the heat, perhaps put on a kettle of water for hot chocolate and make Joseph feel welcome.

I put the key in the lock and turned, opening up a floodgate of memories. There was the wooden ramp Dad had finally conquered on his walker after breaking his hip. Over there, in the corner, sat his empty wheelchair he'd used after the hip operation. And there, in his Lincoln, was the vacant passenger seat where he'd worn the velour upholstery threadbare on his many daily rides over the country roads with his helper Henry at the wheel. I looked at Dad's unused things and remembered the lines from one of his favorite hymns, "Oh Death, where is thy sting?" Here, I thought. Death stings from a million different places. Choose your flavor.

"Mom?" Joseph's voice startled me. He stumbled into the garage. "I'm freezing." I went to him, held his arm and pulled him up the ramp and into the house, out of the cold.

"I'll get a blanket," I said. I grabbed my father's old afghan off the sofa, wrapped him in it, went into the kitchen and quickly filled the kettle and turned on the burner. He stood wrapped in the afghan watching me. Suddenly he burst out laughing.

"What is it, Joseph?" I asked.

"This blanket," he responded.

"It was Grandpa's," I replied.

"I know," he said, holding up a pair of false teeth that had somehow gotten stuck in the afghan's stitches. I started to take the yellowed teeth from him, afraid he'd break them, not that it made any difference now, but he clacked the old teeth together and made them talk.

"Hi, Joseph, good to see you," he ventriloquized. "You too, Avie. I'm starved!" I warmed to his imitation, thick southern drawl. It was perfect. We laughed together. I was so glad I'd brought him along, my own antidote to death's sting.

Later, after I'd tucked him into bed in the guest room and slipped into my pale blue cotton eyelet gown Michael loved seeing me wear. I forced myself to open the door to Daddy's room, expecting to feel fear or emptiness, but instead finding a comfort as I looked around, noticing the familiar objects of his everyday life. On the dresser was a tray holding several old coins and a couple of small penknives, which he was never without. I picked up one of the coins, a buffalo nickel, looked at it a moment then slipped it into the pocket of my nightgown as a memento. I walked over to his closet and stared at his wardrobe: mainly jeans, golf shirts, sweaters and several old flannel plaid shirts. I ran my fingers over the sleeves and bent down to smell his lingering scent, Old Spice and cigar smoke, mixed together. Once I had read that almost half the impressions of conscious life come from our sense of smell, that many of these smells send hidden messages. Redolent of Dad, the closet unleashed images of my father as a younger man.

In his prime Dad had been a sturdy and fearless man. One humid summer night when I was six or seven, I was scared out of my brass-railed bed by the deep boom of thunder. I hated lightning. I rushed towards Dad's room but he met me in the hall, scooped me up in his powerful arms and pressed me to his chest. Together we smelled ozone, and Dad told me the lightning had probably struck the barn, but we would be fine. In his arms I was safe, protected from everything, even the lightning that continued to flash outside.

As I thought of my father I knew the right thing to do was to sleep in his wooden bed, still the most secure place in this place, his home. Clutching one of his old flannel shirts, I climbed in under the sheets and fell into a deep, healing sleep.

CHAPTER 2

Early the next morning, I awoke to two squirrels chittering on the ancient walnut tree outside my window. They jumped from branch to branch chasing each other. Behind them the sun was just rising over Taylor's Ridge, bringing all the hope and promise of a fresh new day. The sounds of the squirrels, the doves calling to each other, and the sound of a human voice from just down the hall.

"You ain't still in bed, are you?" the voice bellowed. My heart pounded in fear. Had someone broken in? I pulled on the old flannel shirt and headed to the kitchen where I found Uncle Earl measuring out coffee into the basket of an aging Mr. Coffee machine. Years of farm work had made him a stocky, powerhouse of a man.

"Time to wake up California," he said in an accent so thick I wanted to scrape it off and splatter it against the wall.

"Did I forget to lock the door?" I asked.

"Nope. I used my key, business as usual," he said, jiggling the plug in the socket, trying to get the coffee maker to work. "Thing's about to short out, I tell you."

"Maybe you could come back later," I yawned as I spoke. "We're on West Coast time."

"Folks around here done ate breakfast and's pokin' around lookin' for lunch," he declared. He watched the coffee as it started to brew. "You hear them gunshots across the road this mornin', down by the creek?" he asked. I shook my head and thought, how could I? I was asleep. I remembered gunshots on another morning, about five years ago, when two prisoners escaped and made their way down along our creek in our huge ridge land pasture. Dad said he could hear the gunshots as the state troopers chased them through our property, almost a quarter-mile wide and several miles deep. They finally shot the escapees in the legs and captured them on the next farm over.

Earl's barging in unannounced left me feeling shaky, and I felt my emotions starting to get away from me. I nervously reached into the pocket of my gown and grabbed onto Dad's old buffalo nickel and began rubbing it between my forefinger and my thumb.

"A little early for huntin' season," Earl droned on. I noticed his hands, overworked and weather worn from years of farm work, but still strong. Uncle Earl and my father were like the two sides of the nickel. Earl was the buffalo, his strength obvious for all to see. It was a raw form of power, dangerous. A person had to watch herself around a buffalo, and Uncle Earl. My father, on the other hand, was the proud silhouette of the Indian chief, also a forceful figure, perhaps on the surface less intimidating than the huge beast of the plains. Yet the Indian chief, in fact, had outwitted the even more powerful buffalo by using his intelligence to hunt down the beast for food and clothing. I stared at the back of Uncle Earl's thick neck.

"You ain't been back there in years, have you?" he asked.

"Back where?" I responded.

"You sound like you been takin' too many them sleepin' pills," he pointed at the small pharmacopeia I'd unloaded on the counter the night before.

"Joseph's asthma and allergy medications," I replied.

"He wouldn't need that junk if you'd get out of that dirty air," he shot back.

"What were you saying a minute ago, have I been back where?" I asked him. He stomped across the kitchen, his dirty boots leaving prints on the linoleum, over the wooden floors of the living room and pointed through the big picture window to the rolling land that started on just the other side of the road.

"There."

"You mean Daddy's back pasture?" I asked.

"Yes Ma'am," he replied.

"As a matter of fact, I was going to walk it tomorrow," I said.

"Walk it?" He looked down at my bare feet, my pink-painted toenails as he spoke. "Why'd you want to do that? There's cow pies back there. We got a mean old bull, too. It don't take much to set him off. And rattlesnakes." I pulled my toes back under the hem of my lace eyelet nightgown and buttoned up Daddy's old shirt. "Your Aunt Cottie dern near got bit last July when we was out lookin' for one of our cows droppin' a calf. And your aunt, she knows that land." I thought of Earl's wife, a country woman with gold caps on her front teeth and proud of it.

"She does?" It was all I could think to answer.

"Yes, Ma'am. And you remember that old grove of trees down by the creek?" he asked. I didn't.

"No."

"Where the line of cedar fence posts stops, just past the second rise?" he asked. I shook my head no. Earl continued, "It's the highest point on your Daddy's place. We was up there on Labor Day and Darnell swears he smelt a copperhead."

"I didn't know you could smell a snake," I said. He sighed in exasperation.

"There's a lot you don't know. There's old wells you could fall down and break your neck. 'Bout ten years ago, a hunter went out alone somewhere's down in Walker County and was never seen again. Sheriff said most likely fell down in one of them old wells. No Ma'am, you don't have no business trampin' around that land. What you want to do that for, anyway?" he asked.

"Well, I was thinking I'd size it up, you know, before the appraiser comes out," I said.

"Appraiser?" Uncle Earl asked, waving around the pot of hot coffee in the air as he prepared to pour into the cups. "You don't need to pay no stranger to tell you what that land's worth. Not even two thousand an acre, that's what. Old James place down the road brought sixteen hundred an acre last April, and it has road frontage." I stroked the old Buffalo coin between my forefinger and thumb. I noticed it had grown hot from the friction. I looked down at the mud~ no, I realized, cow manure~on the linoleum.

"Were there cows grazing there?" I asked.

"What?" he responded, pouring out a cup of coffee for himself, and then one for me.

"I mean, was the old James place leased out for cattle grazing?" I asked, taking the steaming cup from him. He stared at me like I was talking spaceships and aliens.

"Daddy always said cattle could tear the land up," I continued.

"It's horses does that," he responded. I stared down at his boots. He shuffled his feet a bit and stepped back.

"Cows or no cows, don't make no difference," he said, but he looked at the window as he said it. I sniffed the air now noticing for first time, the pungent smell of cow manure. I remembered that Dad had let Earl graze his cows on his land for years, for free.

"Probably not," I replied, sipping my coffee. "Um, tastes good, thanks." Earl took a sip of his coffee, swallowed, then made a face. He spat out any residual flavor, and saliva, directly onto the white enamel of the previously clean kitchen sink.

"Bitter," he replied. He reached in his pocket for a plug of tobacco and tucked it up in his jaw. He ambled towards the kitchen door that led to the carport, then outside. "Time's a wastin, gotta get to my chores."

"That's true. See you," I said.

"Yep," he answered. I shut the door behind him, and then peeked out the curtained window of the kitchen door to watch him leave. He stopped in the carport right by Dad's brass coat rack. It was a sly, quick movement, but I saw it. He took the Bulldogs cap out of his pocket and quickly hung it on the rack. Aunt Ardelia had been right about the cap, but was the rest true?

I reentered the kitchen, pulled out some bleach from under the counter and dumped half a cup into the sink. I ran scalding hot water over that, watched the steam drift lazily up towards the gauzy white curtains that framed the kitchen window. I stared at the spot in the sink where he'd spit. There was only clear white enamel remaining, but Uncle Earl had left his mark.

I picked up the phone and dialed Michael. He would empathize with me, especially when he heard Uncle Earl had just barged in unannounced. I'd tone it down a little, so as not to make him worry. The phone rang a long time before he answered.

"Hello," he sounded groggy. I imagined his light curly hair spilling over his bedroom eyes as he spoke. Then I looked at the clock and realized it was only five a.m. in L.A.! I knew then, that I shouldn't bother him with this. With a big trial brief due that day, he needed his sleep.

"Hi, honey," I said.

"Is something wrong?" he asked.

"No, not really. I just wanted to say we're okay." I sounded awkward as I talked, even to myself.

"Thanks for the early bird report. What time is it anyway?" he asked.

"I don't know honey," I answered. "Uncle Earl stopped by. It kind of took me by surprise. I think he has his own key."

"Well, get the locks changed," he suggested.

"Great idea! Good luck on your brief," I said.

"Yeah, wish me luck on getting back to sleep." He never sounded the same on the phone, and besides, he wasn't a morning person.

"Sorry, love you." It was all I could say.

"Me too," he hung up the phone. I could see him rolling back over, pulling the pillow over his head to cover his ears. I remembered our final kiss as I'd walked out the door on the way to catch the plane. A light brush of his lips on my cheek, a perfunctory kiss, a Yankee dime my grandmother would have called it. I had wanted more.

I sat down to make a to-do list but found myself staring at the walls around me. The upper half was done in a glossy medium

12

blue, my stepmother's favorite color while the lower half was pan-eled in a glossy, white bead board. Dad said it would look prissy but my stepmother had prevailed in a final effort to please herself. She hadn't had much time to enjoy it. Sad and overwhelmed, I opened up my note pad and wrote a list.

Change locks. Call appraiser. Call surveyor. Sort through Dad's things in house and barn. Buy groceries. Call Joseph's teacher. I took the nickel out of my pocket and set it on the table. I stared at it. I wondered if you rubbed it hard enough, for long enough, would the friction eventually melt it away? The sooner I could finish this job and get the hell out of here, the better.

"Mom, did you hear that?" I looked up to see Joseph coming down the hall, into the kitchen. He rubbed the sleep from his eyes, but I could see his lips had not a hint of blue.

"What?" I asked.

"Like scraping against rocks down by the little stream," he pointed to the sliding glass door, to Dad's yard that lay between the house and the highway. We walked over together and peered out the kitchen window. Above some bushes, a clump of dirt flew up in the air. We heard the scraping sound again, saw another clump fly up.

"Someone's digging out there," I said.

CHAPTER 3

Still in our pajamas but wearing jackets, Joseph and I snuck up on him from behind. The digger was so absorbed in his task he didn't hear us until we were a few feet behind him.

"Excuse me, what do you think you're doing here?" I addressed the back of the dirty blonde head. He stopped mid-shovel and turned to face me. It was a boy, about 11, whom I'd never seen before. His eyes had dark circles around them, and he was so thin he reminded me of a Depression-era black-and-white photo in his faded coveralls and torn t-shirt.

"I'm diggin' for treasure. Wanna watch?" he spoke in a nasal tone that made me think of a deserted hollow. He started digging again.

"Did you know this is private property?" I moved a little closer to him. He dug harder at that hole.

"Yes, Ma'am. I promise I'll share the treasure with you, when I find it, that is," he answered. I looked over at Joseph, who was now peering down at the shallow ditch.

"What kind of treasure?" Joseph asked. The boy kept shoveling but spoke.

"There's this girl at school. She done this report on the Chero-kee. Her granddaddy, he got Indian blood, he said them Indians buried silver somewheres 'round here long time ago. Got another shovel?"

Joseph looked at me. "Do we, Mom?" he asked. I shrugged.

"I don't think so. What's your name?" I asked the boy.

"Tyler," he answered, still not looking up from his task. "Tyler Reed."

"Well Tyler Reed, you'll have to look for your treasure some-where else. This is my Dad's land," I said, "and you didn't ask permission."

"Your daddy, was he the old man with the Bulldogs cap and the limp?" he replied.

"Yes," I responded.

"Well, Ma'am, not to be disrespectful, but he told me I could dig here, long's I gave him half of what I found, yes he did." He confidently pitched up a shovelful of dirt as he spoke of my father. "I always keep my word. If I find somethin', I'll do the same for you, give you half." I didn't need, or want, this boy digging holes in my yard, treasure or not. Who would want to buy a home with a yard filled with unsightly holes and piles of dirt?

"Well, I'm sorry, but you'll have to stop," I spoke as I took a step closer and thought about placing my hand on the shovel to still him for a moment. Then I felt Joseph's hand on my arm.

"Mom, it's okay," he said. "He's not hurting anything, and be-sides, it sounds fun."

"Joseph, we can't have these holes here. The appraiser's com-ing out soon and we've got to keep things nice," I responded. Jo-seph looked at me like I was from another world, Planet Adult.

"Mom, Granddaddy gave him permission," Joseph said. "It's what he wanted." He opened his eyes wide and his nose twitched a bit, and he looked like he might cry, but I had seen this look before. My son, the great manipulator. Then he added the kicker. "This could be my project, you know, for school."

"What? Turning the yard into Swiss cheese?" I responded in my best parent voice, mature and sarcastic.

"No, Mom." He was using his frustrated tone. "The treasure.

15

I'll learn more about the lost treasure, get pictures of us looking for it, and do a report."

"Joseph, the appraiser will be coming out here~"

He interrupted me, "We'll fill the holes up before then." He moved over to stand beside Tyler, who had finally stopped digging.

"Yeah," said Tyler. "We'll take turns."

"You can't dig, not with your allergies," I said.

"I'll wear a mask," Joseph answered.

"A mask?" asked Tyler, "Like at Halloween? I hadn't thought of that."

"A surgical mask, to keep me from having asthma," said Joseph. I touched his arm and pulled him towards me.

"Speaking of which, it's time for your morning meds." I led him away from Tyler, back towards the house. He looked back over his shoulder.

"I'll be back," Joseph called. Tyler answered by throwing another shovelful of soil into the air. Joseph looked at me.

"I know you're going to let me do it Mom. You know I'm right," he said. And it was true.

Back at the house we didn't discuss the subject anymore. He'd learned, I suppose from years of experience, to back off and let me think about things a while before renewing his pleas. I would give in, but I had to appear to be thinking about it. I couldn't make it look like I'd given in too easily; it would undermine my authority. We began our morning ritual with air levels. He blew a strong puff into the gauge. I was surprised to see his score was in the low 400s, for him an excellent reading. The day before in Los Angeles, his morning level was 350. Constantly cleaned by the surrounding greenery, the air here was much better than L.A. I could leave off the yellow inhaler this morning. I watched as he took two puffs of his pink inhaler, the one that prevented asthma, followed by his antihistamine pill and a multi-vitamin.

We both got dressed so we could walk over to the little general store down the road, or so I thought, to get something for breakfast. Then Joseph came into the kitchen fully dressed with the surgical mask dangling in his hand.

"I'm going to watch Tyler," he announced, and started out the back door. I stopped him. "You've got to eat first," I said.

"I'm not hungry." We locked eyes for a moment. I noticed his lips, warm and pink.

"Okay," I backed down. "But let me show you something first. Just in case." I led him out the side door to the old bell that stood next to the driveway.

The bell was at least 50 years old, or so Daddy had said. It was black, cast-iron and hung about seven feet high from a thick, half-fence post that lay across the top of two tall poles. The cord that rang the bell was much too high for a smaller child to reach, but within reach of a short adult. I had only heard it rung twice in my entire lifetime. Once, when Mama cut her thumb and looked like she'd bleed to death and again when my brother Griffin was hit by a ricocheting "B.B." in his eye and fell off his pony. The sound of that bell meant one thing to me: get help and quick. Daddy taught us to only ring it in case of a true emergency. I reached up and placed the pull cord in my hand.

"Joseph, if anything goes wrong, if you need your medicine~"

"Ring the bell. I know, Mom," he replied. "You've told me a hundred times."

"Well, this is a hundred and one," I said. "And you can tell Tyler too. I'll hear the bell, just ring it." He turned and walked away, his voice came to me over his shoulder, in the crisp, clean morning air.

"I'll be fine, Mom. Get me one of those honey buns, okay?"

Housed in a small, unassuming old rock building, it is hard to imagine Elmwood's Store is the heart of the small Taylor's Crossing Community, but it is. Its location is part of the store's appeal and longevity; it sits across the highway from the church on a bend in the highway and just next to East Nickajack Road that runs up the side of Taylor's Ridge. Its real draw is, it's the only store in town. Passersby and locals alike are attracted to its small inventory of groceries, soft drinks, cigarettes, chewing tobacco, snuff, video rentals and candy. An old wood and glass case holds boxes of Fleer bubble gum, candy cigarettes and candies sold by the piece. In the olden days, a pot-bellied stove sat smack dab in the center of the store along with castoff, battle-scarred school desks, usually filled with old-timers discussing weather, crops and the latest gossip. A few years back, the proprietor, Mrs. Xylia Elmwood, had removed the pot-bellied stove when her husband, Leo, passed on. At the time, she announced that with her own Vulcan gone, it was time for a more practical approach. A ceramic electric heater now sat in the center of the store, although the school desks remained, offering rest and friendship to an ongoing stream of visitors. A schoolmistress to adults with time on their hands, Xylia Elmwood never seemed lonely.

I pulled up out front next to the gas pumps, under a bare-limbed tree that stood out for its lack of leaves. As I entered the store, the friendly, vacant face of Ernie Elmwood looked up at me and nodded ever so slightly. He sat in a chair too small for him, holding a green spiral notebook in one hand and a dull pencil in the other. Mildly autistic since birth, and later brain-damaged in an accident, Ernie at 30 was over six feet tall. He had a full head of dark hair, and a thin mustache on an almost unlined face, except for the light trace of frown wrinkles on his forehead between his eyes. He resumed his stare out the window, scrunched up his eyes to concentrate on the car passing by on the highway. He mumbled the word "36" to himself and scribbled on his pad.

Behind the counter, his mother, Xylia, struggled to put some cartons of rifle shells on the top shelf next to the heavy duty flashlights. Even on tiptoes, she couldn't reach that high. She turned around and grinned at me. Her silver hair was haloed in morning sun that minced through the lace curtains covering the window behind her.

She was a filled-out woman, her large bosom barely contained by the fluid lines of a green-flowered, flannel blouse. She could be a poster child for the dairy council: her robustness was a testament to years of consumption of milk, cheese, cottage cheese and possibly hundreds of gallons of ice cream. Her personality matched her body. She brimmed over with enough good energy to counteract the mean-spiritedness that cropped up too frequently in this tiny, sometimes claustrophobic, community. The last time I had seen her, Xylia appeared to be thriving in her widowhood like a tree pruned of excess branches.

"Morning young lady," she said in her full, deep voice. And suddenly, although I am 42, I felt light and free as a teenager. "Good to see you girl," she said, walking over to hug me. Her embrace was strong, and her big breasts mashed up against me. Her hair smelled like bacon and musk perfume. She pulled back from me, ran her hand over my hair. "Your hair's as thick and luscious as ever. And with a hint of red like your Aunt Avie's. And you do look like your mother, God rest her soul." She looked me in the face, assessing. "You all right being here? I know you miss your daddy."

I nodded. "As well as I can be, thank you. How are you?" She gestured at her surroundings. The fully-stocked shelves, the spotless whitewashed walls, the donation jar for the teenager shot in the hunting accident and another jar filled with cut-up slips of paper.

"Business as usual. I can't complain," she said. I reached over and picked up the jar with the paper slips.

"What's this? A contest? What're you giving away?" I asked. She pointed at a chalkboard behind the heater which I hadn't noticed.

"Quotations. That's the favorite sayings board. Folks write a quotation on a slip of paper and put it in the jar. They can write down a famous person's quote, or make one up themselves. Every few days I draw one out, and then write it on the chalkboard. Gives the customers something to talk about."

"What a great idea, Xylia," I said. I moved over and read the quote she had written in her neat, flowery cursive.

"Nothing endures but change. Heraclitus. Wow, who submitted this one?" I asked.

"Yours truly," she said.

"I'm impressed."

"Glad you are. Old man Porter wanted to know when this Heraclitus fellow was coming in again. He wanted to give him a piece of his mind." We both laughed. Then she continued, "You bring that cute husband of yours?"

"I left him back home. He's in trial, and he hates to travel." I

19

talked as I kept picking up things: bread, milk, orange juice, cereal and honey buns. "I brought Joseph along."

"What is he now, 12?"

"No, thirteen and five feet ten inches tall. Hey, do you know who that dirty blonde boy is, about 11? Looks like he moved here from a mountain hollow. I never saw him before."

"Sure do," she responded. "He's Trent Crimmel's stepson. His wife ran off with her boss down at the carpet mill. You know Trent? Lives in that trailer down at the end of Ridgeview?" I nodded. "His wife was never the same after her daughter was killed in that wreck." She led me over to the window and pointed south towards a simple wooden cross covered in weathered silk flowers. "You remember?"

"The crash over there? Daddy told me a deer ran out in front of the girl's car. She swerved to avoid it and ran head on into another car." I remembered it well. During my annual visit a few weeks after it happened, Uncle Earl had taken great pleasure in describing the details of the crash scene, even though I really didn't want to hear.

"I can see it like it was yesterday," Xylia continued. "Leo had just closed up and we were finishing supper. I heard the cars slam into each other and felt the ground shake. For a moment I thought a semi-trailer tractor truck was about to smash into the side of our house. We both jumped up and looked out the window. As soon as I saw the two cars, or what was left of them, I dialed up the sheriff and Leo ran out and tried to help, not that he could do much. The cars were so tangled up and he couldn't see much. He called out and no one answered. The fire truck arrived a few minutes later and worked to get them out. They told us what we already knew. Both died on impact. After the mess was cleaned up, Leo and I went out and sat on the front porch, watched the stars and talked some. We both felt completely cheated by death. She'd just come in and ripped the life right out of those poor folks and we couldn't do a thing. And you know what, Avie?" I shook my head no. She lowered her voice so her son couldn't hear. "We went right back into our bed and made love. Two times." I nodded, careful not to smile as I thought about her reed-thin husband and wondered who was on top, or did they do it side-by-side? "I know what you're thinking," she said. I could feel my cheeks burning. "And let me be the one to tell you, there's good loving to be had even when you've been married forever. It runs slow and rich, like honey from a jar." I nodded again, unsure how to respond. She continued. "Later in the middle of the night when we woke up thinking about that horrible wreck, we reached out to each other and did it again. Every time we did it, we told off that whore, death. Each time was us saying 'we're alive.' You ever make love after someone died, Avie?"

"No," I answered, not completely truthfully. After Daddy's funeral, Michael had taken me in his arms and made love to me until the pleasure he gave me left no room for sadness. He seemed to know it was exactly what I needed.

"Well, that's a shame. Let me tell you, the best love is after death, or a close call with it," she said as she reached down into a jar of cinnamon fire balls. "Of course that is, until the death whore comes and snatches your man across the River Styx."

"Witch," I responded. She looked at me and burst out laughing and handed me a handful of candy. "For your boy. From a spunky old lady." We laughed together as I took the cinnamon fireballs. I noticed a huge silver-plated ring on her middle finger. I expected it to have her initials inscribed, but instead the flat face bore something that looked like petroglyphs I had seen in the Nevada desert once. I almost asked her about it.

"Thirty seven," interrupted Ernie's voice, loud, overbearing, rising over our laughter, demanding attention. Perplexed, I looked towards Ernie.

"He's countin' cars girl," Xylia informed me. "Every day for about a month now. From daybreak till dusk."

"What for?" I asked, realizing after I asked what an inane question it was.

"The Learjet's in for repairs," she retorted. I smiled at her. She was really a lot of fun, and reminded me of how my own mother might have ended up at 70, had she not died so young.

"Do you sell shovels?" I asked.

"Nope, but I'll loan you one," she answered, "for a favor." She walked out the back door and came right back, holding a well-worn shovel.

"What kind of favor?" I asked, taking it from her.

"Send that tall son of yours down to help me put stock up later if he's free. I'll bet he can reach the highest shelves."

"Sure, he'd love it," I said. "And speaking of Joseph, he's probably starved. I'd love to visit all day, but he's waiting for breakfast." I headed for the door, but stopped and turned around when I reached the door, noticed the stark limbs of the tree that had provided shade during many a humid Georgia summer.

"Xylia, what happened to the tree? One of those beetles get it?"

"The beetles attack the pines. No, that's an oak and it was struck by lightning last spring. I aim to have it cut down one of these days, once I can round up the money for the tree cutter."

"Why not leave it there?"

"Well, it's like this, Avie. Eventually it will rot out and tip over and fall down and hurt someone. Once a tree's dead, you need to get rid of it."

"Next time I'll park on the other side," I said. "Or wear a helmet." She laughed. "Now shush up there Avie, before you get rumors started. It'll be a while till the tree keels."

"Okay," I said, and waved goodbye. "See you later."

"I'll be here," she answered. "Count on it."

CHAPTER 4

I returned to the yard behind the house to find Joseph and Tyler laughing, covered with mud, and still digging. As I approached, Joseph held up what appeared to be a small skull. He mumbled through his mask, "Rabbit?"

"Yep. Must be gettin' close," Tyler speculated. "My daddy says the Cherokees ate them a heap of rabbits, fur and all."

"Actually," I found myself chiming in, "they skinned the rabbits and threw them into a hot cauldron of water and cooked it up like a soup, or stew. They added squash, roasting ears, deer and squirrels. My grandma told me stories about her great-great-grandmother being invited by the Cherokees for supper."

"Yuck!" Tyler responded.

"Did she eat it?" I noticed Joseph staring at the skull in his hands as he asked. "No. She always declined their invitation politely, of course." Joseph looked at the bag in my hand, and motioned for Tyler to come along. We went inside.

I served the boys' honey buns on Mama's china at the old oak table, and they talked about their next step in the silver mine hunt. They conversed easily and enthusiastically, like they'd been friends forever.

I sat down at my stepmother's cherry desk to make my calls. First I called Rebecca, my closest friend, to cancel our lunch date. In my hurry to get off, I hadn't had a chance earlier. When I reached her secretary, I was told she'd been called away to a shoot in Prague and wouldn't be back till the end of the month.

Rebecca and I had a long history together. We had worked at the same magazine in our 20s; she was an assistant in advertising, I was in editorial. About the time I had landed my first writing assignment, she left the magazine and moved into film production. I'd married Michael and had Joseph. I scaled back to part-time and when his asthma set in, I had quit. She now traveled extensively from one international production to the next. Although we sometimes didn't talk for weeks, we made up for it with our long-winded conversations. With Rebecca, there were no pretenses, no social niceties. We were close enough to simply cut to the chase and serve as each other's sounding board.

Next, I tried to call the local lawyer. He was tied up with real estate closings but might be free next week, check back. The locksmith agreed to stop off on his way home at six to change the locks. The appraiser was friendly but suggested that I first get the land surveyed, "so we'll know what we're looking at." But when I reached the surveyor, I found out he was booked for several weeks.

"Well, I'll just have to get someone else," I told him, and wondered why he answered only, "Good luck." After calling four more surveyors, I knew why. They were all booked for weeks, if not months. Real estate was picking up it seemed, and sub-divisions were sprouting up like mushrooms on cow pies. I quickly called back the first surveyor and booked him for two weeks out, then called Michael to fill him in.

"You might as well stay on," he advised. "The trial's been continued but I'm working sixteen-hour days, seven days a week. Anderson has just slammed us with three new motions and the response is due Monday."

"Then I should come back to help you edit," I answered.

"Got it covered. You go ahead and take care of business. I'm fine," he said. I could hear the other line ringing in the background. "Got to go, talk to you later." The line clicked off abruptly and although I knew how busy he was, I wondered if he was still mad about our geraniums fight which had happened the day before I left.

Michael had given away my geraniums without asking me. They weren't just any old flowers. I'd grown them from cuttings, and dirt, I'd taken from Daddy's yard in Georgia. The cheery pots of red sat on our townhouse porch, and whenever I was homesick, I inhaled their earthy dill-like smell or put my hands down in that Georgia dirt. Without consulting me, Michael had given all four pots of flowers to our gardener. When I found out, I'd asked him if he was out of his mind, but he never answered. He had turned and walked out of the room.

Tyler interrupted my thoughts.

"Bye Miss Avie," he said. "Got to run help Daddy mow the lawn." He waved as he headed for the door and said to Joseph, "See you tomorrow." Joseph started for the sofa and the television but I stopped him.

"No you don't. Xylia needs you to work down at the store," I told him.

"Doing what?" he asked, somewhat nonchalantly, yet I could tell he was interested because he hadn't refused flat out.

"She needs someone tall to put up stock on the high shelves."

"Will she pay?" he asked.

"She already has, Joseph. She loaned us the shovel." He shrugged.

"Sure, why not. Maybe she'll give me some candy too."

I dropped him off at Elmwood's, leaving Xylia with full instructions on what to do in case of an asthma attack. As I handed her the inhaler and portable nebulizer, she promptly put them aside.

"We're not gonna need this junk. Joseph is big and strong and we have chores to do. Now you scat, girl. Tend to your business." She took Joseph's slender hand into her plump palm and led him to the back room where unopened boxes of stock sat waiting. She handed him a knife. As I walked towards the door, I could hear the knife ripping through the cardboard.

"Like that?" Joseph asked.

"Excellent, just excellent," Xylia answered. As I passed Ernie, I heard him mumble, "Sixty three" as he watched a red convertible pass. His endless counting was as much a part of the landscape as the whooshing of the passing tires on asphalt.

The wind had picked up and the day had turned colder. Wearing hiking boots, leather gloves and Dad's Bulldogs cap, I walked across the highway, down Ridgeview and past Uncle Earl's. I moved quickly, hoping to avoid another round of his nosy questions and unwelcome comments. Although the doors and windows of his house were closed to keep out the chill, I could hear the mid-day news report. I quickly opened the latch to the gate, closed the gate behind me and moved up the grassy slope.

The cattle glanced up at me as I walked by. I was simply another human, one without food, something to be ignored. For the most part, they are peaceful creatures.

As I moved up the first gentle ridge, I could feel my thoughts swirling around like dervishes, trying to sort them selves out. I ran through the list of annoyances—Uncle Earl, the unavailability of the surveyors, my apparently lengthening trip. The geraniums fight. He'd never explained why he'd given them away. And then there was the phrase he'd used on the phone.

"Got it covered," he'd said. I chanted the phrase over and over as I watched my feet move over the grass. And then I thought of her, Lily, the temp Michael had used a year earlier when I'd been tied up with Joseph at the hospital. "Got it covered" was one of her phrases.

I hadn't seen her for a while. I hoped she wasn't holding up well. Perhaps her trendy thinness had turned to gauntness; her perky nipples to shriveled nothingness. But Michael didn't notice these things, I assured myself. I wondered if, being in a pinch, he'd hired her again. Despite my resentment of her whippet-thin body, she was a good proofreader and editor. In my absence he might have called her in to help, especially since his associate, Sam, was a poor writer. In fact, she'd probably end up hitting on Sam, a hard-bodied, 30-year-old who'd just broken off with his girlfriend. Yes, she was his type. They could go pump iron together in their spare time, or each other, for all I cared.

With that worry put to rest, I finally relaxed into a steady gait as I moved over, up and down the ridges, breathing in the clean, crisp air and listening to the leather of my hiking boots brushing against the tall, sweet-smelling grass. Ahead I saw a familiar stand of trees. Behind them lay the Little Chickamauga Creek and the swimming hole.

When I was eight, Aunt Ardelia gave my brother Griffin and me new bathing suits, mine a one-piece that consisted of bottoms only. I remembered being embarrassed to wear it, but Dad teased me and said, 'what did it matter, anyway?' I looked like a boy. My embarrassment over the suit proved to be a minor discomfort compared to what transpired. It seems that on this particular day, Daddy was planning to teach me to swim. Even then, I was aware of the low curl of fear that has lived in my stomach as long as I can remember. But on this day, as I stood by the creek, I watched Griffin dangle off the rope swing and drop into the creek. I saw my cousins cheering me on. I felt the curl turn into a thousand fishes swimming inside me. I stared at the murky creek, imagining the real fishes that swam around the swimmers' legs. Uncle Earl yelled out, "Come see the water moccasin, girl." I crossed my arms tighter over my naked chest and shivered. Daddy came over and took my hand.

"Let's go in, together. You can hold on to me." He took my cold hand into his warm one, and led me into the muddy water. I hesitated to descend into the chill and darkness.

"I'm scared, Daddy," I whispered to him so no one else could hear.

"Aw come on, Indian Pony, I'll hold on to you." He picked me up under my arms and held me from behind and we entered the cold water, which sliced into my parchment-like alabaster skin. "Go ahead, dog paddle like your brother." I looked over at Griffin's awkward splashing and imitated. I churned the muddy water and was beginning to feel safe when I felt Daddy's warm hands slipping away from my slender body.

"You can do it!" My father shouted as I panicked and began kicking and fighting the water. I gulped murky water as my head bobbed up and down under the surface and I knew I was dying. In the background, from along the shore, I heard Uncle Earl laughing wildly.

"Daddy!" I choked out his name as my mouth briefly surfaced. I locked my desperate gaze on Griffin, who encouraged me.

"Just kick and paddle. You're okay," Griffin yelled across the creek. But I was in high panic now. I was going under.

"Let her do it, Tommy," Uncle Earl snarled out. Didn't they see I was drowning? My throat burned as the water started to fill up my chest. I kicked back hard several times and felt my toes graze something soft, oozy. I flailed my hands wildly, pushing water away from me, propelling myself back, into the muddy creek bed. I lengthened my trembling legs to touch the bottom. I tilted my head back and gasped for air. Only the lavender-blue circle of my mouth remained above the water line.

"Look like a snappin' turtle to me," Uncle Earl said. As everyone laughed, I felt Daddy's strong hands wrap around my middle and tug me back to the creek bank. He had been right behind me the entire time.

I have thought about that day many times. In that one swimming lesson, I experienced sheer terror, betrayal, abandonment, ridicule and surprise. The other feelings passed, only to surface on the rare occasion, but the fear of abandonment has stayed with me. It didn't make sense and, in fact, seemed cruel to me.

Three and a half decades had caused the old swimming hole to shrink. It now looked like an extremely large mud puddle. Or maybe I had grown bigger, and it had stayed the same. An old tattered rope hung off the limb of an elm tree. I walked over to test it, placing my gloved hands around the thick, yellowed strands to see if it would bear my weight.

"I wouldn't risk it," a strong, confident male voice came out of nowhere. I whirled around to see a dark-haired man standing about six feet away from me. He looked in his late 30's with chestnut eyes and long, raven hair brushed back off his face. He held a short cylinder of wood in his right hand and wore a red-and-black checked hunting jacket and a self-assured attitude. Suddenly I was furious to see him looking right at home on Daddy's, no, the estate's land.

"I'm sorry, but this land is posted," I told him. He stared directly through me, it seemed, his were eyes fixed on something beyond me. He took a slow sidestep to the left, loaded a shaft of some sort into one end of the cylinder, and pursed his lips around the other end and blew hard. A pointed-shaft, or arrow object, flew out and whizzed past me. I heard a tiny thump and turned around. On the other side of the creek lay a bird, either stunned or dead. He moved past me, gathered speed and leapt over a narrow part of the creek and retrieved it. He cupped the bird in his hands for a moment, and then placed it into the pocket of his hunting jacket. My anger was starting to bubble up as I realized not only had he hunted here, but he had killed a bird on my family land!

"This is private property," I told him. He turned and faced me, with a determined gaze in his deep-set eyes.

"I've been hunting here for years," he said evenly.

"I don't see why. This land has had no trespassing signs for as long as I can remember. My family has owned this farm for ages." I was waiting for an apology, but instead I saw his lips turn up a bit, into a smirk. He let out a tiny laugh. I was furious. Before I could tell him to get the hell off my property, he turned and strode away, back into the deep woods.

I took a few steps after him, tried to follow him, but there was no way I could catch up. His pace was quick and he moved through the woods like a scarf passing through the hands of a magician.

As I watched him disappear, I felt the anger rise up hot and red in my face. The nerve. But maybe he wasn't from around here. Maybe he'd been lying. People in the valley respected each other's property rights, cherished their land, their valley that gave of herself daily, yearly, perpetually. Her soft, rich belly lay under people's homes, while her fertile ridges nurtured the grass that fed their livestock.

This cherishing of the land had been a fact for as long as

I could remember, and I imagined since the first white settlers, who were our Williams ancestors according to Daddy, had arrived in the valley in the early 1800s with their property rights notions. It was common family knowledge that my great-great-grandmother, a Bryan, and the Cherokees had shared farming tips and, for the most part, coexisted peacefully. On my father's land, now the pasture by his yard, once stood a Baptist church. Today the only thing left of the church were 36 graves tucked underneath the grass in Daddy's pasture, and a row of redbud trees planted by the Baptists. Several of the graves were marked with aging tombstones bearing the names, birth dates and death dates of the Rev. Humphrey Posey's beloved wife and some of his flock. But most of the graves, some of them possibly Cherokees, remained unmarked, hidden underground, anonymous and safe for eternity.

When I'd seen the stranger on my land, my stomach churned with anger, reacting to this man's intrusion. This primitive child-like emotion was tinged with something else, a little, familiar tendril of excitement that stirred in the corners of my mind. Overwhelming curiosity. Who was he and why did he hunt with what appeared to be a blowgun?

I looked up at Taylor's Ridge. The green, gold and orange trees swayed as the breeze passed through. The wind wove its way through the branches, up the ridge and disappeared over the top of Taylor's Ridge. There was no trace of the curl of smoke from the night before. Only the forest and the soft rustle of leaves remained.

By the time I got back to Elmwood's to retrieve Joseph, it was almost lunchtime. I entered the store. Ernie was exactly as I'd last seen him, except now he had a fat, half-eaten, white bread sandwich perched on one knee, and the spiral bound notebook on the other. Joseph and Xylia were seated at the school desks, drinking chocolate milk, eating and talking.

"Then the blacksmith would smelt the silver into trinkets for the Indians' horses," she said. She glanced up at me. "Come join us, Avie. Your son is almost as curious as you are."

"Michael says I'm nosy," I said, taking the half cheese sandwich she offered. I sat down in one of the school desks and joined the circle.

"Well, Joseph was asking about the legend of the lost treasure. I was explaining how the Cherokees used to ride up the side of Taylor's Ridge and come back with silver in their saddlebags from a hidden mine," she said. "They took the silver to one of your Williams ancestors, a blacksmith. His shop was located near a spring, 'bout a mile down the highway, there."

"When was this?" I asked.

"Oh, before 1838," she answered.

"Let her go on, Mom," Joseph scolded me. "I need to hear this. I'm going to do this for my school project." I took a bite from my sandwich, and settled back in the school desk chair to listen.

"Everyone around here knew they had a secret mine hidden up there over Taylor's Ridge, but the Cherokees were real secretive. Some folks thought the Baptist minister, the Rev. Posey, might know. After all, he saw more of the Cherokees than most folks. But apparently he was more interested in making Christians out of them than in finding out about the silver. They didn't trade their silver with the white folks, but it was common knowledge." She stopped to take a bite of her sandwich.

"Where is the mine?" Joseph asked. She laughed in response.

"Wouldn't I like to know?" Xylia stood up and walked over to a high shelf behind the phone. She reached up towards a dusty, blue volume and pulled it down.

"This is the official history of the county. Now why don't you read it for yourself, maybe you can teach me a thing or two." She started to hand him the book, but I intercepted, taking the book from her.

"This is filled with dust mites. He'll have to put his mask on first." She smiled indulgently at me.

"Okay, Mama," she said.

"I already knew about the dust mites, Mom," Joseph spoke up. "I'll get a plastic bag for you." He started over to the counter. I started to ask Xylia about the hunter I'd encountered, but we were interrupted by the loud clanging of a bell. She looked sur-

31

prised and puzzled.

"I hadn't heard that thing since Henry found your Daddy dead in his bed," she said. I grabbed Joseph's hand and ran out the door.

CHAPTER 5

I arrived at the old bell to find my half-sister Jolene with a Salem in one hand, and her daughter, little Sammie, in the other. Her cotton candy hair was now a brassy orange that spewed from her head in a mass of tangled curls. Sammie was a miniature version, with brown curls and dark eyes as empty as the smoke rings Jolene blew into the air.

"I figured I'd get your attention," she said, motioning to the bell. "Come here, sweetie pie." She held out her freckled, rail of an arm. I stepped over to her and allowed myself to be hugged. I hadn't seen her since her 30th birthday when she was passing through Georgia on her way to Nashville.

"I thought something was wrong, Jolene. You shouldn't have rung the bell. It's only for emergencies. The neighbors will think something's wrong." She released me from her embrace, and her face screwed up and she looked like she'd just tasted a sour tart.

"You haven't changed, have you? Always worried about what other people think," she shot back. "You haven't said hello to my little Sammie. This is your Aunt Avie. Isn't she a cutie, Avie?" Sammie blinked her bovine-like eyes languidly. Had Jolene taken drugs when she was pregnant?

"She looks a lot like you," I answered, half-truthfully. "Especially the hair." Jolene proudly ran her hands through Sammie's thick tangle, and then noticed Joseph.

"Come here Joey. You don't look a thing like nobody. You hook up with the milkman Sis?" Joey held back from her. I interceded.

"He's allergic to smoke, Jolene," I said. She threw her cigarette out toward the pasture, still lit.

"Well as long as you ain't allergic to your Aunt Jolene." She grabbed him around the neck in an elbow lock and planted a moist, pink kiss on his cheek. He squirmed. "Why you're a cute little thing, not at all like your mean old Daddy. Now come along, I'll let you carry my bags in, if you're nice." She shoved Sammie over into my arms and I almost dropped her. The girl remained silent and docile and appeared to be accustomed to being shifted around like a sack of potatoes. I called after Jolene.

"What do you mean, mean? Michael's nice as can be," I defended my husband.

"All lawyers are mean, don't you know it?" she responded. Joseph spoke up.

"Dad's not mean. He has to be tough. Sometimes he deals with some real buttholes."

"Joseph, watch your language," I scolded.

"Well he does Mom," Joseph replied.

"Hey guys, lighten up a bit. I was kiddin', okay?" she said. I had forgotten that Jolene was born with her foot in her mouth, and wherever she went, disharmony followed. Disharmonic convergence, I thought. Her visit would be a long one.

After Joseph had unloaded her four old suitcases, Jolene wanted to visit Daddy's grave, which I had thus far avoided. Cemetery visits are best done in the company of others, in this case, my flaky sister, and I was easily persuaded.

The mound of dirt on Dad's grave was settling and except for a few already fading silk arrangements, most of the flowers had been removed. Jolene, the children and I ringed around the reddish-orange dirt, stared at the temporary metal plaque listing

Dad's name. Sadness stabbed at my heart. My father and mother and stepmother were gone and I was now an orphan. Parent-less.

"Well I'd say he's in hog heaven about now, wouldn't you Sis?" she asked, placing plastic yellow flowers she'd brought along at the head of the grave. Joseph looked disturbed and confused.

"It's an expression, Son. He's really not with the pigs. It means someone's really happy. Why do think that, Jolene?" She pointed to the graves on either side of Dad's tombstone, my mother's and my stepmother's.

"Lord girl, lookie there. He's finally got two women and it's legal, at least here in the cemetery. Come on kids, let's mash this dirt down some." She grabbed their hands, pulled them onto the dirt and began stomping on the grave.

"Don't do that, Jolene," I snapped.

"Why?" she asked, still clomping her boots down on top of Daddy's grave.

"It's not proper to dance on people's graves," I said. Joseph moved away from her, off the grave, towards me.

"It's not dancin'. Soon as the dirt flattens out we can get some grass planted on top and get things back to normal." Jolene looked anything but normal. How easy it must be to think so simplistically, to move ahead with confidence, towards a stasis based upon the mere presence of grass.

"Besides, who appointed you Miss Manners?" she asked, stomping with renewed vigor. "And there's no one around here who cares, in case you haven't noticed." Intrigued enough to watch but not participate, Joseph stood to the side. I walked back to the car and waited. Perhaps my husband had been right in his assessment of her when he called her gypsy fingered. And was I really related to this grave-dancing woman who had apparently missed out on learning standard operating procedures? It was time for a frank discussion.

Back at Dad's house, we settled in the living room and I laid out some ground rules. After an intense discussion, Jolene agreed not to smoke in the house, or make long-distance phone calls. If I paid for them, she'd buy the groceries and cook for us. Joseph and I would do the dishes. She'd watch the kids while I sorted through Daddy's things. It would be hard, but it could work. For a while.

We all made out a grocery list, and compromised somewhere between Jolene's grease and sugar diet plan, and my California light style. After all, I was in the South. We were all going to the Piggly Wiggly together until the locksmith knocked on the door. It was only a quarter to three, and he apologized for being a little early, as he pulled out his tools. His last two appointments had been no-shows, and he wanted to stop by and get his oil changed on the way home, and he sure hoped I didn't mind if he was a little early. I had forgotten how southerners like to share every detail, particularly when it relates to their ability to keep a schedule. They are often late, sometimes early, but never arrive when expected. Jolene insisted on taking Joseph with her to the market so he could carry all the bags. He also wanted to buy some supplies for his school project. I handed him his emergency inhaler and reminded her not to smoke. They climbed into my smoke-free car and pulled off. Sammie and I watched the locksmith remove the old locks and replace them with the new ones. He left us with several master keys that opened all the doors.

Sammie didn't communicate much, perhaps it was simply because with Jolene for a mother, she couldn't get in a word edgewise. So I was surprised when she pointed at my gold wedding band and tugged at my finger.

"Ring. This is a ring, Sammie," I told her. I let her trace her tiny, damp finger along the shiny, gold band.

"Wing?" she asked.

"Yes. Ring," I responded.

"Mama no ring," she said. Maybe she was smarter than I had first thought. She seemed so sweet and vulnerable, but I couldn't help myself. While she was distracted by my ring, I gently slipped up her stained t-shirt and looked at her pale, blue-veined stomach. Her navel was slightly pooched out, but certainly looked normal to me. Perhaps Jolene had made up the hernia story. It wouldn't be the first time.

Then I heard a scraping noise. It sounded like it was coming from the garage door handle. I caught my breath in fear for a moment, and then realized it must be Jolene, trying to use her old key. I put Sammie down on the kitchen chair and went to open the door to Uncle Earl, looking dumbfounded.

"This dern thing needs some graphite." He held a key in his hand as he took a step to enter. I blocked the doorway.

"It's the wrong key. I got new locks all around. The locksmith just left."

"New locks? Weren't nothin' wrong with the old ones. Just a wastin' money."

"The lawyer said the estate should pay for new locks. And only I should have the key, from now on," I told him.

"Lawyer? If you don't watch yourself, your lawyer's gone spend up all the money 'fore you even have it. Ain't you gonna invite me in?" He inched closer to the doorway. I stood my ground.

"Actually, it's not convenient right now. I was in the middle of something. Maybe you can come back over after supper and see Jolene. I'll see you later." He mumbled under his breath, but backed away from the door. I gently but firmly locked the garage door. As I walked back to Sammie, I heard the loud slam of the exterior garage door. He was angry, but I had my limits. I had to stop his unwanted intrusions.

I settled Sammie out on the front porch with a big bowl of salted peanuts and cup of milk, and we enjoyed being outdoors. A squirrel approached shyly, looking for a handout. Sammie tossed him a nut, which he quickly picked up with his tiny, handlike paws. Soon his mate joined him and we tossed nuts her way. Sammie laughed as the squirrels chattered. A light breeze picked up and I buttoned up her jacket, and pulled my collar tight around my throat. It wasn't really that cold, but I felt a chill as I suddenly knew someone was staring at me. I glanced up towards the ridges and saw no one. The only signs of life were Uncle Earl's house and Aunt Ardelia's next door. Uncle Earl would already be back home, complaining to his wife, Aunt Cottie, about my rudeness. I stared towards Aunt Ardelia's windows, and I thought I saw something move, but it could have been the late afternoon light, or the shadows from the blowing tree limbs, playing on her window panes. I scooped up Sammie and the nut bowl. Suddenly, I wanted to protect my quiet, innocent niece.

"Come on, let's go out on the deck on the other side. The squirrels will find us." Maybe it wasn't so bad after all to have Jolene staying with us.

Jolene and Joseph returned with 10 bags of groceries, and she began slicing onions and beating up eggs for meatloaf while Joseph became acquainted with Sammie. They sat on the living room floor where he rolled a tennis ball back and forth to her while asking Jolene if she remembered anything about the Cherokee silver mine. The phone rang and I grabbed it, thinking it might be Michael. But it was Xylia, asking if she could stop by to drop off the book as soon as the store closed. Jolene motioned for me to put the phone down, and suggested I invite her to supper, too, so we could catch up on the gossip. Xylia said she would pop in a video for Ernie at her house—he would be content to watch "Forrest Gump" for the thousandth time.

She appeared a few minutes after 6, and Joseph ran to let her in the back garage door. She was a carrying the book encased in not one, but two plastic bags. Joseph wanted to read it right that moment, but first we all sat down to eat, sampling Jolene's steaming dishes: hot meatloaf with ketchup, fried okra and a cheesy squash casserole. Xylia told us who had married and divorced, and I saw Jolene make a mental note about Trent Crimmel, Tyler's father. I excused Joseph from the table so he could read the history book, and it was a cozy feeling with him reading in the next room by the light of the antique brass lamp and us three women and my niece gathered around the table. Sammie couldn't seem to get enough of Xylia. She was fascinated by Xylia's large arms and jiggled the dangling fat, which delighted Xylia.

"Finally, a good use for my excess flesh," she said, and we all laughed. Later, Sammie screamed out, "Wing, wing" when she spotted the silver petroglyphs ring on Xylia's chunky finger. Xylia let her touch it and I asked her where she had gotten a ring with such an unusual design.

"I found it the week after Leo died, in his old jacket. He was always taking things in trade when some of the poorer customers couldn't pay their food bill down at the store. He didn't like to tell me, though, because I was the one who had to figure out how to pay our suppliers." I looked at it closely. A wavy line ran across on the left side, on the right were two vertical lines with three smaller lines protruding from above, like a carrot with the tops. A half-circle sat at the top of the ring face.

"Weird," said Jolene, as she leaned over my shoulder.

"Looks old," I said.

"Not as old as I feel girls," she said, crossing her fleshy arms over her chest and rubbing her shoulders as though they ached. "I'm having the time of my life, but I'd better be moving along, get back home and put myself down for the night. The sun'll be coming up Taylor's Ridge before you know it and I'll be opening up again. I tell you it's like Chinese water torture, the way my days fall out. Open, work all day, close. It goes on, and on, repeating itself every day. Sometimes I think about taking Ernie, moving down to Jackson with my niece and slowing down a bit."

"Jackson?" Jolene asked.

"For Ernie, eventually. My niece has agreed to let him move in with her, once I join Leo down the road." She tilted her head to the right, in the direction of the cemetery.

"That's a long way off," I said.

"And honey, not before you try my cobbler," Jolene added. She got up to serve us dessert and coffee. I reached out and patted Xylia's full, freckled arm.

"You and the store, you're the heart of the community," I said. "You can't leave here." She looked at me with her clear, hazel eyes and smiled.

"Thanks, but you don't have to worry. I said I'd think about it. I don't have the money to retire here in the valley, or for that matter, anywhere else." I squeezed her arm.

"I'm glad," I answered.

"You like me broke, that's a pleasant thought," she taunted.

"I meant—" I continued but Xylia laughed and stopped me. "I know what you meant. Thanks." Jolene smiled at her, and I did too, and for a moment, I felt like we were a family.

The spell was broken by the sound of someone's footsteps coming through the back door. I had thought it was closed, but apparently Joseph hadn't closed it all the way after letting Xylia in.

"I'm here," bellowed Uncle Earl. Xylia stood up.

"I really do have to go. He can have my place." I reached out to stop her, but she was already in motion. Jolene opened the door and Uncle Earl stepped in.

"What you doin' stayin' out so late?" he asked.

"Hello, Mr. Earl. Just dropped off a book for the boy and these girls forced me to sit down and have a bite." It seemed she acted different around him, patronizing. But, I thought, he is one of her customers.

"Uh huh. How'd you like that cobbler?" he asked. Had he smelled it the minute he set foot in the house?

"I tell you, Jolene ought to open herself a restaurant," said Xylia. "Thank you girls, for including me." She moved towards the door.

"Bring that boy of yours over Saturday afternoon to see them Bulldogs on my big screen, Miss Elmwood," Earl said.

"I'll do that," she replied, as she attempted to squeeze by him in the narrow kitchen. And as she stepped back to get past him, I saw him cast his eyes down, towards her hand and at the ring. It was then that I knew Uncle Earl had sneaked in and eavesdropped through our entire dinner.

"Evenin'," he said, his eyes still fixed on that ring. Then he looked up at me. I quickly shifted my glance so he wouldn't catch me staring at him. I decided to keep the eavesdropping information to myself, but intended to ask my husband what he thought. Later, after everyone else had turned in for the night, I climbed into bed with the portable phone and called Michael, who I imagined would still be at the office. He picked up after the second ring. At first, he sounded happy to hear from me, and I told him about our day. But when I asked him what to do about Earl, he snapped at me.

"Ever think about using the lock you had put in today?" he asked.

"Well, of course," I said. "Joseph must have forgotten."

"Yeah right," he answered. "Listen, is there anything else? I've got a ton of paperwork to finish before I go home."

"I'm sorry I'm not there to help," I responded.

"I told you I've got it covered," he answered, defensively it seemed. "Just try to take care of your business and I'll take care of mine." I had forgotten how stressed out he could become during heavy litigation.

"Sure, okay. I love you," I said.

"Me, too," he answered and I heard the line go dead. I imagined that his associate must have been in earshot and remembered Michael just wasn't good on the phone. I'd have to get busy tomorrow and get this estate business moving along. I wanted to get home.

There's nothing worse than a night of little or no sleep with no dreams. Perhaps it was eating too late, or Jolene's oily fried okra, or being bothered by Michael's sounding so distant. But all night long I tossed and turned just on the crest of sleep with my worries rolling in one at a time like waves on a choppy ocean. By the time the morning sun had come up over Taylor's Ridge, I was exhausted. I felt overwhelmed as I dragged out of bed after I heard Jolene's tap on my door, bringing my coffee.

My sister knew me well enough to keep her mouth shut until I had my first caffeine fix of the day, and she didn't take it personally when I went out and sat on the east deck to drink my mug of hot coffee. Perhaps the crisp morning air would clear my head.

To my left was the old walnut tree which stood next to Dad's bedroom window. A squirrel busied himself running up and down a branch, waiting for a handout. I remembered my last visit, when Dad was sleeping about 12 hours a day.

I went in to check on him one morning and found him in bed staring with wide-open brown eyes at a squirrel. Although he claimed he couldn't see without his glasses, he wondered where the other squirrel was, he saw only one. He wanted me to go into the kitchen and find some peanuts to see if we could lure out the missing squirrel. He was like a boy trapped in an 84-year-old body. I smiled as I thought of my father, and a burst of nostalgia hit me, knocking away all other sensations. I missed him terribly. A sense of deep loyalty washed over the nostalgia, and I was left determined to get through this day, devoted to settling his estate.

I'd just have to tackle one thing at a time.

A light morning mist turned to a drizzle. It was a good day to work in the barn. I left Joseph with Jolene and Sammie, donned some old jeans, grabbed a flashlight and ran out across the pasture to the huge, creaking gray wooden old building.

I opened the double doors and adjusted to the darkness and the musty, sweet smell of old hay that lingered although Dad hadn't kept any animals here for two decades. I switched on the flashlight and saw small bits of dust swirling in the beam of light. I was glad Joseph wasn't here, but that I was. I had always loved the barn. If you don't have allergies, barns can feel very safe.

The barn was built in 1894, the year before my grandparents' farmhouse was built up the road. As was often the custom at the time, farmers would build their barn first before putting up their own residence. This one was made of long oak timbers and was two stories high, with hay storage on the top level and cows and horses on the bottom level in stalls. The stalls still contained some old straw on the floor, but the second story was used as a storage area for old furniture and antiques.

I opened a door into a small side room where Dad had kept his tools and tack for the horses. I picked up a small black bridle with long, decorative tassels and immediately recognized it as belonging to my first pony, Tommy. I remembered the first time I'd seen him. Dad had surprised me during my seventh birthday party when he drove up towing a trailer and unloaded the fat black-and-white spotted pony. I looped Tommy's black bridle over my shoulder. This I would keep. I started up the creaky stairs that led to the second level.

A small bit of pale light filtered through the cracks between some of the long boards that made up the side of the barn. I pointed my flashlight beam around the large area and saw that it was packed. I walked towards the center of the floor, picking my way through 80 years of Dad's belongings and things he and my mother, or his second wife had inherited from their parents. I finally found a long, grayish string and tugged it, flooding the area with light from the bare bulb above.

There was a huge amount of stuff, more than several hundred items, and no order to it. An old oak porch swing lay atop a glass top table. A box of bullets was thrown into a box of old apothecary jars. A washboard from the 20s, or earlier, lay next to snow tire chains. I stooped down and picked up one of the apothecary jars. "Marijuana" was painted on the side of it, and a spider scurried out. I almost dropped it, and then I heard a sigh. I whirled around to see Uncle Earl staring at me.

"Whatcha gonna do with this junk?" he asked. "That jar there you're holdin' will bring you $40 at the swap meet."

"How did you know I was here?" I asked him.

"I figured with the rain there was nothin' else you could do today," he said. Actually, I thought maybe he could be of help, for a change. I pointed to two metal rings lying on the floor and asked what they were.

"Wagon wheel rims," he answered. "Worth maybe $20." I wrote this down on a piece of notebook paper I'd brought along, tagged each item with a yellow sticky note. We sorted through 20 or so more items, putting down Uncle Earl's best estimate of what the items were, and what price they'd bring. Occasionally he'd ask me what I wanted for an item. He held up a grinder, and I stepped in closer to look. He explained it was a corn meal grinder, and assured me was worth about $10. Another time, he held up a black-lacquered jewelry box filled with costume jewelry that had belonged to my stepmother. He held up a rhinestone necklace he wanted for his wife, Cottie.

"She loves trinkets and such," he said. "And her birthday's comin' up. Why don't you let me take it off your hands for a fair price?" I explained that I couldn't really sell anything yet, that I had to first get an appraisal.

"What in the Sam hill is it with you and your appraisers and lawyers and whatnot? Same as the land. I offered to buy it from you for a fair price, and take it off your hands. You could make it easy on yourself, get on back to that husband. I'll give you $1600 an acre, and an extra $1000 for all this junk." He swept his hand out, indicating all the things in the barn.

"I've already told you, the lawyer recommended I get every-thing appraised," I replied. I had explained this before, and I hated having to repeat myself. Besides, asserting myself inevitably led to conflict, which was, after all, Michael's department. I could hear my uncle muttering under his breath so I ignored him, pretending to dust off some old dishes. Eventually he'd quit pestering me about how I was handling things. Suddenly, something cracked just in front of my face, a small brush of air flushed my cheek. He'd almost whipped me with an old riding crop! I held my hand up to shield myself and stepped back. He laughed.

"Like a rattlesnake, ain't it?" He tossed the whip in a box. "You think about my offer. Got to get on home for dinner." He headed for the stairs. I was frightened and furious and my heart was beating so hard I felt it pounding in my ears. I wanted to tell him how much I hated him, how I didn't want him in my life, but not here, not alone in the barn. I heard the thud of the barn doors closing behind him.

Furious, and feeling somewhat powerless, I picked up the riding crop and tucked the handle in my pocket. Next time if someone was going to whip something, it would be me. I stepped around an old steamer trunk and headed down the stairs.

Outside, the storm had broken and all that remained was an overcast sky. It was too early to call Michael, and besides, he'd probably just snap at me. But I was much too angry to go back to Dad's house just yet. I was afraid of what I might say in front of Joseph and Sammie, so I headed for Elmwood's. I walked briskly down the side of the highway and leapt over puddles of water. I looked up towards Taylor's Ridge and spotted a curl of smoke rising in the fog and I wished I were in a safe place, far away from my uncle.

At the store, Ernie was in his usual spot with his notepad of numbers. We were alike, Ernie and I. We both kept lists. I opened the door, smiled at him. Xylia was busy with a customer at the register. I moved toward the soothing heat that radiated from the ceramic heater and glanced up at the chalkboard. Patience endureth forever. Hunnicutt family motto, courtesy Miss Anne Hunnicutt."

Xylia hurried towards me and enveloped me in her warm voluptuousness. I hugged her back, and we both looked at the chalkboard.

"Thought it was about time for a new quote," she said. "What do you think?"

"I'd say Miss Hunnicutt must be psychic. The estate's a lot more work than I'd imagined. I hope my patience can last through what it takes to get things squared away." She motioned me to take a seat, but then noticed the riding crop in my pocket.

"You're not thinking of going riding in this weather, are you?" she asked.

"It's a long story," I answered. We took our seats at the old school desks and I told her how Earl had been acting towards me.

"Let me give you some practical advice," she said. "I don't claim to know what's going on inside of that man's mind. He seems nice enough to me. Fact is, since my Leo passed, he's had Ernie over to watch sports on his big-screen more times than I can count. No one else has taken an interest in the boy, and I'm grateful. But if I were you, I'd try to avoid him. For some reason, you bring out his mean streak."

"I always have, I think. He never cared for my mother and I think maybe I've always reminded him of her. And one time, when I was eight or nine, Mama and Daddy had to leave Griffin and me with Earl while they went to Atlanta to see my grand-mother on her deathbed. Mama normally didn't leave me with Daddy's family, but she must have been distraught when the call came in the middle of the night."

"I didn't care for my in-laws much myself."

"No, it was worse than that. Earl had a bad habit of ridiculing Mama for being too citified. And when Daddy was out of earshot, he always made fun of us children. When we were left with him that time, I did my best to behave. But the first morning we were there, he cooked up cow's brains for breakfast, which I refused to eat. At the time, I wasn't eating meat of any kind. I'd finally figured out where it came from."

"Well, I can't blame you for that," Xylia said. "I don't touch cow brains myself."

"Anyway, after breakfast, he put the cow's brains in the refrigerator in a little plastic bowl covered with wax paper and pulled them out again for lunch and then again for supper. He taunted me and asked who did I think I was, anyway? He didn't allow me to eat anything else, thinking I'd get hungrier. All day I kept opening the refrigerator and looking at that bowl but I couldn't do it. Later in the evening, he loaded Griffin into his old truck and went into town to get supper without me."

"I hope you snuck a piece of fruit, or something," Xylia said.

"No, I couldn't. He made sure the refrigerator was bare, except for those cow's brains. Being single, he didn't keep much food. So there I sat, alone, hungry, waiting for them to get home. I just stayed in the house with the doors locked and turned up the TV real loud. I was starving, not to mention scared. I kept hearing noises outside all night and was afraid to fall asleep, afraid the boogey man would come in and kill me like they did in that "In Cold Blood" book Griffin had told me about."

"That's a shame. Your Daddy must have got all over Earl when he got back."

"I never told."

"Why?" Xylia asked.

"Earl threatened me. He said if Griffin or I told, next time he'd serve up pony brains for breakfast. He meant my Tommy." Xylia shook her head.

"I never suspected he would do anything like that."

"Well he did. And ever since, I can't help feeling edgy around him."

"I imagine so. My Leo always thought he was jealous of your Daddy, since he went to college. Then married an Atlanta girl. Earl never got off the farm."

"I know. And now he's mad at me because I won't sell the land to him at bargain basement prices. I haven't even had it appraised yet."

"Well, I don't know much about the cost of land, but you should do whatever you think is right," she told me. "After all, your Daddy left you in charge." She poured me a hot cup of coffee and as I sipped it, I realized I hadn't felt this warm and taken care of since I'd landed. Xylia was a blessing.

I asked her about feeling watched all the time, and she told me how Ardelia had taken Neighborhood Watch to a new level. Apparently, several years back, some rambunctious teenagers had egged Ardelia's windows on Halloween night. Ardelia had driven down to the store and quizzed Leo to find out who he thought the culprits might be, and when he said he didn't rightly know, she eyed him suspiciously and left in a huff. About three weeks later, the UPS man had arrived at the store and left a package for Ardelia. The return address was a binoculars' company. When she picked up the package, she didn't answer when Leo asked if she were going to do some stargazing. Sometimes, Xylia said, when the wind blew right, if you were walking down Ridgeview Road, you could hear the static crackle of her police scanner. About once a week, the boom of her shotgun pierced the peacefulness of the valley. No question, Aunt Ardelia was prepared for the next invasion of Jehovah's Witnesses or chain gang escapees, or God forbid, Yankees and Californians. It was good to hear this, and realize that my imagination hadn't been playing tricks with me.

"Why do you think she's like this?" I asked Xylia.

"She's been this way ever since I've known her, which was after I married Leo and moved here," she responded. "Folks tell me she changed after her husband was killed up on the interstate, right after it was opened in the early sixties."

"I was too little to remember."

"She got all bitter, drew into herself, pulled away from the world. Earl's the only person she talks to much. He takes her shopping at the Wal-Mart once a month."

"Well, that makes me understand her better, but I still don't like her," I said. Xylia nodded.

"I know," she said. Then I asked her about the stranger I had encountered up in the ridge lands, but she couldn't offer much help.

"Avie, we get so many hunters down here, I wouldn't know this fellow from the next one, unless I saw him," she said. "Now the part that's interesting is that he had a blowgun. I always felt that a real hunter wouldn't use a gun, it takes the sport out of it, throws off the odds for the animal. Sounds like your friend respects the animals enough to give them a fair chance."

"My friend he's not," I answered. "He's a trespasser. He acted like he owned the place." Xylia, seated across from me with her coffee cup clutched in her hands, leaned forward and lowered her voice.

"What'd he look like?" she asked, with a slight raise of her eyebrows. In the men department, Xylia was ageless, the spark in her blue-green eyes said it all. "Was he good looking?" I thought about it for a moment.

"Yes," I answered. "But that doesn't excuse him."

"Of course not," she answered. "Was he tall?"

"Over six feet," I answered. "I just hope I don't run into him again. I hope he stays off my land." Yet I can't say I wasn't curious about that blowgun.

CHAPTER 6

Back at the house, as I passed through the garage, I thought I heard the deep sounds of a male voice. Before going inside, I hesitated at the kitchen door to determine if it was Uncle Earl. I didn't think I could stand seeing him at the moment. Thankfully, I recognized the voice wasn't Earl's low drawl. I pulled the riding crop out of my pocket and propped it in the corner and proceeded into the kitchen.

The heavy scent of Canoe aftershave filled the air, not really surprising because when it came to attracting men, Jolene moved like a short-order cook at lunchtime. Seated across the old oak table was the lately abandoned, solidly single Trent Crimmel, Tyler's dad.

He was a product of the valley and as predictable as the bread route he had called his own ever since graduating high school in the 80's. He kept his ash blonde hair cut short and his plaid shirt neatly tucked into his jeans. His voice was evenly modulated and he droned on in a not unpleasant, but not very stimulating, tone. In short, Trent was about as boring as a piece of the Mother's Best bread he delivered, a plain dull slice with no butter, mayonnaise, mustard or other condiment.

Apparently his predictable lifestyle had served him well, or at least that's what I'd always heard. Although he lived a modest life in a double-wide modular home and drove an older model Dodge Ram, Trent had at least three quarters of a million dollars invested in the stock market, this, courtesy of my late stepmother who had "accidentally" opened one of Trent's brokerage statements and shared this information with a wide-eyed Jolene during Christmas dinner a few years back. Apparently, Jolene had filed this information away, and after being soured on phony record producers, she aimed to find out more about the local pickings.

"You remember Trent don't you Avie?" she purred sweetly as she poured him a cup of coffee. "He just dropped off Tyler to play with Joseph." Her voice had taken on a strange sing-song quality, the sound you might expect a Barbie doll to make, if she could talk.

"Yes," I said. I remembered him all right. Once during a hay ride sponsored by the Taylor's Crossing Methodist Church for the middle school set, we'd wound up packed into the back of a tractor-drawn wagon, bumping along a back road on an inky night. He carefully placed his arm around me and leaned in for a kiss. His lips were spongy, clammy and entirely too soft. I felt absolutely nothing when he kissed me, except I remember wiping my lips with the back of my wool sweater sleeve as soon as it was over. I had been expecting something more, to turn to a helpless puddle of passion but there was absolutely no chemistry. I'd felt more passion when I'd brushed my adolescent lips against my pony's downy nose.

Trent stood up to shake my hand, apparently standing on ceremony. I shook his hand back, although I'm not sure why we were acting so formal since Jolene, after all, was still wearing her shameless hussy, lime-green nightie that showed off a good portion of her long legs. She positively pranced over to the cabinet to pull out a cup for my coffee, demonstrating her superb domesticity and her downy thighs as she reached up. I saw Trent steal a glance at her and he hitched his knee up, ran his left hand down his blue-jeaned thigh, no doubt trying to control more than just his imagination.

"Did you have any luck out in the barn?" she asked, whipping down the coffee in front of me and scooting her chair closer to Trent than was necessary, presumably to make room for me at the table.

"There's about a thousand things out there, Jolene. I don't know how we're going to ever get it sorted out," I told her. "I don't even know its value, although Earl has given me his best estimate, for what that's worth." I could feel my cheeks flush as I thought about the near-miss with the riding crop.

"Have you thought about having an auction?" asked Trent. "I pass right by the auction barn on my route every other day."

"I think that's a brilliant idea," Jolene said, blinking her eyes at him and looking at him like he'd found the cure for cancer. He scribbled out the name of the auctioneer and said he had to get back to work. Jolene walked him all the way to the garage door and was gone for at least five minutes, long enough for more than a simple handshake.

I checked on the children. Tyler and Joseph were reading the history book and Joseph, who had remembered to put his mask on, was actually taking notes. Sammie was parked in front of the TV, mesmerized by a cartoon. I called the auctioneer and set up an appointment for him to come by and take a look at the junk in the barn. I looked at the clock. It was only seven in Los Angeles. Michael would still be asleep.

When Jolene came back in, she announced that she was going to ride into Chattanooga for a drink with Trent Crimmel at six that evening and would I watch Sammie? I agreed because I could see how her whole persona had changed, and she did appear to be "floating on air" since she had returned from showing Trent out. I knew she'd given him more than a peck on the cheek, and that having a drink was, for Jolene, a euphemism for taking someone to bed. It was better if she fawned all over Trent in private, rather than in front of the children, not to mention me.

I was happy for her, but watching the chemistry between her and Trent, not that I wanted any part of him, on top of my encounter with my uncle, had left me feeling restless and edgy. With my sister soaking in a heady gardenia bubble bath and the children occupied, I decided a brisk walk was in order. I wanted to see if I could locate the property line on the western edge of Dad's land.

The weather had turned to a fine mist, and I headed down the road, passing under the redbud trees planted by the Baptists. I walked by the long driveways of Ardelia and Earl, who would be inside sprawled out in front of the TV digesting his lunch like a fat snake who's just been fed a helpless mouse. My grip tightened on the riding crop, which I carried in my left hand. I entered the ridge land pasture through the old metal gate and headed up the gentle slope.

The creek was swollen with opaque-brown water heavy with sediment stirred up by the rain. I looked down at the saturated red clay banks and saw a tiny pointed rock. I leaned down and tugged it out of the soil. An arrowhead. I cupped it in my gloved hand for a moment, and closed my eyes, and thought of the Cherokee who had once held this relic.

I could feel a tingle start from the ground, running up my legs and into my palm. I was calm and completely connected to the earth for a moment through this ancient hunting tool left behind by the original inhabitants of this area. Had this arrow torn through the warm fur of a rabbit one morning? Or through an enemy's chest? I heard a noise. My uncle, the rattlesnake himself, must have followed.

I raised the riding crop as I quickly opened my eyes. I turned in a circle, looking all around me, and then I saw him, crouching behind a tall sycamore tree by the water.

"Why are you following me? You don't scare me one bit," I said, snapping the crop in the air, just as he had. The figure stepped out from behind the tree, but it wasn't Uncle Earl.

His hair was tousled and damp and he had the blowgun in his hand and a slight smirk on his face. It was the man from before, the hunter, trespassing again. He approached me.

"I'm the one who should be scared. You look like you could do some damage with that whip," he said. I let the crop fall to my side. "I wasn't following you. I was just passing through." He started to walk away.

"Good," I said. "I really don't want any hunting on my land." He turned around and stood defiantly awaiting my lecture on trespassing, I imagined. Perhaps it was because I was relieved he wasn't my uncle, or maybe I was overcome with curiosity, but I didn't want him to leave, not just yet.

"Is that a blowgun?" I asked. He handed me the smooth and straight wooden shaft. About three feet long, it was hollow down the middle with just enough space for the dart to pass through.

"I made it myself," he answered. "From river cane. It's America's oldest weapon and all the southeast Native Americans used it to hunt small game." Remembering the arrowhead in my hand, I gave him back the blowgun and held out my palm.

"I thought they used these," I said. He reached out and brushed his fingers along the arrowhead's carved surface. I briefly felt the touch of his fingers as he picked it up out of my hand. His touch was as delicate as a pony's muzzle grazing a palm for a carrot.

"They used these too," he said, studying the arrowhead. "This is flint."

"I remember finding these when I was little."

"After it rains is the best time to search, after the top layer of soil is washed off," he said. "The Cherokees shot game near watering places like this creek, the Little Chickamauga."

"How do you know so much about Native Americans?" I asked.

"My grandfather was half Cherokee. He taught me. He hunted here for years. Mr. Williams told him it was okay, as long as he didn't use a gun and didn't hurt the cows. It kept the rabbits and beavers from overpopulating."

"Have you ever seen any rattlesnakes over here?" I asked.

"Not here, no," he said. "They prefer Taylor's Ridge. My grandfather used to say they don't cross the Alabama Highway."

"Probably afraid of getting run over, I know I am," I said. "The traffic really flies through." He nodded.

"I've heard the rattlers are lobbying for a regular traffic light," he said. We both smiled and I studied his face. His nose was strong, and his cheekbones were high, and although he was probably only an eighth Cherokee, that eighth had been clearly etched into his features. Suddenly the wind picked up, rustling the leaves all around us. He looked up at the trees, closed his eyes and appeared to be concentrating. The wind blowing through the leaves crackled lightly, like the noise a bubble bath makes settling down in the tub as hundreds of tiny bubbles disintegrate all at once. It was a calming sound and I felt myself ease into it.

We stood side by side listening to the leaves, not moving for a minute or two. Then he turned to me and held out his palm, offering back my arrowhead. I plucked it off his palm, put it in my pocket.

He started to walk away.

"Wait," I said. He turned around and faced me, his chestnut eyes filled with curiosity.

"What were you listening to a minute ago?" I asked.

"I was listening to the trees talk," he said, dead serious. "Grandfather taught me that, too. My ancestors thought the plants and trees could talk."

"What did they say?" I asked. He smiled and answered.

"I saw you listening. What did you hear?" He stared at me, waiting for an answer, and smiled again. "Keep practicing. You'll get it." He turned and walked away. I watched the back of his buckskin jacket ripple under his wide shoulders as he grew smaller in the distance. Although the wind had died down, I stood there for a few minutes listening for the sound of the leaves. There was nothing. Suddenly, a loud clanging came from the east, by Daddy's house. The bell!

I turned around and ran down the soft ridges, breathing hard as I rushed to return to Dad's. At this very moment, Joseph was probably suffocating while I had been standing in the woods, waiting for the trees to talk. If God meted out punishment for idiots like me, then Joseph would surely die of an asthma attack. I ran over the slick grass until my side hurt and arrived at the foot of Dad's driveway. Uncle Earl stood ringing the bell. Jolene and the children clustered about him and it looked like my sister was arguing with him. Joseph was alive and well!

"What is it?" I called out as I neared them. "Is something wrong?"

Earl let go of the rope and the dongs of the bell diminished as he spoke.

"While you was messin' 'round in that back pasture, your brother Griffin called," he said.

"So you rang the emergency bell?" I asked. I could feel my ears start to burn as my blood pressure rose.

"I told him, Avie. I tried," Jolene interjected. I pointed to the house.

"Do me a favor, Jolene," I said. "Take those kids back in. I'll be there in a moment." I didn't want Joseph to be upset by the confrontation. His doctor had once said emotional upset could bring on the asthma. They walked back towards the house.

"Don't you ever, ever ring this bell again," I scolded Earl, "unless it's a real emergency." He ignored me.

"Griffin's comin' to town, thank the Lord. From the looks of you, it's gonna take a man to get things in order 'round here," he said. It occurred to me to pull out the whip and beat the hell out of him. Instead, I slid my hand along the smooth wooden handle of the crop and my fingers twitched to pull it out and use it. He saw and glared at me, almost daring me. But why stoop to his level?

"I can take care of things by myself," I said.

"Is that right? Then what's that Injun boy got to do with it?" he asked, spitting out a huge wad of tobacco onto the clean, gray cement of Dad's driveway.

"What do you mean?" I challenged him.

"Gall dernit, gal, your Aunt Ardelia can see for miles with them spyglasses. And it's a good thing. You gonna get yourself in trouble back there in that pasture. A city girl like you ain't got no business out there."

"Why? There's nothing to be scared of back there. There are no rattlesnakes, no abandoned wells, and I think you know it. Mind your own business," I shot back, surprising myself with my firm tone.

"Fine with me," he said, turned and walked away. Watching his dirty overalls retreat towards his house, I suddenly realized he'd been watching us all along, the stranger and me. The thought of Uncle Earl and Aunt Ardelia spying on me made my skin crawl. I shivered with disgust and headed back inside.

CHAPTER 7

I dawdled with the pimento cheese sandwich Jolene had laid out for lunch. I think she could see I was upset, so she was unusually quiet for her. Joseph and Tyler were full of chatter, sharing with me all they'd read that morning in the big history book. It confirmed what Xylia had told us earlier.

Before the Trail of Tears in 1838, the Cherokees had lived peacefully in the community alongside the white settlers. Thomas Williams, our ancestor, the blacksmith, had made friends with the Cherokees and had often asked them the location of the silver mine. The Cherokees trusted Williams with smelting their silver, but not with the location of the silver mine. They closely guarded their secret until shortly before they were forced to leave the valley for the Trail of Tears. One of the braves came to Williams late at night and stood before him, intending to tell him how to find the silver mine. Suddenly an arrow flew out of the darkness and pierced his heart. He fell to the floor, and died there right in front of Williams. Apparently the other Cherokees, realizing he was going to reveal the secret of the silver mine, felt they had to silence him.

"So the secret died with him?" I asked.

"Not necessarily, Mom," said Joseph. "Maybe there's someone left who knows."

"I know," said Tyler. "I betcha that mean old lady across the street would know somethin'." He pointed out the window, towards Ardelia's house.

"Isn't that Aunt Ardelia's?" asked Joseph. I nodded.

"Your aunt? I'm sorry, I didn't know she was blood," said Tyler.

"That's okay, Tyler. She's old and cranky, alright," I responded. Jolene snorted.

"That's an understatement," she said. The phone rang and I grabbed the receiver. It was Michael, calling to check in. I could tell by the sound of his voice that his nose was stuffed up, and he admitted he might be getting a cold. I told him we were fine and I handed the phone over to Joseph, who was eager to share the story of the silver mine. By the time I got the phone back, he said he had to hang up, he was trying to get some papers prepared for filing the next day. It was just as well, I really didn't want to tell him about my morning lesson on arrowheads and leaf listening.

The boys were about to drive me crazy pestering me to take them to see Ardelia, and obviously I wouldn't. Before she merely had an unjustified, venomous attitude about me, but now after spying on me, she possessed real ammunition. The next time I intended to see Ardelia was laid out in her coffin, at the funeral home with her mouth shut for eternity. Of course I realized this might be in another two decades, but I could wait. Patience endureth forever.

Jolene wanted to paint her nails in preparation for her big date and I offered to take the children down to see Xylia, who could steer us to someone who might know the history if she didn't. Besides, I needed to get my mind off myself, to totally immerse myself in something for Joseph. I knew how to be a good mother, if not an ideal wife.

The weather had finally cleared and it was beginning to look like a fine day. A light wind rustled in the redbuds as we passed. I carried little Sammie, who was sleepy and sucked her thumb.

The boys skipped along in anticipation of finding out more about their treasure.

Ernie was in his usual spot, waiting for the next car to pass so he could log it in his notebook. Xylia was seated at one of the school desks chatting with an old-timer who was dressed in dusty, faded denim overalls. She beckoned us to come closer and we each took a seat around them. In his lap, the old-timer held a clipboard with some attached papers. He kept pointing at it.

"Fifty, count 'em, houses in the next year, I heard," he said. "Now you tell me, Mrs. Elmwood, how we gonna fit them cars on this road, here?" She shook her head. "They've got to be stopped."

"You can leave your paper here Hank. I told you I'll be glad to set it out on the counter," she said.

"Well, I appreciate that but I wanted you to know so you could explain it to your customers," he said. Tyler piped up.

"Sir, do you know anything about the Cherokees' silver mine round here?" he asked. The old-timer fixed his rheumy gaze on both boys.

"How old are you boys, 12, 13? When I was your age, my friends and I spent a whole summer lookin' for the treasure. Tramped around the ridge, up yonder, and everywhere in between. My own pappy swore it was down at the blueberry farm, just down from the Moon-Jones Cemetery. My grandpappy had told him the Indians covered it up with leaves and brush so it wouldn't stand out. All we ever found was three or four rattlers."

"Did you get bit?" asked Joseph. The old-timer laughed.

"No sir, or I wouldn't be sittin' here tellin' you," he answered. "You know the Indians lived all around here when my granddaddy's granddaddy was a boy. This part of the country was considered west. Them mountains, like Taylor's Ridge up yonder, was a natural barrier. Indians was here in the West, and the white settlers was down on the coast. Now in the winter, when the creeks overflowed, the Indians lived in them mountains, up on the ridge, to keep from getting flooded out."

"Until the Trail of Tears, right?" asked Joseph.

"Right. It was a shame, what they did. My great-granddaddy said the Indian women, they screamed and hollered somethin' fierce. You could hear them all around the valley. The Indian men, though, they was real quiet-like." We all sat in silence for the moment, imagining the screams echoing around the valley.

"That's all I know boys, but you might want to go check down to Red Clay State Park. That was the center of it all, before they was forced to leave to Oklahoma. Me, I'm goin' to lay down a spell before supper." He rose from his chair, pulling his overall straps up as they tried to slip down his frail shoulders. He tipped his Georgia Power cap at us and asked, "How you like my lid, boys?" Joseph laughed and Tyler responded. "Mighty fine, sir." The old-timer smiled a toothless grin and set his petition up on the counter next to the donations and quotations jars.

"Much obliged, Mrs. Elmwood," he said. As he shuffled to the door, a sharp pain stabbed my heart. From the back, he looked just like my father. Joseph tugged at my sleeve.

"Please, can we go there?" he begged.

"Now what did you all need today?" Xylia asked.

"A map," I said. "Looks like I'm taking these kids to Red Clay." The boys whooped and hollered and Sammie clapped her hands and almost wiggled out of my grasp.

As Xylia had advised us, we took the back roads to Red Clay which was located beyond the state line in Tennessee. We traveled past farms and through valleys on a curving country road. The rolling landscape was covered with a symphony of trees of all types. Tall evergreens that had witnessed the Civil War stood next to a stand of densely clustered, ash gray trees. All along the road, bare branches arched against the powder blue sky.

Time seemed to have slowed down here. A Rebel flag was tucked into a trailer window. Another home had old-fashioned, bleached gourd birdhouses strung across a line running over the backyard. And another modest home was covered with red Christmas decorations no one had bothered to take down.

We arrived at Red Clay about half an hour after we set out from the valley. We parked in a paved lot and climbed out under the shade of some tall old trees. I put Sammie in the stroller and stopped off at the Visitor's Center where we looked at historical exhibits.

Red Clay became the Cherokee seat of government in 1832 after the state of Georgia banned Indian political activity. Not allowed to hold their usual councils anymore at New Echota, Georgia, the Cherokees moved their capital north to Tennessee, and Red Clay. From 1832 until 1838, once a year, up to 5,000 Cherokees had gathered at Red Clay. There, they discussed the ways to fight the government's plan to relocate them to Oklahoma and their precarious future. Ultimately, the Cherokees lost their battle to remain on the land that had been their home for years. They were forced to travel the "Trail of Tears," and their lands were given out to white settlers in a lottery.

In a somber mood after learning how unfairly the Cherokees had been treated, we were silent as we headed down to the Blue Hole Spring, or Council Spring, used by the tribes. Located at the base of a hill, the spring is reached by walking down stairs. I left the stroller at the top and I took Sammie in my arms. We walked down the stairs alongside the split rail fence that bordered the spring. Surrounded by bare ash trees, the spring was a pool of water ringed by a rock shelf. It seemed set apart from nature, or mystical, by its almost turquoise color. Dotted with an occasional bunch of watercress, the surface of the water reflected the sky's bright blue, and the lacing thin, gray tree limbs that hung above. Underneath the clear water, the blue-green rock bottom was shiny in places, like a fish's scales, and reflected upward. The effect was startling and it was easy to see why the Cherokees had thought this place sacred.

Squatting down on some large boulders in the middle of the narrow stream that flowed out from the pool, Joseph leaned over. He dipped his hands into the deep, cool water and splashed his face. Neither he nor Tyler could believe the Cherokees had once stood at this same spot and done the same. Sammie wiggled to get down in the water, but since a raw wind was starting up, I kept her in my arms, and we headed on to see the rest of the park.

With spiky gumballs crackling underfoot, and sometimes thick, dark walnuts, we moved past the Council House, similar to one where the leaders of the Cherokees had held their last councils. We saw a log and mortar farmhouse and a corn crib.

"Where are the tepees?" asked Joseph.

"They were just like us," said Tyler, reading from one of the brochures.

"The Cherokees emulated the white settlers. They owned farms, grew corn and raised pigs and beef cattle. They went to school and had a government modeled after the federal government. Many of them married white settlers and had children and were Christians. They even published a newspaper for several years. Some escaped the Trail of Tears by hiding in the hills, and later some returned to the area."

"The hills, like Taylor's Ridge?" Joseph asked me.

"Or the ridges," I answered, thinking of the hunter I'd encountered earlier. On the way out of the park we stopped off at the Visitor's Center again so the boys could ask the park ranger about the silver mine. Although she said she'd been asked that question before, she had no idea if there had ever been a silver mine, or where it would be. She wished the boys luck and handed them some more pamphlets.

By the time we got back to Dad's place, the sun was hanging low, about to tuck itself in for the night behind the farthest of the ridges. Its last rays washed over the land as it disappeared into the west, just beyond the Little Chickamauga, and suddenly the air grew chilly. I shuffled the children along into the house.

Dressed in a short bright purple mini-skirt suit, her orange hair ratted up and lacquered with spray, Jolene left for her evening with Trent. Jolene had cleverly arranged for Tyler to spend the night with us and I knew she'd probably slip in right before the sun came up the next morning.

Later, after I'd put the children to bed, I picked up the phone to call Michael and see how he was feeling. It was only seven in Los Angeles, and it wasn't unusual for him to work this late. His line rang nine or 10 times and I was about to give up when suddenly I heard someone pick up the receiver. There were giggles, a throat clearing and finally a hello. It was a female, but not one of the secretaries. Could it be a client? While I was trying to figure it out, the voice said hello once again, and then, "There's no one there." I heard a click and the line went dead. As I cradled the receiver in my hand, I realized it was Lily.

I felt dinner begin to curdle in my stomach as I thought about her. As I suspected, Michael had hired her. And why not? She knew her grammar and spelling like an English teacher. She was the type of woman my mother would have called a professional spinster or old maid. That's what I thought myself until I came into Michael's office late one night to photocopy Joseph's school assignment.

As I walked down the long hall, I heard their conversation punctuate the silence.

"Must have turned off the air conditioner," Michael said. As I rounded the corner, I could see her peeling out of her sweater, pulling off her wire-rim glasses, batting her eyes at Michael. She looked positively vampish; he looked perplexed.

"Absolutely burning up, like a woman with hot flashes," she said, and directed her gaze my way at that very moment. "Oh, hi, Avie." She put her glasses back on and resumed her clacking at the keyboard, thrusting out her perky, definitely non-menopausal breasts.

"Honey," Michael looked relieved as he reached out for my hand. "I was just about to leave." I held up Joseph's ant colony drawing. He pulled me into the photocopy room and we smiled at one another as the machine hummed out the copies. "Glad you stopped by."

Later that night, in the safety of our kitchen as we munched on oatmeal cookies and talked about Joseph's ant project, I asked him about Lily. At first he denied that he'd even noticed her coming on to him.

"So I imagine you didn't see her little size A nipples protruding from that thin, cotton tee top?" I'd said, realizing even as I spoke how catty and insecure I sounded.

"Okay, so who wouldn't notice? I'm not blind, you know. But I didn't like it."

"Them," I retorted. He looked confused. "There's two," I clarified. "Nipples, I mean." He shoved the plate of cookies away.

"I'm not talking about the freaking nipples. I meant I'm uncomfortable with her behaving that way."

"Well, why don't you get rid of her, then?" I asked. And he had. I had agreed to come in part-time on Saturdays and to do some proofing and editing at home. Thus, we had gotten rid of the grammatically perfect, hard-nippled Lily, or so I had thought.

I walked out on the deck facing Taylor's Ridge and looked up at its dark, looming height. No wonder Michael said he had it covered when I asked him about the editing. With Lily he had it covered or uncovered if he wanted. And if something happened between them, what could I do about it? Not a bloody thing, not here, more than 2,000 miles away. I looked up in the violet-sable sky. The moon was a smoky, pale white, covered with a haze. It was so full and heavy it looked like it would burst.

CHAPTER 8

I awoke to the smell of bacon frying and Jolene's laughter in the kitchen. I poked my head around the corner and saw Trent squeeze her around the waist. She was still wearing her purple mini-skirt and a big grin.

Nothing feels as good as new love, at least to the people who think they're in it. And observing them made me want to check the pulse of my own relationship to see if it was still breathing. I looked at the clock. It was too early to call, only 5:00 a.m. in Los Angeles. So I got up and took a long shower and gave Trent time to leave for work. As the hot water cascaded over me, my mind wandered.

Are human beings supposed to stay in love for the long haul? Or was modern marriage simply a marketing tool for dress designers, florists, caterers, jewelers and tuxedo rental shops? Despite the heavy use of deodorant, armpits and relationships eventually started to stink, at least some of the time. Living in such close proximity brought great intimacy with one's spouse, his bathroom habits, health issues, emotional problems and sleepless nights. In the beginning, a man and woman couldn't get close enough, lay like two spoons, listened to each other breathe. A few years later, the double bed inherited from grandmother was outmoded, not by time, but by too much closeness. I winced as I remembered it was I who had suggested the purchase of our California King.

I stepped out of the shower and my eye was drawn to the sand dollar on Dad's dresser. I'd picked it up on the beach at Daufuskie Island, South Carolina a few summers ago and brought it to Dad as a souvenir. On my last visit here, when Dad was lingering in bed after his customary afternoon nap, I'd held up the sand dollar, admiring the five-petal flower that appeared on the front, and then on the back.

"Look, isn't this fascinating?" I held the sand dollar up for Dad to see.

"No, Ma'am," Dad had replied curtly.

"But it's beautiful," I protested. I held it close up to his face so he could see the thin designs etched by nature. He shoved my hand away, and I almost dropped the fragile treasure.

"I've looked at that thing every day for a year now and it looks average to me," he said. At the time, his refusal to see the shell's obvious beauty had bothered me, but now it made sense. Day in and day out, exposure to something beautiful diminishes its value. But if you put the cherished object away, and look at it only on special occasions, it takes on a rare quality.

I picked up the receiver and dialed Michael. He answered on the second ring.

"Yes?" he said, and "what do you want now?" Who did he think I was?

"It's me, Avie," I said. He coughed, and I remembered his sinus problem.

"Oh," he said.

"I was thinking of you," I said. "About how—"

"What time is it?" he interrupted.

"It's early, about six your time. You have court again today, right?" The line was silent. I continued, "I mean you were waking up, weren't you?" I heard him sigh.

"We're on second call this morning. I worked until two a.m. and I was trying to sleep in a bit," he said.

"Oh, I'm so sorry," I replied. "I'll call you later, then." He coughed again. He really did sound sick.

"I hope you feel better," I said.

"Me too," he said, and hung up the receiver.

I gently replaced the receiver on the cradle and wondered how I could have been so stupid. Not only to call this early, but to think he would want to talk about my feelings during the middle of his trial. Besides, he never was good on the phone.

As I slipped out of my terry cloth robe and into my shirt and jeans, I felt the warm sun pour through the window as it made its way over Taylor's Ridge. The heat intensified as it penetrated the glass window, and it felt good on my shoulders. I felt alive and content with myself. I looked in the mirror, brushing my copper-colored locks away from my forehead, and then leaned in and took a good look at my 42-year-old face. The nose was Mama's, long and aristocratic. As she always said, not cute or pretty, but elegant. My skin was still relatively unlined, smooth and pinkish. Like Mama's, my eyes were bright and full of their blue-green tint. Irish eyes, Mama had called them, saying we had been blessed with a natural beauty. Not unlike the sand dollar, I thought. I would make myself rare, at least to Michael. I wouldn't bother him any time soon. If he wanted to talk, he could pick up the phone and call me. I was busy too. I had an estate to settle.

Out in the living room, Jolene was dancing in her nightie, holding a broom in her hand like a microphone and singing, "Stand By Your Man." I didn't have to ask her how the date went, but I thought I'd be polite and inquire. She told me she hadn't had this much fun since high school. Trent absolutely adored her and appreciated her for what she was.

"And he loves my singing," she said. "I think he can get me a gig at the Barn. The owner's on the bread route." She skipped over and hugged me. I was happy for her, of course, and remembered how simple love was at first blush. The phone rang and Jolene picked it up.

"I'll tell her," she said, and hung up.

"It's the lawyer in town. They had a cancellation. Why don't you run on up while I watch the kids?"

"Great," I said, rushing back towards the bedroom to quickly change. "Now you be sure to give Joseph his morning meds. There, on the counter."

"Okay. The secretary said to be there in 15 minutes, what are you doing now?" she asked, following me into the bedroom. I reached for my jewelry case to put on my pearls and my blue sapphire ring.

"I've got the perfect complement for my royal blue suit," I said, but Jolene stopped me.

"You're going to Ringgold, not New York," she said, grabbing a tweed blazer and black slacks out of the closet. "Besides, you don't want to look too rich. He might charge you more."

"Right," I answered, glad to have a sister who cared, and I slipped into the slacks.

Jim Johnson was the best lawyer in town. His office was located in the most prestigious building in Ringgold, an 80-year-old brick building, right across from the courthouse on Nashville Street, the main drag. I parked out front for free, almost unheard of in L.A., and headed up the steep, narrow flights of stairs that must have seemed au courant back in the 30's, but now looked very worn-out and dated. No elevator was in sight, and I wondered what disabled people did when they had legal problems.

The reception area was spacious and had several comfortable couches placed on a new hardwood floor. A receptionist with teased red hair sat behind the desk chatting on the phone. She hung up quickly and said, "May I help you?" and led me back past several other offices filled with more teased-haired legal assistants wearing business suits. I hadn't seen this many bobble heads since high school. At the end of the hall, the redhead ushered me into the largest office where Jim Johnson rose to greet me.

Jim was in his mid-50's and might have been quite attractive several years back before the work and worry had chiseled into his face, leaving their mark in his gaunt cheeks. He rose to meet me and shook my hand with a warm, firm handshake.

In his soft, comforting drawl, he laid it all out, my "fiduciary duties" as he called them, just as Michael had. As he ticked down the list, I remembered how slowly it was going. Once I got the appraisal and survey done, I had to give copies to Jolene and Griffin, along with a letter explaining what I proposed to do. He suggested that we file a settlement agreement, stating how we planned to divide the assets.

"Is that really necessary?" I asked, remembering what Michael had told me about trying to keep the legal costs down.

"Didn't your father have a daughter from his second marriage?" he asked.

"Jolene," I nodded.

"She lived up the road a ways, wasn't it Nashville?" he asked, spitting out the word Nashville the way I once heard a preacher say, "Sodom and Gomorrah." I imagined he'd heard about Jolene's misadventures. "At any rate," he continued, "when there are two marriages involved, I generally like to do things properly. After I draw up a settlement agreement, Jolene and Griffin will have to sign it before the assets are distributed."

I assured him that was a ways off, since I hadn't even been able to obtain a surveyor yet. He asked me to go by the safe deposit and try to locate some of the old deeds. He walked me to the door and on the way out, introduced me to his paralegal, Susan, who also had teased hair, but in a shorter, more modern version. She wore it like a black helmet. She told me to be sure and call if I needed help. She seemed bright and eager, and as I left, I scolded myself for judging people by their hairdos.

The First Trust Bank is a one-story building on the corner of 41 and Battlefield Parkway. Out front of the bank is a pyramid of gray cannon balls reminiscent of the Civil War, and inside, old-fashioned southern hospitality lives on. One of the bank officers, Betsy Simmons, a friendly, smiling motherly woman, had helped me before with Dad's banking concerns. She helped me to the vault and turned her key to Dad's safety deposit box and instructed me to turn mine. She slid the box out of its slot and carried it to a small room where she placed it on a table. She closed the door, leaving me alone so I could open up the box in privacy.

The cold, drab metal box sat harshly on the table before me. I touched its chilly edge, and ran my finger along the sharp, defined edges. It was smaller than a shoebox, really, yet it contained all of what really mattered in my father's 84 years. Was this all life amounted to in the end? I sighed and lifted up the lid, remembering the last time I had been here. It was about a year before Dad died that he had insisted I see where all the deeds were stored. But we hadn't opened the box that day, merely gone through the motions.

The first thing I saw was a packet of salt, left on the top of all the other documents. It was from Hardee's and as I picked it up, I knew my stepmother, who loved that restaurant, had put it there. But why? Did salt somehow preserve old papers? Or was there something metaphorical going on here? Was the salt to pour in our wounds when we felt the pain of sorting through these last remnants of their lives? Or did she anticipate a fight between the heirs? I pulled the salt packet out and put it in my pocket. Next I found the deeds to the house and to the ridge lands. I put them aside and dug deeper. Just under his birth certificate, issued from the state of Oklahoma, I found a wrinkled piece of aging parchment, a divorce decree from 1928. It dissolved the marriage of Robert Clark Williams, my grandfather, and Catherine Cloud. I had never heard Grandpa had been married before he met Grandma. Why had no one told me? I studied the paper and found out she was half Cherokee and had received a piano in the divorce settlement. He got their mules and wagon. According to the paper, they were married about a year. I moved on to the next paper in the stack, Dad's car title, followed by several cancelled insurance policies and a timber option for the ridge land. At the very bottom of the steel box, I found a color snapshot of me, around 12 years old, climbing a tree.

I swallowed a lump down, trying to hold in my sadness. Of all the pictures Dad could have chosen, he had kept the one of me on the verge of adolescence, before he started to lose me. He hated it when I started to grow up, and had even given me a princess doll for my 13th birthday, when I had asked for stonewashed jeans and pale pink lipstick. He wasn't comfortable seeing me grow up, but he'd managed to preserve me forever, in his mind, as a 12-year-old tomboy. As I looked at the picture, I suddenly realized how hard it had been for him to let go, and how hard it would be for me, one day, to let go of Joseph. Would I also keep him captive in a steel box one day? Stuck in perpetual adolescence? Or would I be able to let go? It was simply too much to think about. I shoved everything into my canvas briefcase, carried the empty box out to Betsy and left in a hurry.

In the car, I turned on the car radio in an attempt to soothe myself. "I Did It My Way" was on. Remembering it was one of Dad's favorites, I sighed again and switched to "Dock of the Bay." Otis Redding was dead, killed in a plane crash I remembered. I switched again. "Unchained Melody," one of the most nostalgic songs ever written. Were the stations rigged to play only sad or nostalgic songs? I switched off the radio, and thought about Dad again. He wasn't perfect, had never been, and Lord knows he could be a cranky old bastard, but I missed him. I tried to wrestle my grief down, but it was a formidable opponent. It was no use, it was like grappling with a pit bull. I quit trying and let the tears rip. I cried all the way back to the lawyer's office, where, hidden behind my sunglasses, I dropped off the titles to the land, and left.

As I pulled into Taylor's Crossing, I felt a strong urge to stop off at Elmwood's and warm myself by the ceramic heater. As I walked in, Xylia looked up from her newspaper.

"Avie, what's the matter?" she asked. I rubbed my eyes checking for tears, but they were dry. "Has your uncle been givin' you hell again?" she asked. I shook my head and stood by the heater, letting it warm my cold feet, and my sore heart.

"I had to go to the bank and empty the safe deposit box," I said. I swallowed, trying to rid my throat of the lump of sadness that had formed.

"Oh," she said. She held out a box of Kleenex. "It's rough, isn't it?" I sobbed and she patted me on the back with her wide, warm hand. She knew about that lump, and also knew her sunny touch would help it melt away. "Go ahead and let it out. It's just us here. I don't mind, and Ernie, well, you know." We both glanced over at Ernie, who was staring out through the plate glass, looking for his next car to count.

"I miss Daddy," I said. "But I know I should be getting over it."

"No, not necessarily," she said, still patting on my back. The lump was starting to dissolve. "It's only been a couple of months, Avie. It takes time to get over a death, I should know. There was something the preacher gave me that helped a lot when my husband died. Just a minute." She walked back over and began rummaging through a drawer behind the counter.

"This is where I keep all the quotations after I've posted them on the chalkboard," she said. She pulled out a slip of paper and handed it to me. "Seems appropriate." I read the saying out aloud.

"'Time passes and rainy days and sunny days and snow, and sadness settles down.' By Thornton Wilder. Oh, Xylia, this is perfect." I tried to give it back to her, but she wouldn't take it.

"You keep it, Avie. And read it every day. I'll jot it down again and throw it in the drawer. One of these days, I'm going to type up all the sayings and make me a book." She wrote it down on a slip in her neat, flowery cursive letters.

"Thanks, Xylia," I said, and tucked it in my pocket.

"The real problem is you Californians don't know how to handle a cloudy day. Most of them are sunny, I imagine. What you need, if we can trust Mr. Wilder, is some rain and snow. Now if you'll stick around here for a while, I can promise you some rain, and maybe some snow, if you'll stay on through the winter." I laughed, and felt grateful to Xylia for her ability to make me do so.

"That's it, Xylia. It's that terrible California sunshine keeping me sad," I said. She laughed, and at the same time, we both reached out and hugged each other and my chest felt light and free. The lump was completely gone.

She picked up the sayings jar and we went over to the chalkboard. She pointed to the words, "Focus on the journey, not the destination."

"Old man Powell said he hates this one anyway. He said, ain't much of a trip left for me," she explained. "Why don't you draw another one out for me?" I put my fingers down in the jar and stirred around through a sea of paper slips.

"Close your eyes tightly," she commanded. "Elmwood's has standards, you know." I chuckled as I pulled out a slip of paper and gave it to her. She seemed puzzled as she glanced at the small slip of paper.

"What do you make of this? It's not exactly a saying, it's more like something you'd expect in a farmer's almanac," she said. I took the slip from her and immediately recognized the tight, small, neat blue letters that had flowed from a fountain pen.

"Feeding squirrels salted nuts causes high blood pressure," I read out loud and burst out laughing.

"I'm waiting for the punch line," she said, looking bewildered.

"It's really very simple," I said. "This is Aunt Ardelia's hand-writing, and she's been spying on me again."

CHAPTER 9

As I drove past Aunt Ardelia's house, I tooted the horn and held my arm out the window. In my hand was a jumbo-size can of salted peanuts Xylia had contributed. I hoped she had pulled away from the police scanner for a moment and was at the window, watching with her binoculars.

I pulled into Dad's drive and saw my brother Griffin's green SUV parked in the driveway. I had completely forgotten he was coming.

Griffin was two years older than I. He had come out of college with big dreams and quickly racked up more than $100,000 in debt and a string of false starts. He had owned and lost a Christmas tree farm, a used car lot, a feed store and a veal farm. His wife had left him after 40 of the calves were wiped out by E. coli. She said she just couldn't stand the suffering any more and it was not clear if she referred to the dying calves or Griffin's repeated business failures. Jolted into reality by her departure, Griffin began working full-time building houses for a contractor and had quickly risen to supervisor. When his boss died, he took over the company and was now known as one of the up-and-coming builders in the Atlanta area.

Joseph ran out to greet him and was admiring his Toyota Front Runner as I pulled up.

"Hunter green," he told Joseph, as he ran his hand over the smooth finish. Griffin turned his huge, curly red head and attempted to give me a hug, but his rounded stomach kept us from getting too close.

"Hey Sis, is this really your boy? I swear he's grown two inches since the funeral," he said. "What you been feedin' him?"

"The usual," I answered. "Steroid inhalers."

"Dang! Oughta try it myself, huh?" He joked, rubbing his soft belly. I had forgotten how corny he could be, but he wasn't a bad big brother.

We went inside the house where Jolene had prepared a vegetable lunch: collards, fried okra, hominy, green beans and hot biscuits with red eye gravy. I didn't have to bring up estate matters because Griffin beat me to it.

"All I want of the stuff, in the house I mean, is the antique dresser and the washbasin, and Dad's pistol and rifle," he said, helping himself to his fourth biscuit. "And I'd like to have Dad's tools." Jolene tightened up.

"Daddy wanted me to have the guns," she said.

"Huh?" Griffin replied. "What in the Sam Hill are you goin' to do with those guns, Jo? Force little Sammie's dad into marryin' you?" She jumped up from the table and snatched the empty biscuit plate off the table.

"I don't have to put up with your crap, Griffin. Daddy told me he wanted me to have the guns and the tools and I'm gonna take them," she said. Griffin looked at me for help.

"Well, technically, since he didn't write down who got his personal things, we either have to decide, amicably if possible, or draw straws," I answered. "Why don't we all make wish lists with our top choices and when there are items we all want, we'll draw straws for it."

"Sounds fine to me," said Griffin.

"Well, not to me," said Jolene. "I know what Daddy told me last time I saw him."

"And we all know when that was," said Griffin.

"About the time your wife walked out on you, wasn't it?" she said. I reached out and patted his arm to urge him to let it pass. Joseph rose from the table and grabbed his inhaler from the bar and took a deep puff.

"Are you okay, honey?" I asked. He nodded as he held his breath, letting the medication fill his bronchial tubes.

"Look you two, we'll work it out, okay?" I said to my sister and brother. "Jolene, why don't you start on the list of what you want while I take Griffin to walk the ridge land?"

"Fine, but be back by five. I've got an engagement," she replied. When I heard Joseph's light wheeze, I felt conflicted about leaving, but he had already started clearing off the table and putting the dishes in the sink. He looked up at me.

"Go on, Mom. I'll be fine," he said. "I want to read some more about Cherokee history."

"Okay," I answered. "But if you need to—"

"Take the nebulizer, I know," he said as he scrubbed a large frying pan. "I'm not Sammie, you know." I wondered when he had quit needing me as much. Griffin had already walked out the door, so I grabbed my windbreaker and followed.

"Dang, Jolene's a piece work, ain't she?" Griffin said as we pulled out in his SUV.

"She's not been too bad on this visit," I replied. As executor, I felt it was important to remain neutral. "Well, until you got here."

"She only wants the guns because I want them," he said. "Didn't you see that?"

"Well, she hadn't mentioned it before," I said.

"I could say I wanted Dad's toilet plunger and she'd want that too," he said.

"You'll have to beat me to it," I responded. He laughed.

"Sis, do what you have to do. I'll take whatever you say is mine. Most of Dad's things aren't worth that much anyway, unless you count sentimental value." He was being amiable. He pulled up a dirt road running off the county road and jumped out to open the gate. He moved with an easy familiarity. Although I had entered the property this way myself only once before, he seemed to know exactly what he was doing. He hopped back in and continued driving up the overgrown dirt road, path really, until the road became so rutted and weedy we had to stop. He got a couple of bright orange vests and caps out of the back seat and we donned them.

"It's almost hunting season and you can't be too careful out here," he said.

"But it's posted," I said.

"You're assuming all the hunters can read. Better safe than sorry." As we passed through the thick woods, he pointed out a hunting stand high up in the tree. It was simple, made of a few wood planks.

"It looks like the forts you used to build, Griffin," I said.

"Except mine had a stack of old Playboys," he said. I laughed. I shared with him what I'd seen in the safe deposit box, and asked him if he knew about Grandfather's first marriage to the Cherokee woman. He told me he hadn't. "A man and woman ought not to stay together if they're miserable," he said, and I admitted he had a point.

A crackling of leaves and some movement over to our right behind some trees startled me. Instinctively, I moved closer to my big brother. He stopped and pointed towards a brown-spotted cow standing behind some trees about 30 feet away.

"It's just a cow," he said. "You always this jumpy?"

"Out here, yes. I'm afraid I'll run into Uncle Earl."

"After all these years, you're not still scared of him, are you?" he asked.

"No," I answered, not wanting to admit to my big brother that I was. "But he is creepy."

"He's harmless, Avie. All talk. Haven't you figured that out?"

"He acts differently around me than he does you. He tries to intimidate me."

"You always let him intimidate you," Griffin said. "You need to ignore him."

"Easy for you to say. You're taller than he is," I said, looking up at Griffin who was almost six three. Suddenly he grabbed my elbow and steered me away from the cow, which was now coming towards us with lowered head.

"Now there's something to worry about," he said. "She's a new mama. If she thinks we're too close, she'll charge. She's trying to protect her baby. See?" I stared hard through the branches and made out a small pinkish-white head trailing along behind the Mama cow. Then we moved away into an area so dense with trees it was difficult to see where we were going.

"I hadn't remembered it being this thick with trees," I said. "It's hard to imagine the Cherokees once filled these woods. And Dad always said the Rebel soldiers hid out here during the Civil War."

"Yeah, I remember all that stuff," he said, and moved ahead to the crest of a ridge and stopped.

"Look at that, Avie." I walked up and stood next to him and saw we had arrived at the rim of a huge dip, or bowl, in the land. Filled with dried leaves, and about 30 feet wide, it was at least 20 feet deep in the middle. Its steep sides made it impossible to enter the bowl because, without a rope, a person would be stuck.

"Is that the meteor crater Dad used to talk about?" I asked. We stared at the entire bowl space, which had shorter, younger trees. "The heat from the meteor must have destroyed the trees on impact."

"Sis it's a sinkhole, plain and simple. Of course we could tell folks it's a meteor crater and charge them admission to see it. Then again, we could hire a couple of bulldozers to fill it up with fresh dirt," he said.

"Why would we want to do that? I've never seen anything like it."

"Leave it like it is then, but make it into a pond. The engineer would know how that would work," he said.

"Why not leave it exactly like this?"

"One, someone could fall in it and get hurt and sue us. Two, what good is a big old hole in the ground?" he said. He walked ahead of me around the rim of the bowl, and as I watched the back of his curly red head, I remembered him as a fidgety child, always in motion, always building bridges over streams, jumps to ride our horses over or lookout posts in trees. Building houses down in Atlanta was the perfect job for him. We walked along in silence for a few minutes as we turned back through the woods and headed down toward the creek. Perhaps when he saw some of the old arrowheads, he would appreciate the land's history and natural beauty.

The pasture was damp and soggy as we approached the creek banks and the swimming hole. It wasn't long before I spotted the stub of a flint triangle surfacing from the red mud. I leaned down and picked it up, handed it to him. He studied it for a moment then threw it down.

"You know, Sis, this gives me a great idea. We could develop a tract of homes here, call it Arrowhead Acres, you know? I can see it now, with an arrowhead forming the two A's on the sign at the entrance. What do you think?"

"I can't see it, really." A gust of wind came through the trees, the leaves shivered and I thought of the hunter I'd met.

"Listen, the trees are talking."

"Dang Avie, that's just the wind rustlin' the leaves." He grabbed a low hanging maple tree limb and snapped off a branch with his hand. "These trees will have to be thinned out considerably before the roads are put in." I stopped in my tracks.

"Roads?" I asked. He sighed in exasperation.

"When we develop, we'll bring in the bulldozers up here to knock some of the trees down and grade the land."

"Griffin, you're getting ahead of yourself. I haven't even decided whether to sell it or split it up."

"Sis, we could put in a hundred, acre lots, and at $15,000 a lot, minus the cost of layin' in the road and utilities. We'd come out with almost a million in profit."

"Daddy's will left you only a third of this land. You could develop your portion, but not mine and Jolene's. Of course I could sell it all off and give everyone the money instead."

"Don't you see? All you have to do is pay Jolene off. Once she's off our backs, we can do whatever we like." He loomed up above me as he spoke and I noticed he had a wild look in his eyes. The development was a reality in his mind. I chose my words carefully.

"I'd have to speak to the lawyer about it. It might work."

"He'll tell you I'm right. This county's booming. They can't build houses fast enough."

"I think," I said, truthfully, "you've got some ambitious ideas, Griffin, but I'll let Jim Johnson help me figure out the proper way to proceed." He bristled until I added, "Michael says it's my fiduciary duty."

"Yeah, okay," he said, and we turned to go back towards home.

CHAPTER 10

Griffin left right after we got back to the house, saying Smyrna was a long drive off and besides, he wasn't about to spend a night under the same roof with Jolene. Joseph was disappointed he couldn't visit more with his uncle, and I imagined at the root of his feelings was the fact he was starting to miss his father. After we said goodbye to Griffin, and sent Jolene off on her date with Trent, Joseph and I talked as he played marbles with Sammie while I prepared some soup for supper. Tyler was busy studying for a spelling quiz with his grandmother at her house. Lonely, Joseph suggested we invite Xylia over to eat dinner with us in the hopes that she might be able to help us pinpoint the location of the silver mine. Over hot vegetable soup and corn bread, I was impressed as Joseph laid out all he had learned about the silver mine thus far, and speculated upon its location.

"It has to be somewhere on top of Taylor's Ridge." He explained that he'd read all the accounts carefully, and in the old history book, had found another story where a settler had asked to be taken to the silver mine by the Cherokees. They'd blindfolded him and carried him away on horseback. He read aloud to us.

"I felt the horse climbing as I clung to its mane. We went for about 10 minutes this way, till I heard the sound of a small stream babbling over rocks. The Indians took off the blindfold, and I was surrounded by tall pines and darkness. I was certain we were up on the ridge for the wind chilled me, and the air felt lighter. The tall one grabbed me by the sleeve, and lowered me down in to a damp, cold cave where I waited. One of them went in and returned with three chunks of silver. They gave one to me, and put the blindfold back on."

We all sat silent for a moment and then Joseph spoke.

"Xylia, do you know of a stream up there on the ridge?"

"My husband once said there was one to the south a little, near that small cabin at the top," she answered. I thought about the curl of smoke I'd seen drifting out from near the crest. She continued, "But I've only passed by there in car, on the way to the other side. Always going by too fast to notice." Joseph looked at me with pleading eyes.

"If we walked it, I know we could find it, Mom. Tyler could go with us tomorrow since it's Saturday."

"It's a thick forest up there Joseph, too many mold spores in the air," I said. "You know we can't." Joseph jumped up from the table and ran into one of the back rooms. The door slammed shut. I started to go after him but Xylia stopped me.

"Wait a minute, Avie," she said. "You can't keep him in a cage forever, away from the world."

"You don't understand. The falling leaves on the ridge will trigger an attack, Xylia. And it can get really bad. He almost died once. I can't stand by again and watch him almost smother."

"And neither can I. Holding him back, keeping him in, that's smothering him too," she said. "Why don't you try and take him up there? He could wear that mask thing, you could take your pharmacy here." She gestured towards the counter. "You could even drive halfway up there so your car will be close." She scrutinized me, waiting for a decision.

"I can't take the chance, Xylia," I answered. "If something happened to Joseph, Michael would kill me." At this, Xylia appeared exasperated.

"Lord girl, nothing's going to happen to the boy. Try it for goodness sake. If the boy starts up with his troubles, you can always turn around and come on back down. It's only a mile to the top from my store." She got up and poured herself another cup of coffee.

"Do you think your son's gonna live at home forever? One day he'll grow up and move on off to college." She reached out and took my hand.

"You remember my Ernie's accident?" she asked. I nodded, and thought about Ernie's falling off a tractor one summer when he was in his teens. A local farmer had offered him a summer job, helping with haying. Although Xylia was worried since Ernie often seemed in his own little world, she'd decided it would be good to let him do something like the other school kids did in the summer. One afternoon, as the clouds grew heavier, he rushed to finish the day's baling for Mr. Thompson before the rain started. One of the Thompson girls' horses had broken loose and bolted over the fence. Mr. Thompson gave chase to the horse, and tried to drive it back into the pasture. Suddenly a large clap of thunder filled the sky, and the horse bolted back, directly into the path of the tractor. Ernie swerved to avoid it, and fell off. The tractor wheel hit a large rock, and circled back, crushing his head, and any future plans for further advancement in life. The trauma doctors said he was lucky to be alive.

"I've thought about that day a million times," Xylia said. "When he came over to get a sandwich at the store for lunch, I'd warned him about the rainstorm, and the lightning. I even suggested he knock off early, but he just nodded. I let him go, Avie."

"Don't you have any regrets?" I asked her.

"If I had it to do all over, I'd do it the same way, but hope that horse wouldn't escape. It's a mother's job to put her feelings aside, teach them the best we can, then let them go." I nodded in agreement.

"But I couldn't stand it if something happened to Joseph," I said.

"You can't hold him back from the world, or the world from him." As she said it, I knew she was right. I walked back to tell

Joseph I'd changed my mind, that we'd be checking out the ridge tomorrow afternoon, when there would be less pollen and spores in the air. He jumped up and hugged me.

Later that night, lying in bed trying to fall asleep, my mind whirled with too many thoughts. Aunt Ardelia's spying, or was it simply another form of insatiable curiosity, like mine? My father's death, and the empty feeling it left in my heart. Michael's distance from me, both physically and emotionally, and closeness to Lily, on some level. Griffin's plans to turn the land into an asphalt jungle. Joseph's ever-constant asthma, and his quest for the silver mine. The handling of the estate matters. Uncle Earl's hostility. Xylia's perceptiveness. And finally, as I drifted off, I thought of the hunter I'd met in the ridge lands and wondered what he was doing on this cold night. I shivered and fell into a deep sleep.

CHAPTER 11

The next morning we got ready for the afternoon drive up the ridge. Joseph wanted to pack his own medicines, and thinking about what Xylia had said, I let him. I'd check over them before we set out, but it was time I gave him a chance to be responsible. I made a few estate calls, in the name of progress, and set up the auctioneer for the next afternoon and managed to reach the surveyor and the appraiser, who both said they'd try to work me in next week. I felt in my bones that if I kept working the estate every day, the end might be in sight within a few weeks.

After cooking up a huge breakfast of blueberry pancakes and ham, Jolene took Sammie and set off for the Hamilton Place Mall in Chattanooga with Trent to buy a new dress to wear that night for her debut at the music barn. I asked her if she could afford it, and she assured me she had a little mad money tucked away for just such an occasion, after all, it could lead to a paying gig. Sammie would stay overnight with Trent's mother who lived a half mile away from the music barn and was delighted to baby sit. They would be out until early morning, but she would plan to come back tomorrow afternoon.

I helped her carry her things out to the car. Sammie pointed at my finger and said, "Wing." I laughed at her attempts to communicate, and realized I was starting to get a soft spot for the girl. I leaned over and gave her a little kiss on the cheek.

When I went back in, Joseph said that Michael had called to say hi. I asked him if I needed to call back, but Joseph said he didn't think so, his dad hadn't asked about me. I felt the little curl of fear start up in my stomach, but I quickly pushed it back when I remembered my sand dollar revelation; I had decided I was going to make myself rare. I didn't need to call my husband.

I checked over the medicine bag and sure enough, Joseph had packed everything. I complimented him on his thoroughness, but he shrugged it off, quickly grabbed his mask and headed out the door. Tyler and Joseph scrambled into the back and we set off.

We entered the highway and drove the half block towards Elmwood's, then turned up Nickajack towards the ridge. As we started to climb, we passed a newer stone home someone had built on the south side of the road. The fields gave way to forest as we ascended and when we were about half a mile up, I pulled over to the side of the road and parked. Without my prompting him, Joseph took a final puff of Proventil, and put on his mask.

"Come on, Zorro," Tyler said, and Joseph climbed out of the car, carrying his notebook and pencil along with his research notes. I grabbed my 35-millimeter camera, slipped on my thin leather gloves and windbreaker and followed. The boys led the way, walking quietly and listening for the sounds of a stream.

We walked past the greens, oranges and golds and I felt a light wind pick up as we got higher. On our right, we suddenly came upon a wide dirt path. We stopped and conferred.

"I think we should take it," Joseph mumbled through his mask. "It could lead to the stream."

"Me too," said Tyler. "Look here. It's wide enough for one of them wagons. My daddy said some of these here paths are Indian trails." It was covered with fallen leaves, and probably a million mold spores. Joseph noticed my hesitation.

"I'm gonna be fine Mom," Joseph said. "Nothing is getting

through this mask." I nodded and we started down the path. As we got farther from the road, the woods grew darker, dense with the tall, looming hardwoods and pines enshrouding us in shadow. Our feet crackled on the leaves and every 30 feet or so, Joseph signaled us to stop and listen for the stream. I smelled it before I heard it, the damp, earthy smell of wet banks and dead leaves, of fern moss and humid air. I held back from saying anything, though, because the boys needed to make the discovery. Joseph stopped about five feet shy of it, and we listened.

"That's it," said Joseph. He pointed to a small stream, about a foot wide and filled with rocks and rotting leaves. He ran and jumped over, Tyler followed.

"Keep looking for the cave," said Joseph. We all stared left and right, scanning through the evergreens, searching, as we headed deeper into the woods, our footsteps muffled by a bed of pine needles. It reminded me of another time with my father.

The snipe hunt was a rite of passage for children brought up in the valley. Occasionally, groups of teens set off on snipe hunts, venturing into the forest with no adult supervision. But in our family, only children of a certain age, young enough to believe in Santa Claus, were allowed to participate with the adults.

The hype began in the late summer as the days grew longer and hotter and tedium had settled in, along with horse flies as large as hummingbirds. Fathers and uncles began talking about the snipe hunt, always within the hearing range of children. Phrases such as "you'll have to find the right size bag to catch it," and, "danged snipe almost tore my head off" were tossed around as the suspense built. Older children who had experienced the snipe hunt wouldn't talk about it much, except to say that snipes were scarier than possums, and that the hike into the woods was a long one, lasting into the night when the bats came out.

The ideal time for a snipe hunt was somewhere after the harvest, but before Halloween, when the leaves crackled underfoot and the chill had set in at night. It was usually on a Sunday afternoon that the snipe hunters pulled on their long overalls and jeans, gathered up the brown paper bags, their lanterns and a jug of water and started up the side of Taylor's Ridge. A favorite uncle would lead the procession, stopping every now and then to proclaim, "Listen. Can you hear it?" One of the fathers would whoop and holler like an Indian. Propelled by the twin emotions of excitement and fear, the children would scatter out into the woods behind the fathers like a flock of lost chickens on the run. More often than not, the children would become separated from the adults and fears were heightened as the woods seemed larger without an adult guide in charge.

"Dad, where are you?" a child would call, but the only response would be silence. The children slowed down their pace and listened, not only for the adults, but also for the snipes, who were said to be quite dangerous if approached the wrong way. Suddenly a branch would snap, and a birdcall sound would penetrate the quietness.

"Whoo, whoo," came from somewhere just ahead in the dense forest. The children stopped and listened.

"Is that the snipe?" they whispered, and "Should we go that way?" and "Will it bite us?" As one, they proceeded carefully towards the place where they'd heard the noise. Suddenly a father would jump out and scream "boo," and the children would all laugh in relief. Inevitably, one would ask, "Did you see the snipe?" The father would hold his hands about a foot apart and describe the elusive snipe, a critter with the sharpest teeth he'd ever seen.

The snipe hunt went on in this manner for several hours, even into the darkness when the cold crept in, and the children's cheeks got pink and numb. The continued bursts of adrenaline being released into the young bodies finally gave way to exhaustion, and one of the children would suggest getting off the mountain before the blackness made it impossible to see. As the parade of tired adults and children straggled back down through the woods, the lantern's glow fading, the adults continued to boast of the snipe they'd seen, and the children were left with hope for better luck on snipe hunts yet to come.

The sound of a breaking twig somewhere off to my right jolted my thoughts. I turned and looked and thought I saw a flash of color moving between the trunks. The children were about 15 feet in front of me, focusing on the area ahead. I reached down for the handle of the riding crop. And then I heard it. A tiny laugh.

I whirled around and spotted him leaning against a trunk about six yards away from me. Even in the shadows, I recognized his raven hair and deep brown eyes.

"That thing's not much use in this neck of the woods," he said, referring to my riding crop. "Not enough room to snap it back." I walked towards him, noticing that the children had stopped to watch us. His feet moved towards me over the soft pine needles. He was carrying the blowgun and wearing light brown sheepskin moccasins, the kind with the white fluff inside, and light cotton tee shirt even though it was sweater weather.

"You're in luck today," he said, hoisting the blowgun in the air. "I'm taking the day off from shooting trespassers." I could see Joseph moving in closer behind the man, his fists clinched and ready if needed.

"Trespassing?" I asked.

"My people have owned this land for years," he said. As I listened, I remembered how I'd treated him at our first meeting on the ridge lands. I had been hostile, and now the tables were turned. I felt a stab of shame. "So how do you like my neck of the woods?" His left hand made a wide circle, gesturing to the surrounding forest.

"This is yours?" I asked. He reached out and let his palm slide over the rough bark of the pine tree. His fingers were slender but strong, and he seemed to be caressing the bark.

"Every tree, every bit of ground it's rooted to, mine to watch over while I'm on this earth," he said. Tyler appeared from the background.

"The silver mine, too?" he asked.

"Rumored silver mine," the man answered. "I hate to disappoint you, but it isn't anywhere around here. Or at least I've never seen it."

"Boys, this is~" I paused, realizing we'd never officially met.

"Will," he said. "Will Green." I introduced myself, Joseph and Tyler. Everyone shook hands and I was the last to feel his strong, firm grip. I explained about Joseph's mask and the asthma. Will said many of his students had asthma, so he understood.

"Would you mind showing them how the blowgun works?" I asked.

"Not at all," he said, reaching into his pocket for a thistle-topped dart. He loaded it into the cylinder's end, held his finger up to check the wind, then aimed at a pine tree and blew. The dart landed dead center in the tree trunk.

"Wow!" Tyler said.

"Bet you could do some damage to my peak flow meter," Joseph added.

"It's not the blowing that counts, it's the aim," he said. As the boys followed him to collect the dart, they peppered him with questions that he willingly answered. Tyler asked him if he'd heard the story of the settler who was blindfolded, brought up the side of the ridge and taken to the mine. Will motioned us to follow him as he spoke.

"I'll show you what he might have been talking about," he said. We walked along behind him. "But think about it, boys. Why would the Cherokees share their secret with anyone?"

"Because he was their friend?" offered Tyler.

"He might have been their friend, but they didn't know if he could keep a secret," he said. He zigzagged us through the tall tree trunks and we started to climb higher. Suddenly we were standing in front of a small cliff, about four feet tall. Just behind a bush, there was a small hole, or entrance. Joseph switched on his flashlight and pointed it inside. The beam of light bounced off the dark walls.

"Can we go in?" Joseph asked.

"Sure," answered Will. "But it's not very deep." I started to stop the boys, but Will put his hand on my arm and stopped me.

"They'll be okay," he said. "You can wait with me."

"Look, I really appreciate your being so helpful," I said. "You're just what the doctor ordered, as far as these boys are concerned."

"No problem," he said. "I was a boy myself once, you know, and it doesn't seem that long ago that I was out here doing the same thing, like last summer." Now that I'd stopped walking, I was beginning to feel the afternoon chill settling on the ridge. I

90

crossed my arms over my chest and shivered. He saw me.

"Why don't you come back to my place and I'll make some hot chocolate?" he offered. "It's not far."

"You live up here?" I asked.

"Right over there," he pointed towards a gray log cabin that I could see nestled in amongst the pines. "I could get us a fire going and get you all warmed up before you go back down. You must be freezing." He sounded concerned, and for the moment, I felt like I was standing down at Elmwood's, by the ceramic heater. I realized I hadn't felt cared for by a man, it seemed, for a long time. I couldn't see any reason not to go with him. The boys came back out, swearing they'd heard a bat, and we headed towards his home.

The cabin was a small, rectangular structure set up on a foundation of stones. It appeared to be a cross between a traditional log cabin and a wooden house. The sides were grayish, brown logs, with mortar in between, like the homes at Red Clay, but the windows and door and porch were done in white boards that appeared to be freshly painted. The roof seemed to be metal or tin. On the front porch were two ancient woven straw chairs which Will explained had been fashioned from rushes gathered along the shores of local ponds. Next to the cabin was parked an old blue truck that had seen a lot of miles. Will went ahead and opened the door and waved us to go in, take off our coats, stay awhile. The boys pulled off their jackets, but I left on my windbreaker and gloves because I didn't want to appear too friendly or comfortable. After all, I barely knew this man.

The living room was a smoky-smelling, cozy space dominated by a stone fireplace that took up almost an entire wall. The mantle was covered with arrowheads and on the wall above was a print of an Indian. Joseph and Tyler ran to check out the arrowheads, and I followed.

"Is it okay to pick up these arrowheads?" Joseph asked.

"Sure, just be careful," Will answered from the kitchen area, which stood off to the side of the cabin. He filled up a pan with milk and set it on the stovetop, then came into the living room and started to work on the fire. The boys peppered him with questions about the arrowheads and he patiently told them how the arrowheads were made, and for what purposes. He scraped one against the rock hearth to show how flint caused sparks. I studied the portrait above the fireplace.

He stood by a tree, holding a sheaf of papers in his left hand, and a long stick in his right. On the ground below him, using the stick as a pencil, he had written something in the dirt, something that looked like letters. He wore buckskin pants with fringe, leather slippers and a long striped jacket or sweater that might have been made from a blanket. Fringe trimmed both the outer garment and shirt under it. On his head, he wore a red turban-like hat trimmed with feathers. His manner of dress appeared to be part Indian, part English. He smoked a pipe. As I looked at the picture, I heard the fire begin to crackle, and felt its warmth start to take the chill off. The boys had taken the arrowheads over to the kitchen table and spread them out. Will stood up from the fireplace and came up beside me.

"Who is this fellow?" I asked, pointing to the picture.

"Perhaps the greatest Cherokee in history: Sequoyah, otherwise known as George Guess. He invented the Cherokee alphabet. Took him 12 years to come up with 85 characters." Will reached into a bookshelf built into the wall and pulled out a scrapbook. He opened it to a page of characters, the Cherokee alphabet. He handed it to me. The characters looked similar to our own English alphabet, but each character was made of several letters while others looked like hieroglyphics.

"It was a complicated process. He had to take the way the Cherokees spoke and turn what they said into a written form. He once said creating the alphabet was 'like catching a wild animal and taming it.'"

"Or 85 wild animals," I said. Will laughed, and touched my shoulder for a second, then turned to go pour the chocolate. I followed him into the kitchen.

"Let me help," I said.

"Not much to do," he said, "but I like the company." He reached up and got the cups out. They were the blue and white speckled enamel type.

"I've always wanted to have some like these," I said, tracing my finger along the slightly raised white flecks. "They aren't practical. You know you can't microwave them." I started to say that at least that's always what Michael had said.

"No microwave, no problem," he said. He stirred some Hershey's chocolate syrup into the steaming milk, and as I watched him, I realized I hadn't seen it made that way in a long time. Michael had always insisted we buy the instant type. He swirled the chocolate around with a large wooden spoon.

"Got to keep it moving, else the skim will form," he said.

"The dreaded skim," I responded. He smiled.

"I know what you're thinking," he said. He locked eyes with me and stared me full in the face. I felt like he was mentally undressing me. I blushed.

"You're wondering what I do when I'm in a restaurant and I find the skim on my hot chocolate, where I hide it, after I've spooned it off," he said. I gulped. I hadn't been thinking that at all.

"Tell me," I answered.

"Nope," he answered. "It's a one of the great mysteries of the world. I'll never tell." He smiled as he poured the hot chocolate into the four cups, and it suddenly dawned on me: We were flirting. I smiled back at him, and didn't know what to say. We handed the boys their cups but they insisted on staying at the table, reading a book about the Dahlonega gold rush they'd pulled down from the bookshelf. We sat in the ancient but serviceable leather recliners by the fireplace.

He explained that he had graduated from the University of Georgia with a history degree and had taught high school American history for a time. After several years, he decided he could make do with less and enjoy his other passion, white water rafting. So he spent long summers guiding groups down the Ocoee River and cold winters substitute teaching. The rest of the time he enjoyed the cabin and the surrounding acreage he had inherited from his grandfather.

"I like my freedom," he said. "And just being in these woods."

"Do you ever get lonely?" I asked, and instantly regretted perhaps sounding too personal.

"I've got lots of company. My squirrel and bird friends come every day to eat the stale bread I put out for them. And of course, as you know, these tall trees talk to me every night when the wind blows. And once in a while, the curious show up in my woods asking all kinds of questions."

"I'm sorry, I didn't mean to sound nosy," I said. Then I saw him wink, and I realized, once again, this man was flirting with me. It had been a long time since I'd experienced the patois of light chatter with a man. He reached out and swept his dark hair back from his face, running his hands over his black, bold eyebrows.

"What about you?" he asked. "Do you ever get lonely?" I felt awkward when he asked, but having asked him first, knew this was unjustified. I wanted to tell him the truth, that my husband was unreachable and I felt quite alone. Since I barely knew him, it seemed too soon to share this intimate detail. I looked into his deep, dark eyes and felt like I was walking through them, into the forest.

"Sometimes, yes, I feel lonely," I answered. "Especially since my Dad died a few months ago. I've been feeling really alone lately, even when I'm surrounded by people."

"In an alone place, in your mind, I mean, and no one else can understand your loss?" he asked. I nodded. How did he know? "When my grandfather died, I felt the same way. The way I see it is this. The death of someone close sets you apart from the world. It sends you off on a journey of grief, a solo journey, unfortunately." As I listened to him, I swallowed hard, and I hoped I wouldn't cry. It wasn't from grief but it was from finally having someone understand what I hadn't been able to articulate.

"It's painful, but you have to go through it," he said. "To come to terms with your own mortality. You see, that's what it comes down to. It's about finally realizing you will die one day." I knew he was right. We sat in silence as the boys chattered in the background. After a minute or so, he spoke.

"It's the natural end of life, you know, but no one wants to talk about it. It's like hiding a bear in the closet, then pretending it's not there. It rattles around, trying to get out, even shakes the cabin, but everyone continues about their business, ignoring it." As the fire crackled, and we sat in silence, side by side, I thought of Michael, who had plunged into his work after we returned from Dad's funeral.

When the call came in the night from Uncle Earl, Michael had held me in his arms as I cried. And he had listened, at first, to the memories of Dad that poured out as I tried to hold on to some part of my father, to let something of him live on. Yes, he had listened, but never said much. It was enough, at the time.

But when we returned to California, he'd jumped back into his work with a new zest. I had thought he was trying to bury his grief, but now I realized, perhaps he was trying to stay away from mine. Maybe he didn't understand how I felt, and was trying to avoid me.

Will's voice interrupted my thoughts.

"I think it's this. When someone close to you dies, you are left with this empty feeling as you personally connect to the life cycle for the first time you can remember. That's why it hurts so much. The sadness of the whole idea, finally realizing, despite your best attempts, you can't control a thing." I looked at him as he gazed into the fire. I wondered how an almost stranger had managed to nail it down, get it right, exactly how I had been feeling. I looked into the fire, not at him, and spoke.

"Nature itself, it can't be controlled," I said. "And that's what's so frustrating." He turned to me, gave me a look of shared recognition.

"Exactly, that's it!" he said.

I nodded. I swished my hot chocolate around in the cup and thought about the many times I'd swallowed down my grief, my fear of dying, since Dad had passed away. Joseph and Tyler came over and stood by the fireplace.

"Tyler has a question he wants to ask," Joseph said.

"Shoot," said Will.

"Well, I was thinking, are you a Cherokee?" he asked.

"I aspire to be," Will replied. Tyler seemed perplexed.

"My great-grandfather was a full-blooded Cherokee, so I'm

only one-eighth. The rest of me is plain old Scotch-Irish.

"See, I told you," said Tyler, poking at Joseph. "I knew it." Then the boys sat down, and began to bombard Will with questions about the Dahlonega gold rush. He brought over several chairs from the table and placed them around the fireplace and began to speak. He told us how it was a Cherokee who had first found gold in 1815 in upper Georgia.

A Cherokee boy playing along a river found a glittering yellow pebble and took it to his mother. It was a gold nugget. The mother later sold the nugget to a white man and gold fever soon led prospectors to the Georgia Cherokee country. Within several years, whites had taken over the land. Thirteen years later, in 1828, around the time Andrew Jackson was elected, gold was found near Dahlonega. The greed of the prospectors and the influence of a president who hated Indians set the stage for the Georgia government to take the land away from the Cherokees. By 1830, the land had been surveyed into lots and distributed in a public lottery to whites. Ultimately, the Cherokees were removed forcibly from their homes, placed in stockades and moved to Oklahoma.

"The Trail of Tears," the boys piped up.

"Exactly," said Will. The boys told him about our visit to Red Clay. As we sat around the fireplace, Will listening to the boys and I deep in my thoughts, I felt content to be right where I was at this moment in time, at the top of the ridge near where I'd seen the moon come up.

CHAPTER 12

Later, Will made us some fried bread from one of his grandfather's recipe. We clustered around him in the kitchen, listened to the sizzling sounds of dough balls being dropped into hot oil. He cooked and talked, serving up tasty, hot morsels of the bread along with the history of the area.

The county name, "Catoosa," sprung from the Cherokee word "gatusi," meaning a high place, hill or small mountain, some said. Before 1838, many Cherokee families had lived in the county, and in particular, in Taylor's Ridge Valley. In fact, the ridge itself had been named for Chief Richard Taylor, who fought along with Chief John Ross, against the removal of the Cherokees to the West.

Through the window of the cozy kitchen, the sky darkened and it was with great reluctance that I announced it was time to leave. Will drove us back to our car in his old blue truck which he called "Eleanor," after Eleanor Roosevelt.

"She's not much to look at, but she gets the job done," he said, as we bounced along, all crammed in the truck cab. His driveway was a long, rutted dirt road that intersected Nickajack

Road higher up on the ridge. We thanked him for the wonderful afternoon, and he promised the boys he'd soon come by to read over Joseph's report to see if he could add anything.

The boys were tired out and agreed to an early bedtime. I tucked them in and went in to change into my nightgown. As I undressed, I felt calm and content as I savored the time we'd shared by the fire. It felt good to have a man pay attention to me. I opened Dad's dresser to pull out my red silk jewelry case so I could put away my gold chain. I unzipped the case, saw only my wedding ring. My pearls, my earrings, my sapphire and diamond ring were gone.

I searched the entire drawer, thinking perhaps the jewelry had fallen out somehow. When that proved fruitless, I searched all the drawers underneath and eventually slid the dresser to one side. Still, nothing. Within an hour, I'd checked out the entire room and most of the house. In the living room, seeing something behind the TV, I bent over and picked it up. It was one of Sammie's fake-jeweled hair clasps. As I looked at it and placed it on top of the TV where she could find it, I could see her smiling face. "Wing," she'd said. Even though she could barely talk, she knew her jewelry.

I had a hunch where my things were. Although I was torn between my growing curiosity and a desire to respect Jolene's privacy, I found myself in Jolene's room, staring at her luggage. Not surprisingly, she still carried the black canvas suitcases Dad had given her for her high school graduation. They'd suffered a lot of wear and tear during her transient life and the canvas was torn and frayed in several places. I opened up the larger one. Inside she had packed every possible gaudy, sexy, trashy item of clothing imaginable, from low-cut rhinestone-covered tee shirts to stretch pants tight enough to fit a cat's ass. Her taste was a combination of Barbie doll and hooker.

Sorting through her things, and finding nothing, I felt a slight pang of guilt. Maybe I had been wrong to suspect her. I moved on to the next two cases, and had to bypass a dozen or more tubes of hot pink lipstick, half-empty varying shades of pink nail polish and several tubes of jet black mascara. Nothing there.

Perhaps she was wearing the "borrowed" items. As a last thought, knowing that Jolene could be duplicitous, I dug through Sammie's Smurf duffle bag. Her clothes were not much smaller than Jolene's, and hers were sadly worn-out and stained, not new. At least she had the usual complement of T-shirts and jeans and hadn't been turned into a Barbie doll, yet. I was about to give up my search completely when I felt something crunch inside one of Sammie's socks. I reached my hand inside and pulled out a pawn slip, dated several days before. In exchange for $450. the bearer of the slip had pawned three items: a ring, necklace and earrings. My jewelry had paid for her new outfit. I took the slip and ran into the kitchen to phone the pawnshop. No answer.

I crawled into bed, although I knew I couldn't sleep. Michael had warned me, and in my need for companionship, I had let my guard down. All three items were worth at least $4,000 and priceless, sentimentally speaking. Michael had given me the pearls when Joseph was born, and the ring had been a gift on our 10th anniversary. I could hear Michael's reaction if I called to tell him. "I told you so. Why didn't you listen? What did you expect?" His words echoing in my head, I drifted off to sleep.

At the pawnshop the next morning my worst fears were confirmed. The pearls and earrings and ring were there, thankfully untouched, due to an automatic 30-day hold that prevented anyone from buying them. I handed the pawnbroker the ticket and cash and got my own jewelry back. Joseph had a hard time understanding, but I explained Jolene had made a mistake; a rather large one. I was furious.

As we arrived back at the farm, I was glad Jolene hadn't shown up. I needed time to cool down. Instead, I found the auctioneer standing in my driveway next to his long trailer truck. In typical southern fashion, he had shown up an hour early.

Mr. Clyde Trotter was a chain-smoking, graying man with leathery skin and an easy, hoarse laugh. He'd brought along his sidekick, a fresh-faced girl of 20 wearing overalls.

"I'm the barn digger, Sue Ellen," she said, pumping my hand. "Dressed to sort through your treasure, and trash."

"I'm glad you're here," I said. "The barn's stuffed. Dad was a big collector. We don't even know what some of the things are."

"We've seen it all. Don't worry, Ma'am, I'll sort it all and tag it. Did you all want to keep anything?" Mr. Trotter asked. I thought about the fight Jolene and Griffin had already had over the items in the house.

"Tell you what, go ahead and tag it all for auction," I said, feeling good to have made an executor decision without bringing in the siblings.

Mr. Trotter snuffed out his cigarette and we climbed up the dusty, creaky stairs towards the mountain of junk. When she saw it all, Sue Ellen remarked, "Good thing we brought the long trailer, Clyde." He agreed and they put on their gloves and began their work. Side by side, they ripped open old cardboard boxes and unwrapped decaying newspaper from jars, dishes, silver and old tools. Roaches and spiders darted out but Sue Ellen was unfazed. She would hold up an item, and she and Clyde would give it a name, then he would set a price. Bellows, $8.50, two sets wooden horse stirrups, $17.50, calf weaners, $3, carving set, $7.50, churn and dasher, $22.50, glass figurines, $20. They had a name for almost every item, and when they didn't, miscellaneous was the category.

We examined an old apothecary jar with the word "Cocaine" written on the side in Times New Roman type letters. I was explaining to Sue Ellen how Dad had said the formula for Coca Cola actually contained cocaine, back in the days when it first came out.

"No foolin'?" Sue Ellen asked. Then we heard a deep cough come from down the stairs.

"They's a marijuana one in there," Uncle Earl's voice chimed in. He thudded up the stairs and sauntered over to the barn digger. I glared at him, but he ignored me and proceeded to plunge his hands alongside Sue Ellen's into the box. She moved her hands over to one side and let him help. In her line of work, she'd probably seen more than her fair share of meddling relatives.

"Watch out for spiders," she warned.

"Gall dernit, gal, no little spider's gonna scare me," he said.

"Uncle Earl, we'll find it. We can handle it. You don't need to be up here breathing in all this dust." I hated having him around. Why did he always have to horn in?

"Missy, it was my brother who died. And I tell you, he tried to give me these apothecary jars last spring but I never got over here to collect them. He promised them to me." Funny how Griffin, Jolene and Earl all recently and suddenly remembered items Dad meant to give them. I wanted to tell him the promise was as good as the paper it was written on, but responded, instead, like I thought an executor should.

"It wasn't mentioned in the will. I have to go by the legal document. That's the way it's done." He spat tobacco juice out the side of his mouth, onto the loose hay covering the barn loft floor.

"Legal, smegal," he curled his lips over his tobacco-stained teeth and laughed, mocking me. "Tell her, Miss Overalls, down here in Georgia we do things the right way."

"Sir, all I know is how to sort and tag," she said diplomatically, and I silently blessed her. She was a smart one, even though she was young.

"What's this 'un worth?" he held up a blue jar. "Your Daddy meant to give this 'un to your Aunt Cottie. Never could find it up here in all this mess." Despite the dim light in the barn, I could tell it was old, although I'd never seen it before. Clyde came over, held it up, turned it upside down.

"At auction, thirty five, maybe forty. I can talk it up, get 'em fightin' for it," he said. Earl reached into his pocket and peeled out three 10 dollar bills.

"I'll give you 30, save you the trouble," he said, thrusting the bills into my hands. He turned and went down the stairs, cradling the jar in his hands. I followed him as far as the top of the stairs to try and get the jar back. This wasn't the way it was supposed to be done. I stopped and watched as he went out the barn door. It wasn't worth it. I stood there, trembling with anger directed at my manipulative uncle. Then I heard him speak.

"Hey, California, forgot to tell you 'bout the mold down in your pasture. Doc says it's a new type, got down in my lungs, it did. He put me on some pills but it ain't workin'." He coughed. "Comes out in the late afternoon. I tell you what he told me.

Mold done killed a feller up the road." He slammed the barn door shut. I hated him.

"Look what I found at the bottom of this chest," Sue Ellen said, holding up a small, unframed painting. It was a still life, done in oil paints. A wooden bowl held three red apples and a green pear, or rather part of a pear. Uncle Earl had stopped by while Mama was painting and helped himself to a bite.

"Ain't half bad," said Sue Ellen, handing me the painting. "Wonder why it was stuck down in this drawer." I didn't answer, but I knew. After the pear incident, Earl had goaded Daddy about his wife putting on airs thinking she was an artist. Daddy scoffed at him but whenever Mama pulled out her oil paints, Daddy suddenly had a craving for one of her fresh peach cobblers or needed her to hold the ladder while he climbed up to the roof to clean the gutters. Her desire to paint led to more than one fight, and finally she only worked on her painting when he was away at work. After she completed the still life, she tucked her paints away with the intention of taking it up again but it never happened. Daddy kept her too busy on any number of household projects until the creative fires within her simply smoldered out for good.

Carrying the painting under my arm, I left the barn diggers to continue their sorting and returned to the house to check on Joseph. When I walked through the garage, the whiff of Jolene's banana nut muffins greeted me. I set the painting down on a high shelf and entered.

"Hi, there, Sis. Trent ran the kids up to McDonald's in Ringgold to get some Happy Meals. I thought I'd make your favorite dessert."

"Yeah, I bet you did," I said dryly. My anger percolated. Having warmed up on Earl, I was now boiling. "Is that what you call an even exchange? My pearls, earrings and anniversary ring for your cheap little muffins?" I picked up the empty box of 99-cent muffin mix off the counter and threw it into the garbage can. She backed away, clutching the potholders in her hands.

"I don't know what you're talking about."

"Big Doug's Pawnshop ring a bell? On Third Street?" She opened up the oven and pretended to check the muffins.

"Look, I had to have a new outfit, Avie. You know how it is. I'm going to get them back, soon's the settlement check comes from the insurance company. It'll be here by Tuesday." She kept her face turned towards the oven and I couldn't stand it. I grabbed her hand and forced her to turn around and face me. I noticed she was wearing a low-cut sheer white blouse and white leather skirt. My ring had purchased this most tacky outfit.

"Look at me when I talk. What did you think you were doing?" I could see the wheels spinning. She was a quick thinker. She drummed up a look of shock on her face.

"Oh my God," she said. "You didn't think I was going to let him pawn it, did you? I swear on my baby's life I was going up there as soon's that insurance check came in."

"The point is, you shouldn't have done that, Jolene. It's not right to take someone's things without asking." Suddenly, a dark, indignant look came over her face.

"Don't you talk to me about right and wrong. What were you doing looking in my things?" She pointed an accusing finger at me. I was trying to think of an answer when she said, "It's your own stupid fault. That's what you get for snooping." I was incredulous.

"What? You're blaming me because I found out you'd stolen something from me? No way, Jolene, this one won't fly. You've proved you can't be trusted."

"Takes one to know one," she shot back.

"It's time you left here," I said. I turned and stomped back to the guest bedroom and started throwing her things in the old canvas suitcases. As I moved on to Sammie's belongings, I felt a tinge of sadness stuffing her toys into her thin little duffle bag. I felt sorry for her, having a flake like Jolene as a mother. My sister entered the room.

"I never did make you that red eye gravy I promised I would," she said. I turned around and faced her.

"Jolene, you wouldn't know a promise if it got up and smacked you in the face," I said, continuing to pack up her things. She bent down and looked under the bed for Sammie's pink sandals.

"Well," she said, "I don't see what the big deal is with your jewelry anyway."

"Michael gave them to me; the pearls when Joseph was born, and the ring was a gift for our 10th anniversary." A loud laugh came from underneath the bed.

"You think it's funny?" I asked. Holding the sandals, she climbed up off the floor and faced me.

"I was wondering what he'll give you for your divorce," she said.

"And what's that supposed to mean?" I asked. She shoved the sandals into the duffle bag as she spoke.

"It doesn't take a genius to see your marriage is shot," she said.

"Get the hell out, now," I yelled. But as I watched her grab the suitcases and rush out of the room, I felt that old, familiar pain stab me in my lower abdomen. And although I despised Jolene, I thought maybe she was right about my marriage.

Chapter 13

After Jolene was gone from the house, but before Joseph came back from Ringgold, I went into the kitchen and dumped the banana nut muffins into the garbage disposal and ground them up. They belonged in the sewer. I filled up the kettle to make myself a cup of hot tea and switched on the burner. Mama had always said that no matter what the situation, a cup of hot tea would make it better. I retrieved the still life from the garage, gently blew off the dust, took it into the living room and propped it up on the bookshelves in front of a picture of my stepmother, certain Mama would have liked that.

The phone rang. It was Rebecca.

She was about to board a plane to Tokyo, she hadn't had a chance to call me on her quick, turnaround trip through L.A. In her rapid-fire manner, she told me what she'd just seen from the taxi window as she drove down Ocean Avenue on the way to the airport. Her words cut the cables that had held up my heart; it plunged like a falling elevator. I was speechless.

"Look, Avie, maybe it's not what we think," she said.

"Maybe," I answered. She told me to hang in there, we'd talk later, and she hung up to rush onto the plane.

The teakettle whistled annoyingly. I poured the scalding amber liquid into one of Mama's Friendly Village china mugs and sat down at the table to cry, releasing weeks of holding back what I had known all along, not in my heart or head, but in my gut. Steam wafted up, passing the tears flowing down my cheeks. The salt tasted good in my mouth; it was tangible proof I was alive and well, and I would go on, despite all the grief I felt at the moment.

The clues had all been there. About two months ago, he'd started working out again and knocked off 15 pounds. "Looks too good for 50," my neighbor Jill had said to me one day after she'd seen him working out at the Y. He had been there for me during my father's funeral, but after, when we returned to California, he had stayed busy working out or at his office. Although we were fine in bed together, when we weren't having sex, I cried a lot, still grieving over Dad. The first few times he tried to comfort me, but I could tell he was impatient with my molasses-like grief. I couldn't blame him. I don't think he understood how I felt; his own parents were alive and well at a Palm Springs retirement resort. After a week or so, he gave up on me when I started to cry. He would quietly retreat to his newspaper or a sports event on TV. I was so caught up in my grief, and settling the estate, I didn't see the marriage starting to unravel. He'd even tried to tell me, in his own way, just before Joseph and I had left on this trip. I replayed his words in my head, "It might be good to get some time away," he'd said, phrasing it perfectly. It was a good idea, but for whom? Me, because I needed to find closure on my grief by settling Dad's estate? Or good for Michael, so he could screw Lily's brains out? Who was the winner here? I braced myself with a sip of the strong tea, and picked up the telephone receiver.

It was lunchtime, but I reached him right away.

"Is something wrong with Joseph?" he asked, his concern evident in his voice.

"No," I answered.

"Well, I'm busy trying to get these papers filed. The messenger's coming at four."

"This will just take a minute," I said. "One quick question."

"Really quick," he said.

"Are you having an affair?" I asked. He was silent for about five seconds. I remembered that he'd once told me when he was discussing witness techniques. A pause, if too long, could mean the witness had to think up the answer. Too long a pause aroused suspicion. Then he spoke.

"Jesus, Avie, no. This is not the time or place for this discussion. I'll call you back—" but I hung up the phone before he could tell me when he could work me in the schedule. I knew I was last on his list, behind the clients, the deadlines, the gym and quite possibly, Lily.

In 15 years of marriage, I'd never hung up on him. It was my way of rejecting him before he had a chance to reject me. It felt good, having abandoned the line before he had a chance.

I picked up the mug and took another sip. I studied the painting on the china, a covered bridge, its roof layered with snow. The bridge was framed with gray-branched trees and it appeared to be the dead of winter. The road to the bridge was deep with snow. The journey over the snow, through the bridge, would be a cold one. High above the bridge, in the background on the horizon stood a mountain, or ridge. I wondered if this is where the snowy road led.

I got up, walked back to the bedroom, pulled out the jewelry case and slipped off my wedding ring. I put it in the case and zipped it shut. I looked down at my naked finger. The area that had been banded for 15 years looked pale and thinner than the rest of the finger, dented in, like it was choked off from its blood supply. I had never noticed before.

I attempted to pull myself together before Joseph returned, and had gotten as far as splashing my face with cold water when I heard him come in. He was alone.

"I brought you something," he said.

"Thank you, son," I said. He put a bag on the table and pulled out two Happy Meals. I looked across the table, saw my handsome, thoughtful son, and the wonderful man he was turning into. No matter what happened to my marriage, I would always have Joseph. I reached out and touched his arm. He didn't pull away in his usual pre-teen fashion, but let my hand rest there for a moment.

Over lunch, I explained that Jolene wouldn't be staying with us anymore, and he didn't seem to mind. He was tired of having to entertain his little cousin. He suggested we invite Xylia and maybe even Will, over to dinner. He wanted to show Will what he'd written on his report, and Xylia's book, especially the part about the silver mine.

"Maybe he can help me figure it out where it is. I've been thinking about it, Mom. How can I do a report on a silver mine if no one knows where it is?" he asked.

"Focus on the journey, not the destination," I answered. "I saw it posted down at Elmwood's sayings board."

"Yeah, right. I'll tell that to Miss Gallardo when we get back," he said. We headed out to the garage and climbed in the car to pick up some supplies for supper and ask Xylia to join us.

We pulled up out front of the store just as Aunt Ardelia hobbled out, leaning her tall frame against her silver-handled cane. She was at least 5'10", and next to her, carrying her groceries, Xylia looked like a midget. Ardelia glanced up at me and scowled, muttered something that sounded like, "Salted nuts, my foot" and pointed her cane towards the back seat of her Buick Le Sabre, directing Xylia to place the groceries there. She climbed into the driver's seat and shut the door. Xylia saw us and waved as we got out. Joseph ran ahead into the store. I walked alongside her.

"She gets around good, doesn't she?" she said.

"She's as strong as an ox," I said. "Like Earl."

"She's more glum, Avie. Remember that movie 'Natural Born Killer'? Well, she's a natural-born pessimist. Most folks celebrate joyous occasions, weddings, holidays and such. Your aunt is just the opposite. She turns every little trauma into a catastrophe. She'll see a lane closed to fix a pothole on the highway here, and the next thing you know, she's telling everyone the interstate is headed our way. It's hard to believe you sprung out of the same cabbage patch."

"Didn't I tell you I'm adopted?" I said. She snorted.

"You wish," she said. We entered the store, passing Ernie, as usual, counting. He didn't even look up. We were walking side by side, and when she saw me under the lights, I knew she could see I'd been crying. She was smart enough not to ask, but to simply hand me a Kleenex.

"So my friend, what do you want for dinner?" I asked.

"Dinner? Why girl, I haven't invited you all over to my place yet. I can't let you cook again," she said.

"This isn't a social invitation, it's business," I said. "Joseph's planning to pick your brain some more."

"And there's this Cherokee guy I want you to meet," Joseph said. She gave me a questioning look.

"We met him the other day up on Taylor's Ridge. He's one-eighth Cherokee and seems to know a lot of history."

"You must mean George's grandson who moved in last year," she said.

"Will," Joseph answered.

"The trespasser, that hunter I met in the pasture that day," I said.

"When you mentioned him before, I thought he was one of those hunters from down in Walker County passing through. Will, is it? He comes in once and a while, but he's not too talkative. I don't think I've seen him but three or four times since his grandfather died. I don't know why I didn't think of him when you described him."

"Me either," I said, holding a jar of spaghetti sauce in my hand. "If I use this, you won't tell, will you?"

"No Ma'am, but why don't you get Jolene to cook something up?" she asked.

"It's a long story Xylia, but Jolene isn't staying with me anymore," I said.

"She took Mom's ring and tried to sell it," Joseph piped up. Xylia waved her hand in the air.

"Don't need to hear it," she said. "What's gone is forgotten." She pointed to several boxes of stock in the back area. "Joseph, want to make a couple of bucks? My arthritis is actin' up and I could sure use the help." Joseph took a deep breath and stood up tall like a man and marched back to the boxes.

"No problem," he said. "Where you want me to put 'em?" She gestured to the almost empty shelves for the canned foods.

"I'd like you not just to unload them, but to arrange them nicely. Okay?"

"Yes Ma'am," he answered. I put my groceries down on the counter and she loaded them in a paper bag as she spoke.

"And after that, we need to change the saying on the chalkboard. Mr. Hank is mad about the one up there. He said, and I quote, 'I don't want to focus on the der-goned journey. And I sure as hellfire ain't focusin' on the destination 'cause any plumb fool can see my next stop is at the funeral parlor.'" We both laughed.

"Can I pick the quote?" I asked. She handed me the jar and I put my hand in and drew out a slip.

"Never look at the moon through trees, an old German saying, contributed by Lisa Bauer. Sounds like Lisa's superstitious.'"

"Or she works for the paper plant that cuts down all the forests around here," she said. I chuckled and handed it over so she could post it.

"I have to drive up and invite Will in person. I don't know if he has a phone," I said.

"Well, would you mind leaving Joseph here for a few minutes? I wasn't kidding about my arthritis. It may be going to rain. My bones are killin' me." She rubbed her hip, then waved me off.

I found myself feeling light and free as I drove up the side of the ridge, like a kid on her way to a birthday party, no parents in sight. I slowed down as I neared the top, looking for his driveway. It was almost hidden by the branches of two low-hanging pine trees on either side. As I pulled in, I heard a light rumble of thunder roll across the valley. I jumped out and knocked on his door, but there was no answer. Perhaps he was still at the school where he substituted. I was just turning to leave when I heard a board creak inside the cabin. The lock clicked open and the door opened about six inches.

He was still dripping wet, from the wedge of him I saw through the crack in the door. His broad chest was covered with dark, damp hair and I could see it moving up and down as he took a breath.

"Avie? I thought you were the postman bringing me a package," he said. "Want to come in?" He swung the door wide open and stood in front of me wearing only a towel, draped dangerously low around his hips. My left hand flew up to my chest, over my heart, but I pretended to fiddle with the buttons on my sweater. I hesitated, looked into his warm brown eyes, then walked over the threshold into his living room.

"I'll just wait while you get dressed," I said, and quickly sat down on the couch and picked up a magazine off the log end table. He closed the door as he went into his bedroom, talking back over his shoulder.

"So what brings you up here?" he said, his voice coming through the crack in the door.

"I didn't know if you had a phone," I said.

"It's old, but it works," he said. It might have been a draft in the cabin, or the wind, but the door to his room slowly swung open, revealing Will in profile. I caught a flash of his strong thighs as he pulled off the towel. He slipped into some jeans and was putting on a flannel shirt as he came out into the living room. He sat down on the sofa next to me. I could feel the warmth rising off him as he ran his fingers through his damp hair and slicked it back. Alone, and sitting this close, it was hard not to feel the possibilities, but I tried to ignore the flush rising up in me. I eased into my flirting patois. Talking was always easier than feeling.

"So where'd you get a name like Avie?" he asked. I touched my reddish-brown hair.

"My dad's younger sister, Avie. My dad always said when I was born, I came out with a full head of red hair, just like his baby sister's."

"I had never heard the name until I met you. It sounds old-fashioned. I like it." He got up from the couch and walked towards the kitchen. I found myself watching the way his slim hips moved. "Would you like some hot chocolate?" A loud peal of thunder rolled over the ridge and the darkening afternoon sky strobed through the paned window. I let out a tiny gasp and clutched my heart. Lightning still scared the hell out of me. He looked at me, walked back over and sat down beside me on the sofa. "Avie?" Concern was written all over his face. He put his arm around my shoulders and patted me like a baby. "Not to worry. The cabin's grounded and this isn't the highest point. It would hit those tall pines about 200 yards up the hill. That wouldn't be so bad, really. You know, the Cherokees believed the wood of a tree that lightning strikes has special powers. A splinter from a tree struck by lightning, for example, was often planted with corn seeds to enhance growth." A bright flash filled the cabin and I shivered. He pulled me close.

The rain began to patter on the tin roof. He tightened his grip on my shoulder, but it wasn't sexual; he was the father protecting the child. I leaned into him and he stroked my hair. The intensity of the rain increased, the patter turned to a downpour and the sound on the tin roof drowned out the sound of my weeping, but I knew he could feel me shake with the force of it.

I cried for my lost marriage, for the early days of sweetness and simple love and yearning turned into the daily grind of familiarity. I cried for the hours I had nursed Joseph through blue lips and empty breaths, alone, waiting for Michael to come home from work. I cried for the young woman I had been, for her hopes and dreams that slowly submerged one-by-one into the sea of motherhood. I cried for losing my own ambitions in the comet's tail of Michael's career. I cried for being fatherless, parentless, for being an orphan with no one on the earth left to love me unconditionally as my parents had. I cried for being stuck with a flaky sister, who betrayed me for a trashy, Barbie doll white-leather outfit. I cried for being blood-related to an ignorant, poisonous uncle who thought he could keep me in line with fear, and I cried for letting him see my fear. I cried for a life that seemed, at this moment, made up of one abandonment after another, in one form or another. And I cried because this is not what I had wanted life to be. I cried for the naïve child I had been, the sweet child who knew none of this, and believed her life would be different. I cried for Joseph, for all the pain I imagined he could have, for his dreams that would be broken.

A handkerchief brushed gently across my cheek. He held me tighter but didn't say a word. He knew the healing power of salted tears. I shivered all over, then suddenly my tear wells were empty, the last bit of bitterness spilled out. The darkness in my soul was replaced by a tiny beam of hope. "Nothing endures but change," the board had read. Life would go on changing, and I would grab onto it, take hold of it, and ride it out. A thick, Indian blanket fell softly around my shoulders, and I heard Will rise from the sofa and walk into the kitchen.

"Young lady, is it safe to say you need something a little stronger than hot chocolate?" I nodded. I heard the clinking of glasses and the sound of pouring. I breathed in the sweet, tempting smell of Tennessee whiskey as he came and sat back down at my side.

"To the restorative powers of a good cry," he said.

"Here, here," I answered. The warm liquor ran hot down my throat and I smiled. He reached towards my face and brushed back my hair with his long, slender fingers, pausing at the nape of my neck, and something shot through me, like an electric jolt. For a moment, I was certain we'd been hit by lightening. It was a scary, heady feeling. He must have felt it too, because he pulled away, but didn't say anything.

I suddenly became aware of the cool chill in the room, the letting up of the patter on the tin roof. We sat there, searching each other's faces for clues. And then I saw it in his eyes, a wariness, or caution, like a horse shying at a leaf blowing by on a trail. And as he looked at me, I wondered if he could see the fear that manifested itself in the tiny flaring in and out of my nostrils. We were two animals who had felt pain. We held the memory of it within our hearts, as a vaccine against intimacy. It was I who stood up, went to the window, looked out at the bulbous water drops hanging on the eaves, too full and ready to fall to the ground.

"It's getting late," I said. He followed me, and stood behind me, looking out the window. When I felt his hot breath on my neck, I knew it was time to leave.

Chapter 14

As I drove back down the mountain, I breathed in the fresh, clean air. The rain had fallen hard, soaked the earth, renewed the soil, left it ready for new growth. The sun aroused itself for a final appearance of golds and pinks, melding into the horizon to the west, just behind the line of treetops that lay on my family's ridge lands.

I arrived at the store as Xylia was putting out the closed sign, and Joseph and I drove home to start dinner. Xylia said she'd drop Ernie off at home, warm him up a pizza, and put on the "Forrest Gump" video. I'd tried to get her to bring him along, but she assured me that he was so uncomfortable being in a strange environment, and so content at home, it was the right thing to do.

It didn't take long for me to make a salad and for Joseph to spice up the spaghetti sauce with some basil and bay leaves Xylia had given him. We set the table. Joseph went into the back room to try and call Tyler. I found myself glancing at the clock, waiting for Will to come. When the knock came at the front door, I ran to let him in.

I came out from the kitchen and he shook my hand warmly, like a friend. When our eyes locked for a moment, I knew we were both thinking of the electric jolt that passed between us earlier up in the cabin. He said he had a surprise for me and reached into his pocket for a small white box, which he handed me. I opened it to find a string of bright multi-colored glass beads, about half the size of peppercorns, interspersed with larger, gray beads that looked like unpopped corn kernels. I pulled the necklace over my head, let it fall down on my chest.

"The gray corn seeds are supposed to be tears, as in Trail of Tears. Legend has it that wherever a tear fell, a Cherokee corn seed plant sprung up. I got it last May when we took the students on a field trip to New Echota, the old Cherokee capital down near Calhoun. I've been waiting to find the right person to wear it."

"Thanks," I said. Joseph came running into the room and interrupted, asked if he could see the beads. I took them off and let Will tell him about the corn seed while I finished setting the table. They moved into the living room and Joseph showed Will his silver mine report, or what he'd written thus far. I could hear Will complimenting Joseph on his footnotes and clear writing.

Xylia arrived and took an immediate liking to Will. She had seen him at the store, of course, since he moved in last year, and even remembered him as a child, coming into the store for caps and bubble gum when he came down from Asheville to visit his grandfather. I served up the dinner and a lively chatter ensued.

"I have a hunch," said Joseph, "that the silver mine has to be down at the old blueberry farm. We've looked everywhere else."

"But remember Mr. Hank," Xylia asked, "down at the store? All he found was rattlesnakes."

"Well maybe he didn't have a metal detector," Joseph replied.

"You don't either," I said. Joseph smiled, and looked up at Xylia.

"She does," Joseph said. "And she said we can use it." Xylia nodded.

"I was sorting through the garage the other day and came across it. Leo went through a treasure hunt phase, right after the

115

golf phase, but just before the bowling phase."

"It works?" Will asked.

"I imagine so," she said. "It's out in the car. May need a battery, or some such. You can go out and get it out of the trunk after we eat."

"Sure," Will said. "Avie, I hope you'll come along with us. The blueberry patch is at the base of Taylor's Ridge. We need you to beat the bushes to scare out the snakes."

"And get bitten first?" I asked. Will smiled at me.

"I'm teasing. The snakes are all down for the winter. But you should come with us. The more pairs of eyes the better."

"I've got some old hiking boots you can wear, Avie. You're about the same size as me," Xylia said.

"And I have some smaller ones that belonged to Grandfather that might fit Joseph," Will said. I served up some dessert, a warm apple pie, the frozen type, but no one seemed to care. Will looked at Xylia's ring and she explained how Leo had given it to her. He ran his fingers over its face.

"Unusual, isn't it?" I asked. He nodded and let her hand go as he reached out to take a sip of the coffee I'd poured.

"Grandfather had a lot of respect for your husband, Xylia," he said. "He said your Leo had a good heart."

"Thank you," she said. "He was a fine man." She twisted the big ring around as she spoke, and I could see she was sad. Instinctively, I reached for my own naked finger, and covered it up. Xylia continued. "Well, not to rush you boys, but why don't you unload that metal detector? I can't stay too long. Got to get on back home before the video runs out."

"Sure. Joseph, want to come with me?" Will asked. Joseph got up from the table, and they went out the kitchen door. Xylia watched Will's slim hips move away from us, then leaned over and whispered.

"He's built nice, isn't he?" she said. I laughed.

"He's young enough to be your son," I said.

"Or your lover," she replied.

"Be quiet, you know I'm married," I said. She grabbed my left hand and held it up.

"Where's your ring?" she asked. She squeezed my hand, and searched my face. I couldn't lie.

"I've decided Michael and I should separate," I said.

"Oh no, I'm sorry," she said. "I was kidding about Will. I thought you were happy."

"I did too, until I came here. Michael seems like he doesn't want to communicate, and when we do talk, he sounds preoccupied, or mad."

"Avie, don't you know men are manure on the phone? I'm sure it will be okay when you see each other."

"I don't know. I think he's having an affair."

"Oh Lordy, he's 50, right?" she said. I nodded. "The same old unoriginal thing. Fearing old age, and death, the husband has sex with a younger woman. These men are as predictable as the sun rising, or the moon coming over Taylor's Ridge."

"Did Leo have one?" I asked.

"Nope, we talked it out when he got to runnin' scared about this age thing. We came to the conclusion that no young lady, or fellow, for that matter, would change the situation. So we faced the mid-life thing together, and amped up our sex lives a notch." I laughed. She asked, "What's so funny? We were good together."

"It's not that," I said. "You just tell it like it is, don't you?" She leaned over and patted my hand.

"I like you like a daughter, Avie. And I wanted to share it with you. Splitting up your family is a big-time decision. Could you find it in yourself to forgive him?"

"I don't know. It's not just the affair thing. Being apart has given me time to think about our marriage. I'm realizing how much we've changed."

"Now, that's different," she said. "That's scary."

"I know," I said. We were interrupted by Will and Joseph dragging the metal detector into the house. Joseph rummaged through the kitchen drawer and found some batteries. After they sprinkled coins on the floor, the detector let out a high beep. Xylia rose to leave.

"Thanks for the wonderful supper, and company," she said as I walked her to her car. "And don't worry, Avie, everything will turn out fine for you." She hugged me, climbed into her car and drove away. As I walked back in the house, I glanced up towards Aunt Ardelia's. I could see her hulking form in the window, illuminated by her living room lamp. And although I could only make out her silhouette, I knew she was watching me with her binoculars. I waved at her, and watched her curtains close rather abruptly.

I looked up to see Will coming out of the garage as I started back in. He had the "Trail of Tears" beads in his hands. He grabbed me by the hand, pulled me over by his truck, out of the large ring of light cast by the floodlight and gently placed the beads over my head.

"I've had a wonderful time tonight," he said, fingering one of the corn seeds that dangled from my neck. "And an even more wonderful time today. Perhaps I'm going to regret this." He leaned in and kissed me hard and full on the lips. I felt a hot surge in my head, and then he pulled away. "See you tomorrow morning." He left in his old truck and I leaned against the wall, feeling as heady and confused as a teenager, and excited about seeing him again in less than 12 hours.

CHAPTER 15

But it was less than that when I heard the light tapping on the front door. I looked at the clock; it was 7:15, and Will was here already. I threw on my pink robe and quickly ran to the door. I spoke as I opened the door.

"Early bird gets the worm," I said, expecting to see a smile crinkling above Will's high, tanned cheekbones. But it was Michael who stood on the other side of the screen, wearing a scowl.

"Could you stop playing games and unlock the screen door? It's freezing out here." I unsnapped the lock and opened the door and he huffed past. I had forgotten how imposing he could seem. He set his bag down and gave me an accusing look.

"Look, I don't know what the hell you're thinking, calling me up like that, making me leave the office at a time like this." I backed away from him.

"Whoa, wait a minute. I didn't ask you to come here."

"You hung up on me, dammit. After accusing me of sleeping with Miss What's Her Name. This is not you, Avie. What was I supposed to do? Sit back and wait for the divorce papers to arrive?" He truly looked distraught, and I noticed he hadn't shaved.

His nose was red and stuffy and I felt sorry for him. I took his coat and steered him toward the kitchen and a cup of coffee.

"Let's try and keep our voices down. Joseph is asleep." He sat down and calmed down a bit as he sipped the hot liquid.

"Avie, are you having some kind of break with reality? I'm busy trying to run a law practice and make a living, and you're down here going off the deep end."

"Not really," I said. "I'm taking care of the estate, on my own, I might add, with no help from you."

"Jesus Avie, is that's what this is about? I thought I told you what to do. How hard can it be? It's not like you're in litigation, with clients breathing down your neck and deadlines or something." His face reddened as he said it, but as I looked at him, I wondered why, even now, it always had to be about his work.

"No, it's not litigation. It's mean uncles and snakes and dirty barn attics and flaky sisters who pawn away your jewelry. It's dangerous molds and spying aunts."

"What are you talking about?" he asked.

"I've told you all this before, but obviously you weren't listening," I said.

"I've been swamped, Avie, I'm over my head with this case. How could you expect me to hear all the details of your life?"

"Details is what it boils down to. Life that is. And when you stop listening, you no longer share a person's life." He heard me but didn't want to understand.

"Can we just get this thing straightened out so I can get back to my case?" he pleaded.

"Put it off for another five, six years? Wait until we have nothing in common anymore?" I felt the anger rising in my cheeks.

"Come back home with me. The estate can ride for a few weeks." He reached out and took my hand, gave it a familiar squeeze. His eyes were sad, pleading. "I need you."

"Miss What's It's Name not enough?" I asked.

"I don't know where you come up with this stuff, Avie," he said. It was not the right time to reveal what I knew, what Rebecca had told me.

"When we've talked, you've been so distant."

"Yeah, two thousand miles distant, to be exact. I've missed you, Avie." He hung his head down and I noticed the grays blended in with the blonde, more than the last time I'd seen him. And when had his hair thinned so much?

"You sure have an odd way of showing it," I said. "You wouldn't even talk to me." He sighed.

"I thought you would have learned by now. That's the way it is when you're married to a lawyer. Remember what I told you when we got engaged?" I did.

He had wedged a quick lunch in between two court appearances. I was between assignments for the magazine, and not in a hurry. We dined overlooking the Pacific, at a Mexican restaurant on the end of the Santa Monica pier. He explained that he loved me, and asked me to marry him. He slipped the diamond and sapphire ring onto my finger. Before I could say anything, he kept talking. I'll always love you, he said, but remember, the law is my mistress. We'd laughed and kissed. At that time, I found his passion for his career endearing.

The week after our honeymoon, his firm took on a big case defending an oil company, and he started working seven days a week. During the week, when we both worked, I didn't miss him much. But as I whiled away weekends in museums, at movies, and lunching with girlfriends, I realized how demanding his job really was. I loved him and when we were together, he made up for the lost time. We laughed and loved and felt we had it all—careers and love and eventually, family. When Joseph was born, it was I who took off from work to care for him, and when his asthma surfaced in his third year, I finally gave up on my career, for the most part. A few bylines in a regional publication didn't seem as important as my son's health. Besides, Michael was worried a nanny wouldn't take as good care of our son as I would. So I stayed at home with Joseph and Michael's career flourished. He kept up his hectic pace and finally branched off and started his own firm. For the last five years, his work had demanded more of him. His work problems had become the part and parcel of our conversations, and in fact, it was impossible to talk about much else. His career had sucked me in like a comet's tail, spreading out, affecting everything it passed over; its trail was so bright, it was difficult to see even the brightest star in its path. All things paled in comparison to the practice of law, at least in Michael's mind, except perhaps Joseph's battle with asthma.

We sat there in awkward silence, my hand in his. At that moment, I felt sorry for him, and even loved him. Perhaps I had been stupid to expect more out of my marriage. We heard a soft thudding come down the hall. Joseph rubbed his eyes as he came closer.

"Dad?" He said. Michael stood up and held open his arms. Joseph ran to him and they hugged.

"Hey, bud, had to come check on you myself. How you been, partner?" Michael asked.

"Great, Dad. We're going to search for the mine today, at the blueberry patch. Will's bringing his metal detector."

"Oh, the kid you told me about?"

"No, Will's part Cherokee. And he's not a kid. About 35, isn't he Mom?" Joseph looked at me.

"About," I said, and cast my eyes downward and thrust my hands into my robe pockets. I could feel Michael's penetrating stare.

"Well that's great," he said. "I'm glad your mom found time away from her fiduciary duties to locate a treasure hunt assistant." Joseph didn't seem to notice the sarcasm in his voice.

"You can come too, Dad," Joseph said. "There's room in his truck. Tyler and I will ride in the back."

"Sure," Michael said. "My plane doesn't leave until tomorrow afternoon. The experts' depositions were postponed for a couple of days."

"Good," Joseph said. "I'll get dressed." He ran down the hall. Michael glared at me.

"What are you doing planning an expedition with these fall pollens out here? You want to kill the boy?" he asked.

"He's been fine, he wears his mask."

"And who's this Will?"

"He's a neighbor, lives up on Taylor's Ridge. He's been very helpful to the boys." He stepped closer to me, and grabbed me on the shoulder.

"Is that all?" he asked. I paused while I thought of an answer. I didn't know myself. There was a knock on the door. I broke away to answer. It was Will.

"Hi there," he said, handing me a long wooden walking stick. "Ready to beat the snakes off?" Michael had followed me, taken hold of my left hand, and loomed beside me. From the look that crossed Will's face, I knew my husband wasn't smiling.

"Will, this is Michael. Michael, this is Will, our neighbor," I said. Will reached out to shake his hand, and I thought Michael would jerk his hand off. His shake was severe and firm, and when Michael let go, I could see the color return to Will's hand where Michael had squeezed too hard.

"Good to meet you," said Will. "You've got a bright son."

"Thanks," said Michael. I ushered Will into the kitchen and poured him some coffee and told him we'd be a few minutes. Michael followed me to the bedroom and closed the door.

"Is that ponytailed wonder your new boyfriend?" he asked.

"No," I answered. "He's a friend." He grabbed my left hand.

"Then where's your ring?" he asked.

CHAPTER 16

I didn't have a chance to answer about the ring; not then, anyway. We were interrupted by Joseph, who burst into the room wearing Will's grandfather's boots.

"How do they look?" he asked, pointing to the old, worn, but clean boots Will had brought over.

"Take them off. I'm sure they're filled with mold and mildew," Michael said. Joseph hesitated.

"I'm better, Dad. I haven't had an attack since I got here," he said. Michael looked at me.

"It's true," I said. "It must be the air. His levels are good."

"And I don't have any other boots, Dad. I can wear my mask, promise," Joseph pleaded his case. Michael sighed.

"Whatever. I'll pack your meds for the trip," he said, but Joseph quickly corrected him.

"I can do it, Dad. Just get ready." Joseph left the room. Michael looked annoyed.

"You don't actually let him pack his own medicines, do you?" he asked.

"Yes," I answered. "I always check over the bag before we leave the house." He shook his head in disappointment.

"Avie, you can't be too careful. This is not something he should be doing," Michael said. "And those decrepit boots. You've got to make him take them off."

"He has to grow up sometime, Michael," I said. "Even if you don't want him to." He shook his head in disgust. I left the room before the lecture started. We had fallen back into old patterns so easily.

In the kitchen, Will sat at the table, waiting, empty coffee cup in hand.

"If it's not a good time today, we could reschedule," he said.

"Today's perfect," I answered, counting out apples into a brown paper sack. "Two, three and four," I said, slamming the fruit into the bag. "I hadn't planned on company."

"So I gathered," he responded, and his voice was cool and even and I couldn't tell what he was thinking. I glanced up at him, and he winked. I laughed. He was easy to be around.

The best thing one could say about Will's truck "Eleanor" was that it still ran. There were dents in the blue paint, and the front cloth seats had worn away at least two decades earlier. Will had covered the seats with soft, functional horse blankets. What "Eleanor" lacked in youth, she made up for with her friendly face, two, partially hooded headlights on either side of a wide-mouthed grill, and her rounded curves, the style of the '50s. She was quite accommodating with running boards on either side of her bed, just behind the passenger doors.

"It looks too old to be on the road," Michael said, staring skeptically at the truck.

"Younger than you, I'll bet," said Will, smiling. "She's a 56 Chevy." Michael bristled, then climbed into the cab with some hesitation.

Will climbed up the running board onto the truck bed and spread another horse blanket in back for Tyler and Joseph. They scrambled in and settled down for the ride. As Will climbed into the cab with us, Michael grumbled that having passengers in the back wasn't safe and probably against the law. Will overheard and reassured him that the ride would be short. The engine cranked up, and we were off.

Wedged in between Will and Michael, with my feet up off the floorboard, I felt cramped and restless. As we headed south, I looked up at Taylor's Ridge on my left and realized I was, at that exact moment, caught in the middle.

On my right was my past, on my left, my present. My future was as unclear as the fog lifting off Taylor's Ridge on this fine October morning. We rode along in an awkward silence, except for the rattle of the ancient vehicle and Michael's deep, exasperated sighs. He kept glancing back nervously to check on Joseph. Will broke the silence.

"During the Civil War, Sherman marched his troops down this road on the way to burn down Atlanta," Will said. "My grandmother told me a roving band of men tried to steal horses from folks who lived around here."

"It's true," I said. "I heard the same thing from my grandma. The Gatewood Scouts they were called. Came to take her mother's fine, gray mare, Snip, who she'd hidden up in the woods near the ridge. She wouldn't give her up, even though they threatened to burn her house. She climbed on Snip and rode along with them, towards Calhoun, into the night. It was almost dawn when they finally realized they'd never seen such a stubborn woman, and they let her turn back."

"You come from a very strong-willed family," Will said.

"Obstinate is more like it, and Avie, you meant to say her grandmother, not her mother," said Michael. "Do the math." I calculated in my head.

"Okay, it might have been my grandmother's grandmother," I conceded, as I slumped down.

"There's a fine line between stubborn and strong-willed, I've found out in my teaching," said Will. "But the point is, Avie, you should be proud of your family history. Your ancestor was a strong woman to stand up to the Scouts and to hold onto what she believed in."

"Thank you," I said. Michael blew out a breath, and didn't say anything but out of the corner of my eye, I saw him studying Will. The truck slowed down, and turned left onto a narrow road leading up the side of the ridge. We passed over a large pothole and our bodies flew up in the air for a second. Michael put his arm behind me on the seat to steady himself, or perhaps even me, but I leaned forward and gripped the dashboard. I didn't need the bastard.

"Take it easy," Michael directed Will.

"Sorry boss," Will answered. "These shocks are gone."

"We should have taken my car, Avie," Michael said.

"And miss this fun, wild ride?" Will shot back. "I don't think so."

The road wound up the side of the mountain, but we went only halfway, pulling off about an eighth of a mile up. We turned into a long driveway and parked beside an old wooden shack.

The fruit stand had long been boarded up for the winter, it appeared. Weeds sprung alongside old unpainted wooden walls. Empty gray baskets were stacked on the side, and a faded "Bring Your Own Pail or Use Ours" sign was propped up along one of the shack's walls. Spreading out behind were several acres of blueberry bushes. Another small sign read, "Watch out for yellow jackets."

Will opened the tailgate, letting the boys out. Michael ran up and grabbed Joseph.

"You have your epi-pen in the medical kit, right?" he asked.

"I think so, Dad," he said. Michael glowered at me.

"If he's allergic to yellow jackets, a sting could kill him," he said. Joseph looked from him to me, and back again.

"Michael, the doctor never tested for it, but we do have the emergency shot, and we'll all be careful," I said, trying to calm him. Will spoke.

"I doubt too many are around this time of year. It's too chilly. Come on, Joseph." He beckoned Joseph forward, and Joseph ran up and walked next to Will. Michael shot me a critical look, and ran to catch up with Will and Joseph.

"Do you own this land?" Michael asked Will.

"Nope," Will answered. Michael said nothing, fidgeted with his hair, twisting a small tendril by his ear, which he often did when he was worrying about something. "Okay boys. Where do you want to look first?" The boys gathered around Will and Joseph pointed up the side of the hill.

"There," Joseph said. "That guy from Atlanta, the geologist, said the veins are in the mountains or ridges, maybe by a stream. I think it would be higher up."

"Yep," said Tyler, "me too." He and Joseph slapped palms in a high-five.

"All right," Will answered. We all started up the slope with Will and the boys in front, Michael and I behind them, bringing up the rear.

"Wait!" Michael shouted. His voice sounded fearful and I wondered if he'd spotted a yellow jacket. We all stopped and everyone stared at him.

"Did you get permission?" he asked. Will looked skeptically at him for a moment, then replied.

"Old Widow Jones won't mind. As long as we don't leave any trash."

"You need written permission," Michael said. Will turned around and came back down and stood right in his face. In California, I'd never seen anyone do this to Michael. He could be intimidating.

"Do you see a no trespassing sign?" Will asked. "Look around. Is there a locked gate?" Michael bristled.

"No, but written permission is required from the owner," he said.

"The custom here is verbal permission. Widow Jones told me I could come here anytime, keep an eye on the place. I think I know what I'm talking about, boss." The tension between the two was so thick you could cut it with a knife and serve it for lunch. I looked at Joseph and saw him reach into his backpack for his inhaler. I knew at that moment he had inherited my distaste for conflict. It got to me in the gut, and Joseph in his bronchial tubes. I had to smooth things out before he launched into a full-blown asthma attack.

"Michael, I think it'll be fine," I said. "Widow Jones is 90, if she's a day, and she's Xylia's friend, so no problem. I remember she always let the church groups come up here in the summer."

But Michael stood his ground and didn't budge. I told Will to go ahead, we'd catch up in a minute. Will and the boys turned and continued up the slope, and even though Joseph was at least 30 feet ahead of me, I could see his shoulders drop down, relaxing, as he moved away from us, up the hill. I turned to face the lecture.

"You've become awfully mouthy," he said. "And careless. Look at this freak you're hanging out with, allowing our son to follow him up the side of a mountain, trespassing, no less. You're acting like a dumb Georgia cracker." His face was grim and he looked at me like I'd committed a federal crime.

Deep down in every woman, under the layers of pretense, resides a witch. Some women pass through their entire lives and the witch never surfaces. In others, the witch rises up every month or so. In some, the witch lies close to the top, bubbling and warm, awaiting the right combination of offenses, in actions or words, to bring it to the boiling point. All at once it shoots out, like scalding hot lava. I felt my face redden and my blood pressure rising as I looked at Michael.

"I'd rather be a Georgia cracker than Woody Allen on steroids," I replied. "There's no excuse for your neuroticism, and criticism. We were doing fine, just fine, before you arrived. I know being here in the country isn't your cup of tea, and I know you are used to calling the shots in your law firm. But we're here now and I know what I'm doing. If you don't want to go with us, if all you can do is moan and groan and worry, then just stay here in the truck because I won't let you make my son sick."

"Meaning?"

"I mean he hasn't had much trouble breathing and just now, he had to use his inhaler while you were arguing with Will."

"That's low and ugly," he said.

"And true," I answered. "If you want to come with your son, and you can act like a normal, civilized human being, not a trial lawyer, then let's go join them. Otherwise, we'll see you in a couple of hours." I turned away from him and followed the boys up. I heard Michael trudging up behind me, and I knew it was not because of me, or what I'd said. It was for his love of Joseph.

It was a long morning. To his credit, Michael didn't say another word, at least to me or Will, although he spoke to Joseph and Tyler a few times. Will largely ignored Michael as well, as we wove our way through the woods above the blueberry patch, and let Joseph and Tyler lead the way. As we combed the area, Will kept snapping off small twigs to mark where we'd been so we wouldn't backtrack.

Joseph remembered reading something about an oak tree being near the mine, so we carefully searched around the trunks of every oak in sight. Joseph told us he'd read that if we actually found silver, the metal detector would go nuts. Several times the metal detector beeped, but we found nothing more valuable than a 1971 quarter.

In the early afternoon, Will directed us to the clearing in the trees that overlooked the valley. He spread down a blanket and pulled out some cheese and fry bread, and I handed out the apples. Joseph shared all he had learned with us, explaining that the ridge and valley were made from folded, faulted rocks. Taylor's Ridge had probably been the valley at one time.

"The silver is probably in veins between other types of rocks," he said. "Of course we could find native silver."

"You mean Native American silver?" asked Tyler.

"No, I mean a silver nugget. The geologist says that's called native silver. Sometimes rocks containing silver come to the surface of the ground."

"That should be easy to find. The sun will reflect off it," said Tyler.

"No, it will be a dull gray, and could be mixed in with another type of rock, like gold or galena," Joseph said.

"You know Joseph, it would be a lot easier if I bought you a silver nugget off the Internet," said Michael. Will and I laughed, but Joseph replied, "Focus on the journey, Dad, not the destination."

"Touché," said Michael. We cleaned up our things and set out to finish a small strip to the south that we hadn't covered. Again, we found nothing notable but we all stopped to look up when lightning flashed across the valley below. The clouds were rolling in over the ridges, and a thunderstorm seemed imminent.

"We'd better get down before the lightning hits one of those tall pines over there," said Michael, studying me to see if I was scared. I smiled back at him.

"Well, if it does, we'll have to cut ourselves a branch from it," I said. He looked bewildered, until Will spoke.

"The Cherokees thought a tree hit by lightning had special powers. Cherokee ball players painted themselves with the charcoal from the burnt splinters in order to get the energy of a thunderbolt when facing opponents."

"Awesome," said Tyler.

A tiny snorting noise came from Michael. The peals of thunder began to drown out our voices. We hurried back down the mountain through the blueberry patch, back towards the ridge lands where I'd first met Will.

CHAPTER 17

Will dropped us off and Michael went into the bedroom to call the office. The boys and I changed clothes. Maybe it was the rain, but the boys wanted to stay in and watch TV, so I ran into town to get some takeout for an early dinner.

As I drove through the storm towards Ringgold, fat raindrops pounded against the windshield and I felt safe and cozy, comforted by the wipers swishing back and forth on the windshield. I wished I could keep riding along in this warm, blissful state forever, never having to face Michael. But the relationship, or non-relationship, had to be moved forward. There was the issue of Lily, not to mention telling Michael why I wasn't wearing my ring. I put it all out of my mind when I pulled into the restaurant driveway and saw a familiar truck parked in the lot.

Sitting just off I-75, the Waffle House is the gathering place for many of the locals. When a stranger or newcomer comes in, gossip stops and all faces turn to stare, especially at folks not dressed in overalls or shirts and caps bearing the Bulldogs, 'Bama or Tennessee.

Through the rain-splattered window, I saw Uncle Earl in his

overalls sitting at a table across from a businessman dressed in a suit. They both sipped coffee as Earl pointed at some large sheets of paper spread out on the Formica table. A bubble-headed waitress with a missing front tooth interrupted them by pouring more coffee. Earl grinned at her and must have said something funny. She threw back her head and slapped him on the shoulder. After she left, Earl opened up a green spiral notebook and flipped through the pages, pointing and explaining something to the man. Using a hand-held calculator, the man punched in some numbers and nodded. Earl folded the papers on the table into a neat rectangle and handed it to the man. They shook hands and the businessman walked right past my car and climbed into a silver Lexus with Cobb County plates and drove away. Earl flirted a little longer with Missing Tooth, and came out. I ducked down on the front seat so he wouldn't see me, but the rain had started coming down so hard and he ran so fast, I don't think he had a chance.

I walked into the Waffle House. A dozen well-fed country faces turned to look at me. Their steaming buttery grits, hot biscuits and hash browns would wait while they entertained themselves by staring at the stranger. I buttoned up my purple, puffy jacket and wondered why their mothers hadn't taught them not to stare. They did it boldly, unabashedly.

A redhead with a blossoming stomach came to take my order, mostly breakfast items, except for the patty melt Michael wanted. I asked for an unsweetened iced tea, and the waitress announced to everyone in earshot, "Unsweet? Ma'am we don't have any made up right now." A low buzz started around the room and I might as well have worn a sign around my neck that read: "not from around here" or maybe even "danged Yankee." I sat down on a stool at the bar and observed the interaction between waitress and the cook at the grill.

"Scattered, triple, smothered, hold the yolk," the redhead chanted. The cook repeated this back to her, "Scattered, triple, smothered, hold the yolk." She continued, "Cheese omelet on the side, bacon, cheese plate, scattered peppers, pecan waffle, scramble," and he chanted it back, word for word, as he scraped the spatula against the hot grill, flipping eggs. She went on, "Double patty cheese melt, hold the mayo," she continued in her singsong voice. The cook echoed back, clanging down the spatula at the end like cymbals at the end of a song. The waitress turned to another customer, a good-looking, silver-haired man with a generous girth.

"Hello honey, how you doin?" she asked in a syrupy voice. She took his order and recited her mantra, and the cook responded again. In the background, the custodian's squeegee scraped against the window. The chanting of the waitresses and the cook, the squeaking noise against the glass and the scraping and flipping clang of the spatula against the grill created a rhythm of its own. Performance art, southern style.

Then another stranger came in. All eyes, and the men's more intently, turned to stare. Although it had to be 40 degrees out, she was dressed in a tight, sleeveless yellow flowered knit tee shirt and wore a clanging silver bracelet. Her breasts showed through her shirt as she eased onto a stool. One old geezer appeared to wipe drool off his chin as he looked at her shapely figure, and one salt-and-pepper haired man next to the girl licked his lips. But then three stick-thin, scantily-clad children burst through the door and hung onto her bare arms. The men looked away from her, retrained their eyes on the aging waitresses that scurried up and down behind the counter. Funny how a couple of kids in tow can turn off most men in a New York minute.

A few seconds later, the waitress called out my "to go" order, and it was with some reluctance that I left the comforting warmth of the always entertaining Waffle House. Watching other people's lives is a lot easier than dealing with your own. Carrying two brown bags of food, I ran out into the light misty fog that had replaced the rain. I drove back to Taylor's Crossing slowly since the fog was thick, and I dreaded what lay ahead that evening with Michael.

I found him sitting at the table with a half-full fifth of vodka in front of him and an empty glass. While I handed out the food, he poured himself a glass. I hadn't seen him drink in years, since the doctor had advised him not to, due to the cholesterol medicine he took.

The boys and I wolfed down the omelettes and waffles, while Michael studied the oil that seeped through the paper around his patty melt. He grabbed some paper towels and made a big deal of blotting the excess oil off the meat before taking his first bite.

"The frigging food down here will kill you," he said, jumping up from the table and throwing the patty melt away. Tyler winced. "What's that they say? Deep fried, fried fat?" He reached on top of the refrigerator and pulled down a couple of Little Debbies. He studied the labels.

"Look at the frigging fat content, will you? Jesus, did you know this has carnauba wax?" He searched the room, looking for a target of his brewing hate for all things southern, and aimed his gaze at Tyler.

"Tell me, do they teach you about the food groups in school?" he asked. Tyler's eyes widened and his body tensed up as he tried to think of the right answer. Any answer would be wrong, and he knew it. He turned to me.

"Excuse me, Miss Avie, I think my Daddy expects me home," he said, and got up from the table. I started to follow, but Tyler assured me he could walk the short distance home.

"Okay," I said. "Call me when you get to the trailer." Michael burst out laughing uncontrollably and took another long sip of the vodka as Tyler exited.

"Trailer trash, this is classic," Michael said, slapping his hand on his knee. Joseph rose from the table and took his asthma and allergy pills.

"I'm not feeling well," he said.

"No wonder," Michael said. "Your mother dragged us out in those woods today."

"Whatever," Joseph answered. "Anyway, I think I'll go read in my room."

"Don't forget to take a shower son," I said. "Wash off the pollens."

"Those that haven't already landed in your bronchial tubes," Michael said.

"Right," my son answered. I moved into the kitchen and

rinsed off the silverware. Joseph came over and made a point of giving me a big hug, unusual for him. He was at that awkward age where displays of emotion were considered childish.

"Night Mom," he said. "Thanks for taking me to look for the silver mine." Michael interjected.

"Hey, what about me?" He held out his arms. Joseph gave him a quick hug and I noticed he had grown taller. The top of his head rose several inches above his father's shoulders.

"Night Dad," he said, and walked down the hall. Michael went to watch TV. I grabbed a scrunchy, pulled my hair up in a ponytail, and began cleaning up in the kitchen. I shook powdered cleanser into the sink, wiped down counters, dried all the dishes in the drainer with a clean cotton towel. I scrubbed the sink, turned on hot water and sprayed out the last vestiges of cleanser. I opened the cabinet and began rearranging the glasses, by height. How many clean kitchens in America are the result of orchestrated avoidance of one's spouse? I wondered. And then the phone rang. It was Tyler. He'd gotten home fine. I could hear Jolene chattering away in the background and as strange as it seemed, I wished I were there, down in Trent Crimmel's trailer, not here. As I hung the phone up, I smelled Michael's alcohol breath behind me, felt his eyes caress the back of my neck.

Everyone has her sweet spot, that special square inch of skin that responds to the slightest touch. Mine is midway down my neck, a nibble away from the ear. A most vulnerable spot, because revealing one's neck opens up one's carotid artery, and the possibility of death. Michael had bitten me there, lightly of course, when he wanted to quickly initiate the lovemaking. He knew I would turn to putty, and in our early years of marriage, he'd coined my sweet spot "the key to Pandora's box."

I felt his finger just below my ear. He traced my sweet spot lightly and slowly and I felt goose bumps rise from his touch. But instead of melting, I stiffened to the core when he jerked the "Trail of Tears" beads Will had given me.

"When did you start wearing dime-store beads instead of the pearls I gave you?" he demanded. A chill shivered down from his fingers, into my neck, my chest, and finally into my heart. He must have felt it. He let go of the beads, then roughly grabbed my left hand and jerked it up, looked at my bare finger. His grip was tight and unrelenting. It was a cruel gesture. "And what's this supposed to mean?" he asked, staring at the white ring of skin that had replaced my wedding band. It was now or never. I took a deep breath and turned around, looked into his bloodshot eyes, inhaled his fetid breath.

"I know about you and Lily and the Shangri-La," I said, and I felt his grip soften, but just a hair. "Rebecca saw you two coming out in the middle of the afternoon." I tried to pull away, but he tightened his grip again.

"I can explain," he said. I felt tears welling up in my eyes.

"Go ahead. Tell me why you kissed her, for Pete's sake, on Ocean Avenue, in broad daylight, coming out of a hotel."

"Jesus Avie, you don't believe that, do you? Rebecca's just jealous of what we have. She'd like us to break up so you could join her in her Sunday afternoon lonely hearts club."

"Don't Michael. You're digging yourself in deeper." I sobbed and turned around and grabbed the sink ledge. The pain of knowing what I had suspected for weeks traveled down my gut, through my legs. My knees buckled as I felt the world as I'd known it slipping out from under me. "Why her? Why now? What does she have that I don't?" He grabbed me by the shoulders, stared in my face for a moment, then replied.

"She's a good listener, Avie."

"I've been listening to you for our entire marriage, haven't I? Doesn't that count?"

"You haven't heard a word I've said since the day your father died."

"No?"

"You were all wrapped up in yourself, too busy crying." As we stood there, looking at each other, I realized he was right. My grief had been the catalyst for our marriage's unraveling. He continued. "It was a lousy kiss, that's all."

"A kiss? Tell me, Michael. What does a kiss mean?" An ugly smirk came over his face.

"You tell me, Avie, you ought to know."

"What's that supposed to mean?" I asked, realizing as I said it, I'd let my guard down around this trained, verbal assassin, and he'd drawn me into his web, like a spider trapping a helpless insect.

"I'll answer for you, with another question. What's worse? A kiss in broad daylight on a city sidewalk or a kiss in a dark driveway in the Georgia countryside? You tell me, Avie." And as I watched the words coming out of his $375-an-hour lips, I realized why he'd left his trial and jumped on a plane. Aunt Ardelia or Uncle Earl must have seen Will kiss me in the driveway and called him. And once Michael realized he had some competition, he came to check it out. Our being apart had been "a good idea"--until he felt threatened.

"You can't have your cake and eat it too, Michael. I'd say that's rather basic."

"And neither can you, my dear," he reached for the vodka, poured another glass. He was smashed.

"I'm going to bed," I said, and started towards the bedroom. He grabbed my shirt and pulled me back. I stiffened my body and tried to pull away, but even drunk, he was stronger. He grabbed my shoulders and forced a sloppy, intrusive tongue through my tightly shut lips. I pushed him away but he started to follow me as I turned to walk away. Then I heard a cough. He stopped and we both stared at Joseph's door. I grabbed the inhaler and went to check on him. Michael followed.

Joseph sat on the edge of the bed, gasping. He grabbed hold of the inhaler and took a puff, then got up and ran into the kitchen for his medicine bag. We followed and Michael tried to help him get the portable nebulizer out, but Joseph pushed him away and did it himself, loading up a small vial of Proventil, a bronchial dilator, into the nebulizer's plastic holder. I watched his bluish lips as he struggled to breathe. He was like a prize-fighter between rounds, wide-eyed and puffing. Finally he clicked on the switch and a fine mist started to come out of the breathing mask. He inhaled deeply and calmed down. The pinkness started to come back into his lips.

We remained there in silence, the three of us, except for the whir of the machine. Michael sat on the bed on Joseph's left side, patting his back reassuringly but glaring at me. I felt uneasy under his critical eye and leaned down to pick up Joseph's jeans and shirt he'd thrown on the floor.

"I think I'll just toss these in the washer," I said.

"A lot of good that'll do," said Michael. "You should have done it an hour ago." Joseph coughed and started to choke. Michael patted him on the back.

"You know, we can talk about that later," I said, and left the room to put the laundry in the wash.

Later, after Joseph had settled down and was breathing easily, and had gone back to bed, we found ourselves sitting in the living room across from one another. The asthma attack had sobered Michael up. He sat in the tallest chair in the room; I had somehow ended up in a hard-backed chair in the corner, and I might have been a child wearing a dunce's cap awaiting the dreaded scolding from the teacher.

"I think it's time you took a serious look at your irresponsible actions in relation to my son," he said. I stared at his lips as they formed a battery of words that he aimed at me like tiny missiles. I ducked into my secret place.

Daddy is screaming at Mama again. The eggs aren't done right. They're too hard, the toast is too soft. Mama murmurs an apology, fueling the fire of anger. And why haven't the children weeded the lawn yet? He has seen the clippers thrown to the side of the house, the children standing under the mimosa tree, stripped down to their skivvies and dressed in scarves. See-through scarves. What kind of a mother is she, to let them behave like this? Doesn't she know dancing will cause the boy to be queer, and the girl to be a whore? And what will he tell the neighbors when they see the children dancing around like heathens, half-clothed, in the moonlight? Mama mumbles, they were staging plays, pretending to be in paradise. He snorts, and the sound of his chair being pulled away from the table scrapes along the floor. A signal for me to escape before my father begins ridiculing Mama's efforts to bring culture into our lives.

I run away from the sounds of fighting in the dining room,

retreat to my secret hiding place. I open the door and tiptoe down two of the basement stairs. I close the door, and shut out the noise. The dirty and splintery wooden stair presses into the back of my bare thighs, but the pain is okay, preferable in fact, to hearing the war on the other side of the door. I huddle in the dark, safe behind the door, away from the fight, where no one will find me, bent over as the tentacle of fear grabs low at my belly.

"I said the molds. How many times do I have to tell you?" Michael demanded. "It started in California with those frigging geraniums. Any rational human being would have realized that further exposure to that trigger would set him off." Michael's lips stopped for a moment while he waited for me to absorb what he had said.

"So you got rid of my geraniums because you assumed they were bad for Joseph?" I asked, rising from my chair and standing. "The fact is that the doctor assured me they weren't, especially since they were outside and nowhere near Joseph's room. Any rational human being," I said, "looks at the facts."

"You're full of it," he spat out, the words. "Your negligence brought on his asthma." We both heard the click of Joseph's door open from down the hall. He yelled.

"Stop it, both of you. Now!" He coughed, and then continued, "Your fighting is making me sick." I turned and went to the hall closet, pulled out a blanket and a pillow and threw it on the couch. "Good night." I didn't even look at him as I headed to my room, where I shut and locked the door.

I sat down on the bed, exhausted. Standing up to my husband, facing conflict, had drained out every last bit of energy I had. And what Joseph had said was true, I realized. Until Michael's visit, he hadn't had any other attacks or used his nebulizer. Something had to change. I lay down on the bed, pulled the covers up to my neck and shook all over until the peaceful veil of sleep overtook me.

Chapter 18

I opened my eyes when I heard low deep voices out in the living room. The sun streamed through the window and I got up to open it. As I inhaled the crisp air of fall, I saw the squirrel scrambling around on his customary branch. It was a beautiful day. I brushed my hair and looked in the mirror, saw traces of my mother in my strong nose. But I was not my mother and would not suffer through a marriage disintegrated into a perpetual battleground, as hers had. I thought of Michael and how I had stood up to him the day before and felt lighter and freer than I had since his unexpected arrival. I pulled on my jeans and a sweater and went out to see what was going on.

Michael lay on the sofa watching the "Today" show. Uncle Earl stood in the kitchen, making coffee.

"That husband of yours snore?" he asked.

"No," I said, passing him as I went to pull out a coffee cup.

"Hrumph," he mumbled, glancing back towards the sofa.

"Don't you need to check on your cows?" I answered. He ignored me and poured two cups of coffee. He walked over and handed one to Michael.

"Someone 'round here's got to show your man some southern hospitality," he said. "Now Michael, I can get you a good $3,000 an acre, guaranteed. Get it down on paper, if you like. Y'all can wrap on up down here and get the little lady right on back home where she belongs."

"Michael doesn't have any land to sell," I said, and came around the corner to join them in the living room. "And you and I both know the land is worth twice that much, if not more." Michael sat up to take a sip of his coffee.

"What'd the appraisal come in at?" he asked. My stomach lurched, and I hesitated.

"You did get the appraisal, didn't you?" he said. "Jesus, Avie, what have you been doing?" Uncle Earl cleared his throat. Michael sighed. "Right."

"The appraiser was backed up," I said. "She's supposed to come Monday. The surveyor expects to start mid-week."

"That's the most backasswards thing I've heard," he said. "Why didn't you get the appraiser out after the surveyor?"

"Gall dernit, gal, you don't need neither one," said Earl. "I can show you them boundaries myself."

"It's okay, Earl. I've walked the land several times. Why don't you butt out of this one?"

"He's just trying to help, dear," Michael said.

"That would be a first," I replied.

"I'll take you out this afternoon and show you. It's thick and deep and ain't good for nothin' but pasture."

"I'll take him myself," I said.

"What about the boundaries, Avie?" my husband asked. Second-guessing me was his worst habit.

"Dad left a map in the safety deposit box," I said.

"Your sumbitchin' map don't show where Jensen put up that fence and took over 'bout a quarter an acre," said Earl.

"Adverse possession," said Michael. "I'd need to see it." He twisted a small wisp of his hair as he talked.

"I can show you," said Earl.

"So can I," I said. "It's on the southwestern corner, near a stand of cedars." Earl hrumphed again.

"That Brangus bull's pretty jumpy," he said. "One of them cows may be in heat."

"We'll be careful," I said. I went in to the bedroom to retrieve something. My uncle drawled on.

"Last time one was in heat, Akins' old bull jumped the fence, gouged my Brangus 'fore I could scare him off. Let me tell you, Michael, a man's got to watch his animals when they're in heat. Keep them other bulls out." I walked back into the room, carrying my riding crop.

"The Brangus won't be a problem." I snapped the whip in the air.

"Touché," Michael said. Earl stomped out into the kitchen and I heard his cup clink against the sink as he set it down. He passed by us and went to the front door, clamped his big hand around the knob and hesitated.

"Y'all think it's funny, but y'all will wish old Uncle Earl was there when one of you gets hurt, or one of you falls down them abandoned wells."

"You have a nice day, too," I said as he left. Michael had a slight smirk on his face but he didn't say anything.

We remained civilized with one another through breakfast and even until we dropped Joseph off at the store with Xylia. We hadn't spoken about it, but I felt we both didn't want to risk another asthma episode.

We parked the car back in Dad's driveway and set out on foot. I wore my Bulldogs cap, hiking boots, old jeans, a thick wool jacket and carried the riding crop. Michael, on the other hand, was dressed in a jogging suit with new white Nike tennis shoes, the only pair he'd brought along besides his loafers. We passed through the gate by Uncle Earl's and started up the grassy slope in silence. The steady rhythm of our feet moving up the first gentle ridge was mixed with the sound of the breeze rustling through the trees and an occasional cow bellowing. I felt myself ease up a bit. Michael might have felt the same way, because at the top of the first ridge, he turned and looked across the valley, towards Taylor's Ridge.

From this view, I could see the mountain had changed since

my arrival. Many of the leaves had fallen and others had been blown off by the wind. Smudges of gold and orange were punctuated with the deep and enduring green of the pines. There was no hint of smoke curling up from the familiar chimney.

"You can see a lot from here," Michael said.

"Yes," I said. "Come on. We've got a long walk ahead." I led, he followed, approaching the tree-lined banks of the Little Chickamauga Creek where I'd first met Will. A herd of cows were down at the edge drinking. A small calf eyed us from where it stood by its mother's side, about 60 feet away.

"Let's go this way," I told Michael.

"That's not a bull, obviously" he said, continuing to walk slowly towards the mother and calf. "There's a narrow part over here where we can cross."

"Michael," I tried to warn him, but it was too late. The mother cow lowered her head, stamped her front hoof and trotted towards him, her calf in tow. Michael spun around and ran towards me. The cow slowed down, but continued following us until we ducked behind a huge sycamore. Losing sight of us, the cow suddenly gave up.

"What the hell?" he said.

"A mother cow is more likely to charge you than a bull. It's her way of protecting her offspring."

"Your uncle never told us that," he said.

"Earl only sees things from the bull's point of view," I said. Michael sniffed several times and we both looked down at his tennis shoes. The toes were covered in brown, gooey cow manure.

"Shit!" he said.

"Shit it is," I said and he surprised me with a smile.

"Now let's just hope there's no dangerous mold lurking in that cow pie," I said.

"Or a snake," he said, and suddenly we were both laughing. He swiped his shoes along in the grass, trying to get off some of the gunk. I watched. Despite his best efforts, the front of his shoes bore the green stains. We turned and crossed over the creek at another narrow spot and things felt better between us. I wondered how long this could last.

We moved up a series of ridges and headed into the deeper woods. I heard his footsteps stop.

"Want some water?" he asked.

"No thanks I've got my own," I answered, pulling out my own bottle and moving over to find some shade.

"I've got a parched mouth," he said.

"That's the least of your problems," I nodded towards his dirty shoes as I stood under an elm tree, facing him. He walked towards me, put his soft, perfect hands on my shoulders.

"Avie, I'm sorry."

"For?" I shrank back towards the trunk of the old elm.

"Everything," he answered. I looked up into his blue eyes. Bedroom eyes, I'd always called them. Bluish-gray today because he was wearing navy blue. Chameleon eyes, chameleon man. His always changing eyes narrowed and his nostrils flared as he breathed deeply and stepped closer to me, gave a slight squeeze to my neck, an invitation.

Something stirred deep inside me and I tried to push it away. But the feeling was low down in my belly, persistent. Did I want to fall into his arms, and see where this feeling took me? But the feeling grew stronger and became what it was: pain. The curl of fear had surfaced. I removed his hand from my shoulder, where it rested awkwardly, heavily.

"Remember when you said it would be good to get some time away? You were right, Michael."

"Yes, and now it's time to come back." He took another step closer to me and I shrank back against the strong trunk of the tree.

"Why? To pick up where we left off? Continue tearing each other apart? No, Michael, I'm not going back now. I'm not ready." A look of disbelief crossed his face, then he stepped closer to me, and I felt his cold fingers tug and snap the string of beads around my neck. I saw his face come closer to mine, saw his hands come towards me. He shoved me hard against the trunk. My back stung as he pressed me against the rough bark.

"No," I yelled. "You're hurting me!"

"It's him, isn't it?" he demanded, his face an inch away from mine. I gasped for air, instead sucked in his stale breath. I wildly flailed my arms, reached for the riding crop propped on the side of the tree trunk, but it was hopeless. He had me pinned.

Suddenly air and light rushed in and he was flung away from me. I gasped for oxygen and stared as he seemed to fall in slow motion. Backwards, into the ground, his head crackled against the dried leaves when it hit the banks of the creek. His arms were flung out to the side, his eyes wide and startled as he landed on solid ground. I sucked in huge breaths of air and was stunned to find Will standing in front of me, his hands balled up into hard fists. His fierce eyes shifted away from Michael's still form, back to me.

"Is he okay?" I asked. He walked over and bent over Michael, slapped him hard in the face. Michael's chameleon eyes opened, startled as he saw Will's dark, angry face and mass of black hair hovering over him.

"Looks fine to me," Will said, turning to me. He reached towards me and I placed my cold, shivering hand into his warm chapped hand, an outdoors hand. He gathered the broken strand of beads off the ground, led me away, down towards the valley. I heard Michael call after us.

"Avie?" But I ignored him, as he had so often ignored me.

CHAPTER 19

Will took me back to his cabin, steered me to the sofa and covered me with a soft Indian blanket and put on some black gospel music. He made a pot of coffee and poured me a large cup. He held up the bottle of Tennessee whisky and a shot glass.

"One?" he asked.

"Two," I answered. I needed something strong. My back smarted where it had been pressed into the bark. A flesh version of bas-relief, compliments of Michael.

Will brought in our coffee and we sipped in silence for a while as I tried to absorb what had happened. I swallowed the hot coffee slowly, concentrated on not letting it burn my throat, although I was having a harder time managing the waves of dismay and anger that assaulted my stomach. I heard Will's voice.

"I hope you don't think I was spying," he said.

"What?" I asked. "Of course not."

"I saw you set off and followed you as far as I could with my eyes. I wasn't going to track you, but after you disappeared over the first ridge, I started to worry."

"How'd you know? I mean, I didn't know myself. He's never-"

"I wasn't thinking about that," Will said. I looked at him sitting there on the fat, overstuffed recliner, his dark hair framing his smiling bronzed face. His chestnut eyes were as deep and sincere as the first time I'd seen him. He lowered them and appeared to study the blue and white flecks on the coffee cup. "To tell you the truth, I was spying. I wanted to see how you two acted when you were alone." He looked up at me, his face filled with concern. "I hope you're not angry with me."

"Hardly. I can't imagine what would have happened if you hadn't been there."

"I can," he said. His right fist clenched the chair's soft, worn leather arm and the color drained out of his knuckles. He got up, grabbed his keys.

"I'm going to set him straight," he said.

"No, I can handle this," I said. I set down my coffee cup, moved the blanket aside and stood up. "I'll talk to him." He came over and gently placed his hand on my back. I pulled away from his touch.

"You're hurt, aren't you? May I?" he asked. I nodded and he slowly lifted up the corner of my shirt and looked at my back.

"Ouch!" he said. "You're going to need something on that." He left for a moment and returned with cotton balls and witch hazel, which he dabbed over the abrasions. The cold wetness stung in places, but it was a good pain, a tactile mantra to keep me focused on what I had to do while I had the courage.

"I've got to talk to him," I said. "Before he leaves."

"I'm coming with you," he said, pulling my shirt down. I thought about showing up with Will and what would happen. After verbally abusing him, Michael would tell him to leave, Will would refuse and Michael would end up getting another dose of those tanned knuckles.

"I think it would be better if you drove me and waited outside," I said. "What I've got to say may take a while. Do you mind waiting?"

"Patience endureth forever," he said, smiling. "Old family motto."

"So you've been reading the chalkboard down at Xylia's?"

"On the rare occasion when I go in," he said. He grabbed the keys off the rack and opened the door. "Ready?" he asked. I followed him.

"As I ever will be," I said, and we got into his truck and rattled back down to Dad's house. Before I got out, he squeezed my hand.

"Good luck," he said. He waited in the truck and I went in to face Michael.

The dirty tennis shoes were placed on the side of the ramp by the back door. I entered the kitchen and heard the shower running from the center bathroom. I went back into the rear bathroom and freshened up. I washed my face, changed into clean pants and shirt. I went into the living room and sat in Dad's old rocker, waiting for Michael to come in. I tried to calm myself, plan what I'd say. I looked out the front window, across the fields up towards the ridges, imagined about how it would look in a month or two with a light dusting of snow. And later, perhaps, how winter rain would freeze onto the branch tips of the redbuds, creating clear icicles that made the branches bend down and creak under their weight. I heard Michael's footsteps at the end of the hall. I placed my feet solidly on the floor and braced myself.

He walked into the living room rubbing his hair with a towel and was startled when he saw me. We locked eyes. Now his were gray, playing off a black turtleneck. Under the left eye was an ugly reddish swollen area. His eyes traveled up and down my body as though he were inspecting me for damage. I was glad Will wasn't so far away. I focused on the puffy area under his eye, not his eyes, and began.

"I'm staying here," I said.

"Okay, until you finish the estate. If you'd stop carrying on with Tonto you might have more time for your fiduciary duties."

"His name's Will and we're not carrying on anything. I've done as much as I could with the estate to this point. Things move slowly down here." I took a deep breath and continued. "We're skirting around the real issue. Tell me Michael, what do you think just happened out there in the pasture?" He wrapped the towel around his neck and simply looked down at the floor, collecting his thoughts. Then he looked up at me with cool, even eyes. His face was shaven clean, flushed with color and he had a hint of Armani aftershave. His shirt was neatly tucked into belted pants. I realized I was still attracted to this handsome man standing across from me. I sighed but as I exhaled, there was my breath again, reminding me how he behaved a mere two hours earlier. The lawyer spoke.

"Your boy attacked me. He's lucky I didn't suffer any permanent damage."

"You're kidding, right?" I asked, but even as I spoke I could see he wasn't. "Michael, you hurt me."

"I was trying to make a point." He stood twisting the towel in his hands and didn't say a word.

"Didn't you hear me yell no? You were hurting me."

"I didn't hear you," he said. And I believed him.

"You haven't been hearing me for a long time," I said.

"Ditto."

"Then I think you'd agree with me, we're just not communicating," I said.

"That's an understatement," he replied.

"We haven't been, for quite a while. The only thing we've done lately is fight."

"Your point being?"

"Joseph is right. Our fighting is making him sick, it has for years."

"That's ridiculous."

"Would you agree it's possible?" I asked.

"Anything's possible," he said, spitting the words out at me. "As you've proven so aptly. If you'd stuck to your estate work instead of going off on these wild goose chases, we wouldn't be having this discussion." He stood in front of the high shelf that held my mother's oil painting. I looked at Mama's perfectly painted apples and half-eaten pear and her art spoke to me, told me of all she had sacrificed to stay in her marriage. I would not allow myself to end up like her.

"I think we should be separate for a while and see what happens," I said. He studied me with chilly, calculating eyes, and I could see the next volley forming in his head. He was, and always would be, an excellent trial lawyer.

"If you insist, Joseph and I will leave tonight."

"No. Joseph's staying here with me until your trial is over and you have time for him, until we can work something out." He kept playing with the towel, which he'd rolled into a ball. He passed it back and forth from one hand to another.

"Who do you think you are? Judge Judy? He's coming home with me."

"I don't think so," I said.

"Try and stop me." He spat the words out, took a step closer to me. I could see the ruddy flush of anger starting up the side of his neck. He would not intimidate me into giving up the best thing that had come out of our marriage. I thought of the mama cow we'd seen out in the pasture, pushed aside my fear, concentrated on forming the words in my mind.

"Tell me Michael, how many hours have you spent with Joseph in the last two months?" He stepped away and glared.

"That's not fair. I've had back-to-back trials. He threw the balled towel into the wall.

"Okay, let's forget the past. How many hours will you have to give him next week? Next month? Does your Miss Lily babysit in addition to her other duties? That's a touching thought."

"You're reaching, Avie. All because of something you think happened out there in your freaking cow patch," he shot back. "I'm sorry you took my firm approach as something else, but your anger with me has nothing to do with Joseph." As he spoke, he twirled a blonde tendril of hair around his fingers.

"You're right, Michael. Why don't I let you explain this to him?" I turned my back to him as I peeled off my shirt, exposing the abrasions he'd created with his overwhelming need to control me. He looked at my back for a moment, turned away so I couldn't see his expression. He mumbled something and left the room. I pulled my shirt back down and straightened my hair. My curiosity propelled me into the bedroom where he was carefully folding up his clothes and placing them in the suitcase.

"What did you say?" I asked. He looked up at me. His face was serious, but all played out.

"This place makes me crazy. The food, the people, the cows and all these trees. I hate the South." He turned to the closet and pulled out the black wool jacket I'd given him for his 48th birthday. He carefully slipped his long arms into the sleeves and then concentrated on lining up the holes with the buttons. I had replaced the original silver buttons with black plastic buttons emblazoned with anchors. We'd often joked that one day, when Joseph grew up, we'd sell everything and buy a big boat and sail to Hawaii. At that moment, I couldn't imagine a boat large enough to allow me the distance I felt I must put between us. As I watched him carefully buttoning, I gulped back remorse over lost dreams. Sadness lay there just under the surface, ready to rise up and crack my fragile composure.

"Would you please call Xylia and tell her I'm coming over to pick up Joseph? I want to spend some time with him before I leave."

"Sure," I answered eagerly, in an overly civil tone. He strode out the door. I picked up the receiver, dialed the store. Joseph answered.

"Elmwood's Country Market, Joseph speaking," he sounded cheerful and competent. I complimented him and told him his dad was on the way. He bargained to stay longer, until I explained Michael had to leave that night. He wanted to know why so soon, and I told him we'd talk about it when he got home. As I hung up the phone, I heard yelling coming from the driveway. In my haste to be conciliatory, I had forgotten Will was still out there, waiting. Michael would try to provoke him into a fight. I ran through the house, out to the garage, just in time to see Michael peeling out in reverse. Will sat in his old truck, his hands on either side of the steering wheel. I stood by the door of the truck, and placed my hand on the window frame.

"What happened?" I asked. He turned and looked at me with a poker face.

"Nothing," he answered, but I had heard the raised voices. I looked away from Will's face, down to see his white knuckles clutched around the steering wheel in a death grip, and I knew. Michael had spread his verbal poison.

"Are you all right?" I asked. He nodded.

"I think I'd better leave," he said, reaching to turn the key in the ignition. I thrust my arm through the window, let my hand rest on the sleeve of his buckskin jacket.

"What did he say? He threatened you, didn't he?" I asked.

"No," he answered. The ancient engine started up unevenly. He hit the gas peddle hard, revving it up.

"He tried to provoke you, then?" He looked me full in the face, searching for something with his chestnut eyes.

"I assumed you were separated, or divorced," he said.

"We weren't, officially, that is. I mean, we are now," I answered. He banged his hand on the wheel. I pulled away from the window, and continued. "I'm sorry. I didn't realize you thought I was~"

"Available? It's not your fault, Avie. I should have known, even though I never saw a wedding ring. If I'd known you were still together, I wouldn't have let myself~" his voice trailed off. I waited for him to finish, but he continued by saying, "I'm not into wrecking homes, Avie. Taking another man's wife away isn't my style. It's not honorable."

"We're separating," I said. He nodded.

"Good," he said.

"And I need some time to figure things out," I said.

"Okay," he said. "Call me if you need me." he said. I nodded and watched him back out of the driveway, thinking of the times I'd chosen not to wear my ring, or worn gloves. The times I'd acted too friendly. I went back inside and stayed in Dad's bedroom when Michael returned with Joseph. I stood by the window, stared out at the bare branches of the tree where the squirrel had frolicked in days past.

The weather had turned ugly. The sky was overcast and gray. The wind scattered leaves across the backyard, past the squirrel, hunched down in a ball, against the chill. Thick charcoal clouds clung to the side of the ridge and the sun showed no sign of reappearing. It looked so miserable outside, that if I didn't know any better, it could have been the last day on earth.

CHAPTER 20

Just before dusk, Michael knocked on the door and came in. He thought we should tell Joseph together, and I agreed. We sat down at the table, and explained it to our son. He didn't seem surprised or upset at all but in fact looked relieved. He asked if he could be excused to go watch a dinosaur program on TV and left Michael and me alone.

Over coffee, we discussed the details of our separation. Our talk went smoothly until I brought up the money. He bristled when I asked if the bookkeeper could deposit a check every week to cover my expenses.

"Oh, sure. I'll continue working my tail off while you and your new boyfriend get better acquainted," he snapped.

"It's for Joseph and me. And I'm not talking about a huge sum, Michael."

"How much?"

"About $ 500 a week, a lot less than I'd spend back in California," I answered. A lot less than your take home pay, I thought, but didn't say.

"I'll think about it," he said, gauging me for a reaction. I hesitated, contemplating what he didn't know. I had kept several credit cards in my own name and I had savings as well. And who did he think he was fooling? California was a community property state and half of all we had was mine anyway. Knowing all this, I remained calm when I finally spoke.

"Okay, Michael, you think about it." He seemed disappointed that I had given him no argument, then went into the other room to call his office.

It was twilight when he left. We walked him through the garage and stood in the driveway, where he hugged Joseph tightly and whispered something in his ear. Joseph nodded and went back inside. Michael then turned to me.

"Take care of him," he said.

"The best." He hesitated, headed towards the rented car. He turned around before he got in and spoke.

"Avie, I'm really sorry. I didn't mean to hurt you." I nodded as he got in the car. I walked back to the garage doorway and watched as he drove away, saw the red taillights disappear in the darkness. I returned through the garage, entered the house and shut the door to the cold and my 15-year marriage. Back in the kitchen, I looked out the window up at the ridge where the Yankees had long ago spilt a wagonload of supplies. The people of the valley had gleaned something good from someone else's disaster. My marriage had wrecked, but like the people of the valley, I would make the best of my situation. My thoughts were interrupted when Joseph came in and asked when the trial would be over.

"A few weeks," I answered.

"I'm going to miss Dad," he said.

"I know, but it will go quickly. You'll be okay." And I knew we both would.

"Can Xylia come over for dinner?' he asked.

"Sure," I said. I called her and she said she hated to leave Ernie. I encouraged her to bring him along, although she had explained he was uneasy in strange places. Joseph promised to let him watch ESPN. She said we could try and she arrived with Ernie shortly after she closed up the store. Ernie shuffled along behind her, and immediately headed towards the flickering light of the TV in living room. Xylia threw a brown sack on the countertop.

"I wanted to make your husband some of my dumplings," she said, pulling out apples. Joseph and I both looked at each other and then I told her.

"He had to leave."

"He's in trial," Joseph said. "Mom and Dad are getting a divorce."

"Joseph!"

"Well it's true, isn't it?" he asked. He and Xylia quizzed me with their eyes.

"We're trying a trial separation, and then we'll see what happens."

"Lord-a-mercy girl, you sure move fast, don't you? Joseph, would you run out and get the other bags out of the back seat? I'll need that flour and what not. I'll make this batch up for you and your mom. And look in the trunk. I found something I think you're going to like." Joseph left and Xylia turned to me.

"What happened?" she asked.

"It's complicated, but the short version is it hasn't been working for either of us for some time. And we finally realized the tension in our relationship was what was making Joseph so sick."

"Well, I'm sorry to hear it, but a person has nothing if they don't have their health. So I guess until you all can straighten things out, it's for the best." I sighed.

"I hope so. I know I'm scared as hell."

"You'll be alright. You're spunky as they come." She reached out her sturdy arms and embraced me. I smelled her scent, the usual bacon and musk cologne odor lingering in her silvery hair, and I was comforted. I knew at that moment that the disjointed pieces of my life would eventually fall into place, like the final pieces of a jigsaw puzzle. When you first opened the box, the task seemed impossible, but with work, patience and time, the big picture fell into place.

Joseph came back with the bags and set them on the counter.

"Is this what you brought for me?" He held up a plastic bag that contained some envelopes.

"That's it," she said. "Leo and his uncle down in Savannah corresponded when he was in his treasure hunting stage. I was cleaning out the hall closet the other day and came across a box of letters. Sorting through Leo's things is like an archeological dig. Anyway, I pulled those out, thought you might enjoy them."

"Thanks." Joseph grabbed his dust mask, slipped it on and went into the living room to read the letters. He lay on the sofa, near the lamp. Ernie sat perched on the edge of a hard-back chair, rocking back and forth as he watched the ballgame. Xylia started cutting the apples, and I diced celery and onions to add to my soup. We were a symphony of chopping.

"When you're ready, I'd like to hear the long version," she whispered, and added, "For therapeutic purposes of course. You'll feel better if you share it."

"Just a minute," I said, and went in to turn up the TV volume. When I returned to the kitchen, Xylia told me she was glad I'd turned up the volume, to give us privacy.

"Little pitchers have big ears, and big pitchers do too," she inclined her head toward the living room as she said it. "Ernie doesn't say much, but I know he hears things, although I doubt he'd gossip." She mixed the flour with some salt and started to cut in the shortening to make the dough.

"Like his mama?" I said. She nodded her silvery head, where she kept at least a thousand of the valley's secrets locked away.

"According to Michael, the trouble started when Dad died. Michael said I was so wrapped up in my feelings that I didn't notice his."

"Is it true?"

"Well, I have been dealing with Dad, one way or the other, since his hip surgery. You know, he got so lonely after his wife passed. I tried to be the perfect daughter, but I guess I didn't realize I was being less of a wife. Since Dad died, Michael and I've been quarreling over every little thing."

"But you didn't before?"

"Well, yes, but not so much. I always made myself available to listen to his problems, which all revolved around his work. The next trial, the last trial, the secretary with attitude, the emergency motion that needed proofreading. There was always some new crisis at the office that seemed far more dramatic than anything going on at home, or in my life. He was, and is, consumed with his work."

"Which provided you with a nice income," she said.

"Yes, that's true. At first, he worked seven days a week, and he said the sacrifice was worth it. He would make us rich. His working was a means to an end."

"I'd have a hard time getting mad about that," she said.

"Yes, but he had made enough money five years ago that he could have cut back, but he didn't. He had become a workaholic. The means became the end."

"He doesn't work as much now?" she asked.

"No, five and a half days a week, we're talking 12-hour days, about 65 hours a week."

"But you're accustomed to it, right?"

"Let's just say I went along with the program until my step-mother died. Then I started coming out here to Georgia more and more, tending to Dad's needs. For the first time in our marriage, I was away from Michael for extended times. I missed him."

"Absence makes the heart grow fonder?"

"No, that's the strange part. I missed him the way he used to be, an early version of Michael, the way he was when we were first married."

"What had changed?" she asked.

"Well, in the beginning, even when he'd had a bad day, he always had time to ask about my day, and he acted like it was important. But the more he worked, the less patience he had for me."

"So he turned from this sweet, attentive guy into?"

"A man unable to turn off his critical nature. He would come in all wound up from work and question how I handled even the slightest things—the way I cooked the fish, the way I managed the gardener, the way I disciplined Joseph. No matter how hard I tried to do things perfectly, he always found some flaw and pointed it out. He's an expert at finding flaws."

"Must have done wonders for your self-esteem." We both laughed.

"I think every husband does this from time to time. I know Leo did. But I knew deep down, he loved me."

"Yes, but then when we were apart, I saw how other people lived life on a day-to-day basis. Every time I flew home, it was a crash course in reality. His negativity and need to control was getting harder to take."

"When you're the boss at your work, it's hard to turn it off at home. That's what Leo always said."

"I know. I tried to be understanding, but we always ended up fighting. This time was the worst."

"Because?"

"His behavior seemed rude and boorish. You know those places where the R.V.'s dump their waste tanks?"

"I've heard of them."

"Well, this last time I started to feel like he was the R.V. and I was one of those waste tanks. He just kept spewing out his negativity. And then I finally realized it was making us sick." I pointed to the living room where Joseph was reading. "Even he said so." She shook her head.

"Folks change, don't they?"

"I'll say."

"But deep down, don't you still love him?"

"I don't know." I took a deep breath. "He was trying to make a point and he pushed me against a tree, out in the woods." I pulled up my shirt and showed her the abrasions on my back. She moved in closer and squinted.

"I don't have my reading glasses, but from what I can see, it looks like you were scratched by a pack of wild tomcats."

"It's abrasions from the bark. He did it right after I told him I wasn't going back with him."

"How horrible," she said.

"It is, it was. Xylia, he's never done anything like that before. Right now, all I want is to stay away from him."

"I'm sorry for you, but you did the right thing. I guess it's a small comfort for me to say at least there wasn't another woman," she said. I rolled my eyes. "Oh Lordy, tell me there wasn't."

"Well, I think there is, or was, but I don't know for sure. "

"You could hire a private detective."

"What's the point? It doesn't matter, really. I don't want to spend my life with a man I no longer trust. I can't stand the daily barrage of negativity, or the fighting that makes Joseph sick. Any one of these reasons would be enough to split up, but taken altogether, I'd say the odds of the marriage working out are slim to none."

"Time heals all wounds."

"Except for the fatal variety."

"Lordy girl, I'm feeling depressed myself."

"Well, you asked."

"Heck, I was hoping for some racy gossip, not a derned soap opera." I laughed. "Is there anything at all for you to look forward to?"

I stared through the kitchen window, up towards the dark, hulking outline of the ridge against the starry night and felt a spark of hope.

"Maybe." I didn't tell her what I knew in my heart.

Joseph charged into the kitchen carrying one of the letters in his hand.

"Listen to this, Mom." He read from the letter. "You asked about the legend of the silver mine. My daddy said the Indian had the map on him all the time and never let it out of his sight. There's an old Indian fellow at the top of Nickajack, up near the crest of the ridge, might know. Lives in a cabin before the road bends off towards Dalton. Mom, he's talking about Will's house." Xylia took the letter from him.

"I think he's right, Avie. Will's granddaddy is who he means." Joseph continued reading. "He's right private, keeps to himself. But if you carry him some pipe tobacco, and ask him nicely, he may talk with you. By the way, what did you do with the silver ring you wrote me about? The one you found down in the field near Temperance Hall?" Xylia's hand flew to her finger and she touched the ring she had found in Leo's jacket. "He's talking about this. And I always thought he'd gotten from a customer, or picked it up at an estate sale."

"Temperance Hall is where the Cherokees cooked the stew,

the one with the rabbits, right Mom?"

"Yes, it is."

"Well, maybe it was a Cherokee ring." We all leaned in to study the ring's face.

"And if it is, these could be pictures."

"Petroglyphs?" I asked.

"Yes!" Joseph said.

"The jagged lines must be the ridge," Xylia said.

"And the squiggly line is Little Chickamauga Creek," I added. We all looked at the wavy lines beyond it.

"The ridges," said Joseph.

"And those two parallel, vertical lines on the right?" I asked. "With the three lines coming out of the top?"

"A tree, that's a tree!" Joseph said. Hearing the commotion, Ernie stood up and moved a step closer to the kitchen, and his mother. Xylia held out her finger, showed off the ring.

"I've been wearing a picture all these years and didn't even know it," she said. Or, I thought, but didn't say it, a map.

CHAPTER 21

The next few days of activity left me little time to think about maps, Michael, or even Will. I had to focus my efforts on settling the estate. The appraiser and surveyor had both finally called and wanted to begin their work right away, with me accompanying them on the ridge land. Although the school had faxed out a fat homework packet to the drugstore in Ringgold for Joseph, he begged to tag along to see how the surveyors did their work. I checked with the surveyor, Ben Blackwell, a lean, redheaded man in his 30s, who was agreeable, as long as we didn't talk too much. Joseph put on his mask and we set out into the crisp air along with Ben and his assistant, and the appraiser, Jeannie Lou Harris, an older brunette dressed in jeans, blazer and hiking boots that showed as much wear and tear as her crinkled face.

We passed Aunt Ardelia's and Uncle Earl's without incident, although I knew Ardelia had probably been watching us with her binoculars ever since the Blackwell's Surveying truck had pulled into Dad's driveway a half-hour earlier. Our activities would provide Ardelia with many hours of entertainment, and I stifled a laugh as I wondered what she'd do if I sent her a bill for watching my goings on, and the changing cast of characters I'd brought into her dreary life. Jeannie Lou huffed and puffed her way up the first slope and then declared she had to stop and get her breath. I politely stopped alongside her, after pointing the crew to the first corner of our property, about a hundred feet ahead, where an old capped iron rod stood. Joseph went ahead with the surveyors, and I was glad he had when I saw her reach into her pocket and pull out a Marlboro Light. "I know," she said. "These durn things are killin' me, but I've tried to stop and can't. I plan to die with an oxygen tank in one hand and a cigarette in the other." She coughed. "Care to join me?"

"No thanks," I said, pondering her demise. Would she blow herself up with the combination of fire and oxygen, or would the cancer kill her first?

"You plan on sellin' this parcel as one piece, or splittin' it up into smaller parcels first?" she asked, bringing me out of my daydream. I looked out towards the verdant ridges rising above us, towards the stand of trees by the Little Chickamauga and the cluster of cows moving along slowly away, up into the woods. It was a difficult question.

"Do you need to know in order to evaluate the price?" I asked.

"Let me answer you this way. There's not much call for the bigger tracts. This is what, about 240 acres?" I nodded. "Let's say you divide it into eight parcels of 30 acres each. These eight smaller parcels are worth more than the big one."

"Kind of like paying more for the small boxes of Tide instead of one large one?"

"Exactly. So how do you plan to sell it?" she asked.

"I'm not sure yet. Can you figure it out both ways?" She snuffed out her cigarette with the heel of her foot.

"Whatever you want, Jeannie Lou can do," she said. "My logo back in the '80s. You ready?"

"Absolutely," I answered, and I followed her towards the men, who were ahead at the first corner of Dad's property.

Ben set up a telescope-type device on a tripod and explained the process to Joseph, who watched. The measuring device was an electronic telescope that measured distance and angles by shooting out an infrared laser beam to a reflector placed up at the next corner to be measured. Ben's assistant walked ahead with the reflector, into a tree-covered area. Joseph pointed at him.

"Can the beam go through those trees?" Joseph asked.

"No, I have to have a line of sight. We'll have to cut down any trees or bushes in the way, if that's all right with you, Miss Williams." I remembered what Will had said about trees talking to you, telling their stories.

"I'd rather you cut as few trees as possible. Is there some way to work around it?" He looked at Joseph.

"This is where the trigonometry comes in, son," he said. "I'll do my best, Miss Williams."

"Her name's not Williams, it's Cole," said Joseph. I liked the sound of my maiden name. If we divorced, I'd change my name back. This pleased me, somehow, and the overriding thought of regaining my old name, my first name, made the thought of permanent dissolution palatable.

"That's okay, Mr. Blackwell," I said. "You can call me Williams, if it's easier."

"Whatever," Joseph said.

"I'll just call you Miss Avie, how's that?" said Ben, shooting a grin at Joseph. I could tell he had experience with teenagers.

"Fine," I said.

We watched them work all morning, and Joseph learned the practical application of the higher levels of mathematics. Jeannie Lou shot pictures of the property as she talked. She was a chatterbox, but filled with information about the area. The county was growing rapidly, with an influx of new residents who would require housing. Many people had moved out to the country, to avoid living in Chattanooga or Dalton, and this had caused land values to go up. There were several housing developments going up in the past three years. The county supervisors were starting to crack down on the developers and many longtime residents wanted a moratorium on development and were circulating petitions like the one I'd seen down at the store. Jeannie Lou thought the county would eventually end up giving in to the developers, because "folks need somewhere to live, after all." There was talk of building new county roads to serve the developments. She talked, smoked and coughed all the way till noon when we all stopped at the top of one of the gentle ridges to have some lunch. I pulled out a blanket and set out some sandwiches I'd made for us, while the men opened their lunch pails. Jeannie Lou left just after lunch, saying she'd seen enough to give her a fair idea of the lay of the land, and she needed to get back to her office to pull comps on recent sales of similar parcels. I warned her about Uncle Earl's inquisitive nature, but she assured me she knew how to handle nosy relations.

Joseph and I got back home just before dark, and we both showered to get off any dust or mold spores, although his breathing seemed excellent. He talked me into going into town to eat pecan waffles and eggs at the Waffle House. The waitresses smiled at me as we walked in. I was becoming a regular.

Back at home, after dinner, he suggested we call and see how Michael was, so I dialed the number for him. Michael answered his private number right away, and Joseph reported on his day. Apparently Michael didn't ask to speak to me because after a few minutes, Joseph hung up and announced he was tired and wanted to go to bed. As I was tucking him in, he asked if we could have Will over the next evening to show him some trigonometry.

"We'll see if he's free," I told him, and kissed him good night. Remembering how Will had said to call him if I needed him, I picked up the phone and dialed, and Will answered on the second ring. He was friendly, but guarded. He had just signed on for a two-week substituting stint; filling in for the ninth-grade algebra teacher's husband who was having open-heart surgery, and he wouldn't have much free time until the end of the week.

"I suppose I could come by Friday evening and bring him a high school textbook," he said.

"That will work. Will?"

"Yes?"

"If you'd rather not come—" I wasn't sure I was ready to see him. "If it's not too much trouble."

"Not at all, not for a good friend," he answered before hanging up. Was he referring to Joseph or me? I wondered. Pondering this, I crawled into bed.

That night, as I stared at the empty and wide space next to me, I thought of the nights Michael had spent by my side. I counted the years, times the nights. More than 5,475. Better than counting sheep. But was it the current version of Michael I was missing, or the Michael I'd fallen in love with? Or was it simply the warmth of a man next to me? Would things ever return to normal between us? And what was normal? I drifted off.

I was down at the Taylor's Crossing Methodist Church social hall at a giant potluck dinner. The church ladies had laid out their finest dishes on rows and rows of tables. Alive and well and apparently not deceased after all, Mama was there. She handed me a paper plate and told me to help myself, but to choose carefully. The plate would only hold so much. I got in the line that snaked from one table to the next, and looked out over the tables to study the variety of dishes.

Two columns of breads and appetizers made up the first table. Sweet cucumber pickles, peach pickles, chowchow, celery sticks, dips and cheese logs were lined up against homemade yeast rolls, corn sticks, hush puppies and a simple loaf of sliced, white store-bought bread that hid shamefully behind its half-removed blue-and-white plastic sleeve. The next table was a platoon of salads: potato and macaroni, lettuce, coleslaw, cold red beets, chopped fruit and bright-colored, too sweet Jell-O molds filled with odd ingredients such as marshmallows and pineapples, cherries and pistachios. The third table was a troop of vegetables, cooked in the traditional overdone, but tasty, southern fashion. Several varieties of baked beans and black-eyed peas stood alongside two squash casseroles and three pots of ham and bacon seasoned green beans. A large pot of turnip greens was flanked by its coarser sister, collard greens, both laced with pork hocks. Two iron skillets of dark brown-green fried okra sprinkled with crispy bits of fried cornmeal brought up the end, next to a lone sweet potato casserole covered with so much brown sugar and cinnamon it could have been at home on the neighboring dessert table, the most crowded of all. Dozens of cookies—thumbprint, sugar, peanut butter, oatmeal and chocolate chip—populated a third of the table, in between pumpkin, pecan and coconut pies. A couple of pound cakes looked naked next to coconut, carrot and chocolate cakes wearing thick coats of sugary frosting. The traditional thick banana and chocolate puddings, adorned with stiff-peaked meringues and creams, captured the attention of even the strictest dieters in the crowd.

I was careful with my choices, taking small servings of the dishes I'd never tasted, such as chowchow, or dishes I really loved, such as turnip greens, cold red beets and fried okra. I couldn't resist a small tablespoon each of the two, stiff-peaked puddings. I sat down at a table next to some older women who chattered about who had made which dish. I listened and ate, savored the earthiness of the red beets, the crunchiness of the fried okra. At a southern potluck, it was not impolite to simply concentrate on enjoying the food. In fact, the women smiled at me and described each bite as I took it: Judy's squash, Emily's corn sticks, Gail's fried okra, Dean's green beans, Ellen's sweet potato casserole and Margaret's black-eyed peas with longhorn peppers. With each morsel, I tasted the care they took in their cooking, the love they'd put into their creations. But even as I enjoyed each new flavor, I kept anticipating the next. I looked at my plate and suddenly realized it was made up of side dishes: appetizers, salads, vegetables, bread and dessert. There was no meat, chicken or fish.

"Did I miss the main course table?" I asked out loud. One of the ladies down the table leaned forward, and I could see it was Mama.

"Girl, there ain't no main course." She laughed, and all the ladies laughed along with her. "Side dishes is all there is to it."

I woke up with a start and sat up in the bed. Could Mama be right? I went over to the window, pulled back the curtain and looked up towards the ridge. I couldn't make it out in the dark and fog but I knew it was there. Sometimes, a person has to be satisfied with what's right in front of her. If Will and I could just be friends, that was fine with me.

CHAPTER 22

"Sorry I'm early," said Will as I opened the garage door to let him in. He looked better than ever, wearing a thick, red wool jacket and a brown Stetson, which he promptly removed. As I took his hat and coat from him, I could feel his warmth as my hand brushed beside his. I quickly pulled my hand away.

"Where's Joseph?" he asked.

"Over at Tyler's," I said. "It's been a difficult week for him. Tyler's in school all day and I've been busy with the estate. Between Xylia and me, I think he's getting bored with female company. I know he'll be glad to see you. He should be back in half an hour."

"I'm glad he's not here yet," he said. "I had something I wanted to talk to you about." He pulled out some papers from his soft, leather briefcase. "You know how I am always talking about Cherokee history? Well, the principal at my school told me about a federal grant I should apply for. I've filled out these forms, but I haven't tackled the proposal itself. I was hoping you could help me?" He handed over the letter explaining what the proposal should include. I glanced over it.

"Sure," I said. "But first you'll have to tell me what you envision."

"Could you be more specific?" he asked.

"Okay, you want some money from the government. Say you get the money, how will you spend it, and how will this teach students about Cherokee history? What age group are you aiming at? And why should they learn about Cherokees, and not some other tribe? And where will you teach it? What tools will you need?" He held out his hand and motioned for me to stop.

"Whoa, wait a minute," he said. "This is great. Let me write this down." He pulled out a notebook.

"Wait," I said. "Write only one question, every other page."

"Why?" he said.

"You'll see," I answered. I grabbed us a couple of cups of coffee, and we sat at the kitchen table together, brainstorming for the next half hour and he ended up with 20 pages of questions. I told him to answer each of these questions with at least three pages of writing.

"And then?" he said.

"Don't worry about that. One step at a time," I said. He smiled at me.

"You're good," he stared at me appreciatively as he said it. "Just what a writing phobe like me needs."

"Thanks," I said, and reached my hand out to lightly squeeze his arm, like I always did with Rebecca when she said something that touched me. I could feel his warm, firm arm through his soft flannel shirt. Again, I quickly pulled away. I needed to make sure I wasn't sending the wrong message. But then he stared into my eyes and spoke.

"Avie, I've been thinking," he said. "A lot. I care about you, I think you know that." My heart thumped hard and fast and pounded in my ears. I didn't want to hear this. I wasn't ready for anything but a friendship. He continued. "The truth is, I don't think you're sure of what you want, yet. You've been hurt. You're confused. It would be easy for me to take you in my arms and help you forget. One day you might wake up and realize you weren't ready to give up your marriage." He reached his palm out and placed it over my hand.

"I want to give you some space, let you think about it, figure out exactly what you want," he said. At that moment, I was torn. One part of me, my impulsive self, wanted to burrow my face in the dark hair of his warm chest; my pragmatic side, the good wife and mother, told me I should be thinking about ways to salvage my marriage.

"The molasses approach works for me."

"One step at a time," he said. We both laughed and when he pulled his arm away from my hand, it was such a natural thing I hardly noticed it at all. But as he got up to retrieve some books from his truck, and I watched his strong, wedge of a back walk away from me, the impulsive nymph in me stirred. Then, as any good friend would surely do, I got back to the proposal.

"Mom?" said Joseph, entering through the garage door. "Why didn't you call me?" He ran to Will and they high-fived and spent most of the evening together trying to work on a few trigonometry questions.

Will was true to his word, and gave me ample space. Joseph spent much of the weekend over with Tyler, Trent and Jolene, and several afternoons with Will, who had invited him to see an arrowhead museum outside of Ringgold. Will also taught him to target shoot with the blowgun. Xylia had come down with a cold and didn't want to venture out after work. I finally reached Rebecca, who simply listened and empathized. She assured me that it would all work out, but meanwhile I should take notes. It would make a really fine screenplay, if not a soap opera episode. We were still laughing when she had to hang up and take a call from Antonio Banderas' publicist.

I spent a lot of time working on the estate. I met with the lawyer to discuss the settlement agreement, but I found myself effusing about blowguns and arrowheads and the hunt for the silver mine. He looked down at his watch, quickly changed the subject back to details of the agreement he would draft. I listened to him drone on, his voice emotionless and businesslike, watched him scribble notes on a long legal pad. What a narrow, restricted world lawyers live in. A world of rules and minutia, a world made claustrophobic by the tight boundaries of the law. I felt sorry for

Jim Johnson, and for Michael, and I did not know if their world was a world compatible with mine.

Afterwards, I stopped off to finalize the wording for Dad's gravestone. I remembered what he'd told me once. "Just the facts," he'd said. So I arranged to have his birth date and death date on the large granite stone which also bore the names of my mother and stepmother. For all eternity, both women would share a headstone with Daddy in the middle. I stopped by the funeral home to pick up a refund check to deposit in the estate account. Back at home, I spent hours sorting through family pictures and started photo boxes for Griffin, Jolene and me.

Until the lawyer got the agreement finalized, and with Joseph off with Will, I had some time to read the Cherokee history books Will had left. For the most part, I was left alone with my thoughts, and the vistas of the ridge land, where I spent hours walking the fields in the crisp air, bundled up in my puffy jacket.

I felt like a girl again as I became lost in my thoughts. For youngsters, hours were abundant, and purposefulness not a requirement. Children were allowed to spend hours in no apparent activity except for simply being and thinking. As they grew up, school and work and society took over more and more hours and left fewer and fewer hours in their possession. Every hour had to be filled with some meaningful activity, work, networking or working out. And when people talked about their weekends, they usually described activities. No wonder our society was in trouble; we simply didn't allow ourselves time to think, only to act. And who could act reasonably, if no thinking ever occurred?

I sat on an old log and stared at the slow-moving muddy waters of Little Chickamauga Creek. I listened to the rustle of the leaves on the sycamores, and watched as a yellow leaf floated down, away from the tree onto the water's surface. It drifted around a bend and into the bank where the creek widened into the swimming hole.

Suddenly, I saw myself as a little girl. I was six and standing in that ridiculous boys' bathing suit at the water's edge. Daddy was standing right behind me, ready to support me with his strong arms, but not letting me know he was there. On my own, I was forced to swim. My father let me suffer a temporary abandonment because he knew, ultimately, I must depend on myself. In the little skinny girl, he saw the future woman, knew what life would deal. The little girl would ultimately be required to take care of herself.

A surge of love for Daddy hit me as I got up and followed the sycamore leaf, which now continued down the stream. It landed by the muddy bank where the stream narrowed, and I smiled as I remembered Michael landing in the cow pie. Michael was competent, but not with cows, or the country. He was out of his element here and had even acted out of character. As he'd said, this place made him crazy. He belonged in the city, behind a desk, fighting other people's battles on paper, in court. Michael could never live here. I followed the leaf as a gust of wind drove it downstream again, towards the red clay banks where I'd found the arrowhead.

As I sat in the chill by the creek, I thought about the feel of Will's fingers brushing over my palm when I showed him the arrowhead. The way he reminded me of the wind, the way he weaved in and out of the woods. He was as much a part of this land as the arrowheads embedded in the ochre stream banks, as the leaves that spoke to him. He belonged here, and would never leave.

And then, as I walked along towards home, I saw the top of the ridge in the distance and thought of Joseph. I remembered the day he had insisted we had to search the ridge for the silver mine, and my reluctance to take him into the thick forest. But his breathing had been fine that day, and his asthma had continued to improve since we arrived in the Valley. Even if it were only during vacations here, my son could experience breathing normally in the pristine air. This was a gift I could give him. I had to come up with a plan to keep the land.

Back at home, I saw Earl's truck parked in my driveway. Cottie waved as I passed, jangling three or four charm bracelets that encircled her wrist. Earl was standing by the back door, like an old hound dog waiting for a handout.

"I'm tellin' you, that Jeannie Lou was born a Hunnicutt, and them Hunnicutts belong in the nuthouse," he informed me, holding up a fat manila envelope. "Mailman thought it was for me. Cottie opened it. Here." He handed over the envelope. "The woman must be on dope. That land's not worth more than $ 3,000 an acre, what with there bein' hardly no road frontage."

"It's a crime to open up other people's mail," I said, and turned to go into the house.

"Gall dernit, gal, it's a crime the way you're tossin' away your husband for that Indian trash," he shot back. I slammed the door behind me, and went in to study the appraisal.

The value of the land was much higher than I had ever imagined. Jeannie Lou had calculated a range of $4,000 to $6,000 per acre, depending on how I divided up the land. I didn't need a calculator to multiply it out; the land was worth almost a million dollars, or more. I picked up the phone and dialed. Griffin answered right away.

"We all need to talk," I said. "Can you drive up tomorrow?"

The next morning I dropped Joseph off with Xylia at the store, made a stop at the bank, and headed to the lawyer's office. Griffin, Jolene and I assembled around the conference table with the appraisal laid out in front of us. Jolene's fuchsia-lipsticked mouth dropped open when she saw the numbers.

"Shootfire, I'm gonna be rich!" she said. "When are we going to get the money?" Her long, purple-leotarded legs fairly danced under the table. Griffin's beefy fingers drummed on the hard, thick oak as he stared at her.

"I could double our money if I develop the land," he said.

"I wouldn't trust you to develop a roll of Kodak," she scoffed.

"Okay, fine. I'll get a bank loan and buy you out," he said.

"Who's gonna loan your ass money? Trent said you never did pay his Daddy back after he loaned you the money to start up the feed store." She clutched onto a fat diamond engagement ring as she spoke. Remembering how my siblings' arguing last time had caused my son's asthma flare up, I was glad I had left him back at the store. I hated conflict myself, and had suggested meeting the lawyer to keep arguments to a minimum.

"If he has something to say, he can talk to me. You tell him that," Griffin said. He turned to me. "I already met with my banker down in Atlanta. He's agreed to give me the loan. In a few years, Arrowhead Acres will make us millionaires." I pictured yellow bulldozers razing the pasture, decimating all the arrowheads to lay down roads, and winced.

"Let's see what Jim has to say," I answered.

"What's there to talk about? It's simple. Pay off little Miss Muffet here and start clearing the land." Griffin could be pushy. I was glad when Jim entered. He came over and shook my hand and I felt comforted as soon as I felt his firm shake and heard his low drawl. Maybe it was his navy blue suit that smacked of success, or his polite pleasantries. He complimented both Jolene and Griffin, saying how neither one of them had changed a wink since he'd seen them at a barbecue 20 years back. My siblings quickly calmed down and both looked fairly eager to be models of cooperation.

"I'm going to be married, Mr. Johnson. Trent and I are planning a big wedding, so I'll be taking my inheritance in cash," she said, folding her hands in front of her and placing them strategically on the table so her flashy diamond was visible.

"And I'll be glad to buy her out," said Griffin. "The bank's already approved my loan." Jim nodded agreeably, and you would have thought he was rooting for both of them until he spoke.

"Avie's the executor, and her job isn't to make deals between the heirs. All she's required to do is distribute the property. Now there's two ways to do that. She can either sell the land, and split the proceeds three ways, or she can divide the land up into three parcels, and give you each one and keep one for herself." Griffin's face reddened as he listened.

"Well, that's an easy choice. Avie and I want to sell it, don't we?" said Jolene. She leaned in towards me, batted her heavily mascaraed lashes. "I know you can use the cash, what with your divorce and all." Griffin looked shocked but, bless him, he didn't say a word. Jim Johnson ignored the remark altogether.

"Avie?" Jim said, holding his pen poised over a legal pad. "What's your pleasure?" We might have been talking about dessert, not a million dollars' worth of land.

"Actually, I want to keep the land."

"To develop," Griffin said, nodding.

"No," I said. "I'm not sure yet. Maybe build myself a cabin." Jolene and Griffin looked at each other and spoke at once.

"No!" Griffin said. Jolene added, "A love nest." I detected a small smirk cross Jim's face and I kicked Jolene under the table.

"Ow!" she said, but she shut up.

"Look," said Jim. "Avie, you can do that. Keep your third, and just hand them the other two pieces, if that's what you want. But you'll have to agree on who gets which parcel, or you'll have to draw straws."

"I want to keep all the land. I intend to buy them both out," I said. Griffin looked puzzled, but Jolene smiled.

"That's fine. How much?" she asked.

"She has to give us six thousand an acre," said Griffin. "Not a penny less." Jim studied the appraisal.

"Actually, as long as she gives you four thousand per acre, she's covered. The six thousand appears to be if the land is divided into 20-acre parcels," Jim said.

"That's ridiculous. I could sell it for twice as much, I know it," said Griffin.

"Maybe so," said Jim. "If you were the executor. It's up to Avie. She's the one in charge." Griffin's mouth formed a hard line, until his lips started to tremble. Pouting, he seemed to be a boy again, an eight year old who's just been whipped by Daddy for bad judgment.

It was a hot summer day and we had been playing in our basement with a couple of neighbor boys who had no baby sisters. Always able to spot a business opportunity, Griffin had told our playmates that, for a quarter, they could pull my pants down. They groped under my dress and quickly jerked down my pink-dotted panties. I had escaped by running up the stairs, into Dad's arms. He put me down and went to the tree in the front yard to break off a switch to use on Griffin.

I imagined when Dad had chosen me as executor, he might have remembered that soured business transaction. I know I did.

"Have you got the cash, Avie?" the lawyer asked. I had stopped by the bank and Mrs. Simmons was, at this very moment, running a credit check on me.

"I expect loan approval by the end of the week," I bluffed. Griffin shook his head with the look of defeat that lottery players wore when they checked the winning numbers against their tickets. There's no limit to imaginary fortunes, or the disappointment that accompanies their loss. For some folks, counting chickens before they hatch is a way of life, but they always seem to forget one point. First you need some hens.

CHAPTER 23

On the way out, my brother let me know what he thought of my blasphemous actions.

"That was just plain stupid back there. You could sell me half of your share and use the money to build yourself a mansion. Hell, what do you need all that land for?" he asked.

"I'm not sure yet," I answered. Jolene interrupted.

"It'll hold a lot of teepees," she laughed. I glared at her.

"What? Can someone clue me in?" Griffin asked.

"She's referring to my friend, who is part Cherokee, like Grandfather William's first wife," I answered.

"Now I'm really lost," he said. I pulled Grandfather's marriage certificate from the estate file and showed it to Griffin. He said, "Dang, I wish we were part Cherokee so I could get some of that stipend money they hand out." Excited about the possibility, Jolene fantasized about changing her stage name to Birdsong or Singing Dove or some other Cherokee-sounding name, after all, it was the "in thing," wasn't it? I nodded, remembering the Salt Lake Winter Olympics and the Native American entertainment.

"I don't see what any of this has to do with our land, my

inheritance," said Griffin.

"Exactly," I said. "Jolene, could you be quiet for one moment?" She stood over to the side and lit up a cigarette and watched. She had never been one to turn away from a good fight.

"I thought you understood, Avie, after the day I showed you where I plan to put in the development. I talked to my boss and he agreed the sinkhole could be turned into a lake at Arrowhead Acres, stocked with bass. He's ready to begin bulldozing next month." We had reached our cars. I turned to him.

"I'm sorry, Griffin. That's not going to happen."

"What do you want to build, then? A shopping center? I haven't done one before but my boss has. There are some zoning issues, but with Jim Johnson pulling some strings, that would work. All these folks moving into the valley will need somewhere to shop." He just didn't know when to quit.

"No," I said. "I don't see a mall."

"What do you see? Tell me." He stood waiting for an answer that would justify my quashing his unhatched dreams.

"I only know what I don't want, and that's more roads and buildings and empty spaces where trees once stood." He stared at me a moment, then replied.

"They're right. You are crazy." He turned and climbed into his hunter green Front Runner and started the engine. Jolene crushed out her cigarette against the pavement.

"What's he talking about?" I asked.

"Aunt Ardelia and Uncle Earl both think you're having some kind of mid-life crisis, or something. You know, leaving your husband, having the affair with Will and all. Hey, but who am I to talk?"

"Jolene, I told you we aren't having an affair. My word, the rumors that get started around here."

"Avie, it's time you knew. Everyone in the valley heard about that kiss. Aunt Ardelia told Uncle Earl, and Aunt Cottie talked about it at the beauty parlor. By tonight, there won't be a soul in Taylor's Crossing that doesn't know you plan to keep the land. I don't blame you. If you plan to stay here, you should put a lot of land between you and Aunt Ardelia. Otherwise, you'll be livin' in a fishbowl." Despite her bad choices in fashion, and sometimes men, my sister occasionally had a valid thought emanate from her brassy orange head.

"You're right," I said. "So tell me. What's the word on Michael? Is he the good guy?"

"You have to ask? He's a lawyer," she said. We both laughed. "You know they always were suspicious, him being from up north and all. I know I knew all along he wasn't as good a catch as you thought he was."

"What? You had a hunch, or something?"

"More than a hunch," she said, lighting up another cigarette. Now I was really glad Joseph wasn't here. "Remember when we all met up at the Choo Choo for my 30th birthday? And Michael made fun of my outfit?"

"And your teased hair?"

"Right. Well, when he and I were at the bar ordering drinks, he asked me if I needed some money."

"And?" I asked. I felt a little stab in my stomach, but I wanted to, needed to, hear this.

"He asked me how much it would take to keep me in Nashville, away from you and Daddy."

"You mean he tried to pay you to stay away?"

"Exactly. I told him to take his money and shove it where the sun don't shine."

"I guess you draw the line at stealing jewelry," I said, realizing even as I spoke how catty I sounded.

"I'm sorry about that," she said. "It was wrong. But you just don't know how to let bygones be bygones, do you? I may not be perfect, but I'm the only sister you have." I looked at her fuchsia, fuzzy sweater, lime-green skirt and purple tights. Despite her 30-something years, she was really just my kid sister with a lot of growing up to do.

"You're right, Jolene. I tell you what. I'll promise not to mention the jewelry again if you'll promise to never wear those tights again with that skirt." She looked down at herself and we both laughed.

We ended up at Aunt Christie's Cafe eating fried green tomatoes and cornbread and drinking sweet iced tea. We had a lot of catching up to do. Her performance at the Barn had been well received, and she would be the warm-up act on Saturday nights next month. She chattered away about her wedding and she asked me to take her shopping for the wedding gown, explaining she wanted something really classy. I agreed. She hoped I wasn't jealous and I told her I wasn't, that I, too, was starting anew. She asked for details, but I didn't have any.

"All I know is endings bring beginnings," I said.

"Like Will?" she asked, scooping into a thick banana pudding.

"Maybe," I said, and for once, she didn't press for more information. We parted amicably, after promising each other to get together later in the week to go shopping, and we left in separate cars to go back to the valley. As I drove back, I was grateful for a sister who had been brutally honest with me. Why had I not noticed my husband's changing values? What she'd told me about Michael made me more certain of what I had to tell him.

If I'd arrived at Elmwood's 10 seconds later, or earlier, it would never have happened. It was overcast and the air was tense with the smell of ozone. I was looking up at Taylor's Ridge, studying the clouds, hurrying to pick up Joseph from the store before the rain unleashed. I pulled in and was slowly passing a couple of parked cars when I felt a jolt. I turned around to see the right rear fender of Aunt Ardelia's car up against my left rear bumper. I pulled forward and got out of the car and walked over to inspect for damage. There was a little red paint dust, but nothing a hard waxing wouldn't remove. Her horn blasted and I saw her passenger window roll down. I walked over to face her.

"It's your fault," she yelled. She was half turned around in her seat, her beet-red face stretched to its limit with rage.

"Actually, it's not," I said. "I had the right of way. There's no damage, though."

"Ha," her snort said it all. I was not to be believed. She opened up the car door, pushed her tall frame out of the front seat and hobbled around to the back of the car to check out the damage herself.

Surprisingly, although she had been somewhat crippled by

an injury in a car wreck years ago, she was quite mobile. She supported her tall self between the side of the car and the cane, and except for a slight limp, she moved well. Even through the nylon of her red windbreaker, her arms appeared thick and well muscled, almost like she'd been working out. She reached the rear of the cars and wet her finger in her mouth. She ran it along her bumper, against the loosened paint.

"It'll rust out if not painted," she said. "You ought to watch where you're going, Missy. Keep your mind on your driving, not on that Indian boy."

"And you ought to mind your own business," I said. She snapped to attention, her back ramrod straight and held her arms against her Buick, using it like a shield between us.

"It is my business, keeping blood relations from courtin' other blood relations," she said.

"What are you talking about?" I asked. Her usual pessimism had apparently metamorphosed into full-blown delusions.

"Your grandpa, my father, was married to a Cherokee woman before he met Grandma Beth."

"I know that," I snapped.

"What you don't know Missy, is that Indian woman bore your daddy and ran off. She was no-count anyway. Then your grandpa married my mother and started a proper family. Had me and Earl." I thought about my dad, and how he always looked so strong and dignified, like the man on the nickel, especially in his younger days. His nickname for me, "Indian Pony," suddenly made perfect sense. And no wonder I'd felt connected to the land. Ardelia continued.

"The Indian woman married again, that feller up on the ridge." She waved her cane towards the top of Nickajack Road, and Will's cabin, and I looked up that way and saw the ridge, obscured by dark clouds. "Let me spell it out for you, Missy. Your beau is your cousin." Her evil grin stretched over her yellowed teeth. She'd smoked for years, until the doctor had warned her the habit might shorten her miserable life.

"I don't believe you, you're making it up," I said.

"Ha," she snorted again. "Why would I do that?"

"You're bored to death and you have nothing better to do than spy on everyone else and spread gossip." A fat drop of rain landed on my cheek and I let it course down my cheeks. It felt good. Her dark eyes turned to slants and her nostrils flared again like a threatened Brangus mama cow.

"You should talk. You're supposed to be down here settlin' up your poor old Daddy's estate, and you run around like a fool, here and there, chasin' after silver mines, lettin' that Indian stick his tongue in your mouth. At least my goings-on don't embarrass the whole family." She jabbed her cane in the air to make her point. I heard a cough behind me and turned to see Joseph and Xylia standing at the store entrance, watching.

"Go away," he shouted. "Leave her alone." Seeing she was outnumbered, she headed back to her car, but gave a parting shot.

"You ought to be ashamed of yourself," she said before leaning over and lifting her body into the driver's seat. She cranked up and pulled away.

"Don't mind her," said Xylia, ducking back into the store out of the rain, which was turning to slushy hail. "I'm going to close up early and go home." On the way back to Dad's house, as I concentrated on seeing through the heavy sheets of icy drops, Joseph spoke in an excited voice.

"Is it true? Are we part Cherokee?"

"And related to Will?" I responded. "Ardelia could be making it up."

"Let's ask him," he said.

"Okay," I answered.

"Mom?"

"Yes?"

"Did you really let him stick his tongue in your mouth?" I cringed. I hated Ardelia.

"Aunt Ardelia has a dirty mind. Will kissed me one night and it was a mistake. That's all." I looked over to see if he was grossed out, but he seemed to be simply processing the information.

That evening, Will came over carrying a burgeoning notebook of grant materials. Almost before he could say hello, Joseph assaulted him with questions about his parents, and grandparents. We all sat down around the table and he drew a family tree, filling in the names of his father and grandfather. I pulled out the divorce decree and compared it with Will's grandmother's name, and found the first name to be the same. But was it true that Will's father had been my father's half-brother? If so, it had been a well-hidden fact.

"So you're my uncle or something?" Joseph asked.

"Cousin, but a half-cousin, or second cousin, I think. I've never gotten those genealogy terms straightened out," Will said. "Let's put it this way, we could be blood, if it's true." We looked at one another through new eyes, familial eyes. We were just becoming accustomed to being friends, and now, in an instant, we had moved into a new relationship. In the space of several weeks we had gone from platonic, to romantic, back to platonic and now to familial. I wished I had never bumped into Aunt Ardelia.

But later, while Joseph and Tyler were playing video games in the back of the house and Will and I worked on his grant proposal notes, I read the material with new eyes: Cherokee eyes. His answers to the questions we'd created the other day were long and full of sadness and anger for what had happened to the Cherokee people, and as I read what he'd written, I could feel how horrible the Trail of Tears had been for my ancestors and others who had been torn away from their land. Perhaps one of my own family had walked along the freezing trail on the forced march to Oklahoma. I must have shivered because suddenly I felt Will's hand on my shoulder, steadying me. I looked up and we stared into each other's faces, reading and studying them for signs we were related. Except for my high cheekbones, I looked Irish and he looked mostly Cherokee.

"It's weird, isn't it?" he asked.

"My having Cherokee blood?" I said. He nodded.

"But I think your aunt's imagination is working overtime. I doubt we're related."

"It wouldn't be the first time she's been wrong."

"Or probably the last," he said, rising from the chair. "I hate to go but I've got an early start planned for tomorrow."

"But tomorrow's Saturday," I said. "No school." He slipped

into his buckskin jacket.

"I've got to run up to Asheville," he said. "I'll call you when I get back." I was about to ask him what for, when the phone rang. I picked it up as he waved goodbye and walked out the door.

CHAPTER 24

"Avie?" Michael said. He sounded friendly. "How are you?"

"Busy with the estate, of course. I was planning to call you later but you beat me to it."

"I wanted to let you know I had the bookkeeper deposit a check. He mailed you a duplicate of the deposit slip."

"Good," I answered.

"Also, I was thinking you might want to reconsider the separation, now you have all the facts at hand," he said, his tone shifting into his lawyer mode.

"Reconsider?" I asked.

"Us, now that Tonto's off the playing field." I could feel the anger rising up in my chest. How dare he make fun of Will!

"His name isn't Tonto. And I would appreciate you're using his correct name, Will."

"Whatever. I know you Avie. You wouldn't hook up with your cousin, or should I call him kissing cousin?" Apparently, Aunt Ardelia had done her dirty work. Or was it Uncle Earl?

"Even if he were off the playing field, why would you assume you're back on?" There was silence on the line, for a moment.

Sometimes even he had to think of an answer.

"One, for our son's sake. He would be better off, in the long run, if we could stay together."

"Not if we were miserable, and fighting."

"We could try to change." He sounded reasonable. He took my non-response as an opening. "I've called James Reiner. He's given me a referral for a counselor. You could fly out next Tuesday and we could go in Wednesday." His intercom buzzed in the background. "Hold on a minute, please?" he pleaded.

"Okay," I said. And suddenly I was alone with the singer's husky, bedroom voice taking me to another place. As he sang of fields of holly, I thought of the big field between Dad's house and the church, covered in Queen Anne's lace and goldenrod every spring and summer. Michael's voice interrupted my thoughts.

"Sorry about that. Where were we?" He was all business.

"Michael, I can't come right now."

"Why not?" he asked.

"I'm in the middle of the estate, for one. And two, I'm not ready to see you yet." There was a brief silence and then he answered.

"Two weeks, Avie. Two weeks."

"We'll see," I said, and handed the receiver to my son.

Later when I went to tuck Joseph in, I wondered. He looked up at me with sad eyes and asked when we would be going back.

"As soon as I finish up the estate," I said.

"I miss Dad," he said.

"I know," I said as I gave him an extra hug. The fighting, and now separation, had been hard on him. He and his father shared a strong bond and always would, despite my own problems in the relationship.

I stayed awake late looking over my estate to-do list and reading Will's history of the Cherokees. At midnight I found myself in bed trying to fall asleep. I kept thinking of Joseph, then Michael, wondering if counseling would make a difference. And even if Michael changed, even if we started afresh, could I forget how he'd hurt me in the pasture that day when Will had intervened? And what about Will? What was he to me? Could he really be my cousin, or cousin once removed?

Removed, removal. The Cherokees had been removed, like exterminators removing pests, like gardeners removing geraniums. Or goldenrod. In golden fields. Down where the Indians gathered. Before their land was taken away. By the land lottery. An unlucky lottery, for the Cherokees, lucky for the white settlers who acquired the land. The land the Cherokees left. Walking away, leaving their land, their game, their farms, their homes, to the settlers. Walking with small, halting steps. A woman, with lustrous hair. A berry-brown woman in the late summer sun, walking through the fields of Queen Anne's Lace and goldenrod, walking, moving, towards the ridges. Beyond the red clay banks, beyond the muddy stream. Into the woods. The noisy woods. The woman weaves through the woods as the leaves chatter. She winds up higher and higher beyond the deep hole in the ground, past the pearly surface of a pond, where a blue heron's cry joins in with the noise of the trees.

"A-de-lv-u-ne-gv," they whisper in unison. She moves onto a path and up another ridge towards a split log house set on a rock foundation. She passes the house, goes beyond, towards a bubbling noise that is a background melody to the symphony of the trees. A heron cries. She stares up through the shafts of light to see a flash of blue-gray pass over.

"A-de-lv-u-ne-gv," the trees beckon. Her pace quickens. She's running now, after the heron, towards a chorus that emanates from the strong branches of a tall oak. A bird shrieks again and she looks up, high into the branches, at the topaz sky.

"A-de-lv-u-ne-gv, a-de-lv-u-ne-gv," oak branches chant and the trees of the forest cry back, "a-de-lv-u-ne-gv." The heron's cry, the babble of the brook, the mantra of the trees, merge into one perfect note that fills the forest. A single feather falls from the heron, floats down through the branches of the oak. Slowly it drifts from side to side. She opens her hands to the feather. Opens them wide to receive the soft, silver wing of the bird as it brushes gently on her palms. She closes her hand around the feather, then reopens it. It is no longer a feather. It is now a silver ring.

I opened my eyes, held my hands up in the dim light, seeking the ring. There was none. Fully awake, I rose to look out the window. It was still dark but almost dawn. Although I had some estate work planned for later in the day, what harm could come from checking out Xylia's ring to see if it was a map, as Joseph had suggested? I would borrow it from her, bring it back for Joseph to study and perhaps spend another afternoon with Will and Tyler searching for the silver mine. Anything to cheer Joseph up, he had seemed so down about Michael the night before and he had been begging to go look for the silver mine.

I pulled on a t-shirt and jeans, checked on Joseph and whispered to him that I had to run to the store for a few minutes. He nodded and rolled back over to sleep. I locked the doors as I left.

Elmwood's opens its doors by 6:30 to cater to people going to or from work. Xylia usually arrived around quarter after 6 to brew the first pot of coffee for her patrons. Ernie always arrived an hour or so later. It was 6:25 so Xylia would be there shortly.

It was a cold, wet morning, about 45 degrees. I pulled up in the store parking area and was surprised to see the door ajar. Xylia always kept the door closed against the cold, and had a hand-lettered "please shut the door" sign hanging on the wall next to the door frame. I walked through a puddle, entered the store and smelled the coffee but didn't see her.

"Xylia, it's me. I think I know how we can find the silver mine. I need to look at your ring. Hello?" I walked across the center floor, already covered with wet footprints, towards the back of the store. I glanced at the chalkboard and read, "You can smell a rotten egg a mile away." I continued into the stock room but couldn't find her. I turned back to the main room and walked across towards the stool behind the counter where she usually sat. Something looked out of place, I thought, and then I noticed. The cash register was half-open. Someone could come in and steal the money. I stepped around to the other side of the counter to shut it and almost stumbled over her.

She was lying on her side on the floor, one hand splayed out on the cold concrete as though she'd tried to stop her fall. A red, heavy-duty flashlight lay next to her. She had probably fallen trying to reach that top shelf. I leaned over her and touched her cheek. Still warm. I felt her wrist and found a weak pulse.

"Xylia?" I tried to rouse her, but she wouldn't move. I jumped up and dialed 911, then went back to her. I spoke to her again, but she didn't answer. I brushed a strand of her pale hair away from her face and felt a lump swelling under her hair on the side of her head, just behind her temple. I pulled apart her thick, silvery hair and saw a small smudge of red blood. Perhaps she'd bumped her head on her way down, but against what? And why was it on the side facing up, not on the hard concrete floor? I reached out to take her cool hand in mine, in an effort to warm her up.

"Xylia, the ambulance will be here shortly. You're going to be okay." I hoped so, I thought, realizing how much I liked, no loved, this woman. Comforting her, I stroked the back of her work-worn, freckled hands, and then I realized something was missing. I picked up her middle finger, the one where she usually wore the ring. It was bare. She'd been robbed.

After the ambulance had taken her away, I called Jolene to come watch the store and Joseph while I went to the hospital. She arrived about 20 minutes later and I left for Ft. Oglethorpe.

Along with other patients' families, I sat for what seemed an eternity. After an hour, a doctor came out and explained that the CT scan had shown some bleeding in the lining of her brain. A subdural hematoma was pushing against her brain and surgery might be needed. Worst of all, she was still unconscious, in a coma. All we could do was wait. I settled back on the worn, upholstered couch with my thoughts, trying to ignore the crackling of cellophane being peeled off snack food, the inane chatter and the slurping noises a teenager made as he attempted to suck down the last dregs of a Coke with a straw.

An hour later I was allowed to see her after she was moved into intensive care for observation. Heart monitors beeped, respirators swooshed and water gurgled humidity into oxygen units. Nurses and the family members spoke in low voices. There were no TVs playing funny sitcoms in this unit. Instead, behind every curtained cubicle, each patient fought his battle against death. When the nurse pulled back the curtain to Xylia's cubicle, I was shocked to see her with a myriad of tubes attached to her arm and hooked up to a respirator. Sticking out of the top of her bandaged head were several inches of steel rod, an intracranial pressure monitor, I found out later. Her mouth was taped open around the tubing, causing her pale face to look misshapen, like a Salvador Dali painting. It was painful to see her like this.

I had heard that the last thing to go is hearing, so I took hold of her clammy hand, spoke to her, told her that Ernie and the store were being taken care of. All she needed to do was try and get better. But as I looked at her bandaged head, saw her chest rise and fall from the forced breaths pumped into her by a machine, I wondered if she would survive. Hovering all around us, death could simply slip under the curtain hem and claim her at any moment.

Somehow, keeping vigil over her might stave it off, I thought. So I sat there for several hours, until Sheriff Young arrived to question me about the robbery. He arrived at the intensive care unit and invited me down to the cafeteria for a cup of coffee.

Dewey Young was a heavyset man, about 60, with good old boy looks that belied his sharpness. He ordered a hot plate and offered to treat me to one, if I was hungry. When I told him I could pay for my own, he protested.

"Your daddy bought me lunch so many times I lost count, Miss Avie. It's the least I can do," he said. We sat over steaming platters of food, and he covered the usual bases: how old was my son, how was the old home place and my uncle and my aunt? Did my husband come along? My answers came easily, until I spoke of Michael.

"He's in trial," I said, preferring not to go into our recent marital problems, "and can't break away right now." He glanced down at my Red Clay tee shirt.

"Um hum," he said. I knew he was an antique collector, like Uncle Earl, and wondered if Earl had gossiped about Will and me. Did gossip travel eight miles up the Alabama Highway, or did simply swirl round and round the valley, like a tornado locked between the high ridge and the ridge lands?

"How'd you get caught up in this mess?" he asked. Which

mess? The robbery? The separation? The estate? Will's kiss? I hesitated. "You know Mrs. Elmwood?" he asked. I nodded.

"Yes, she's been a big comfort since Dad passed away."

"I see," he said, spreading some butter on a flaky, white biscuit. "So you all normally get together this early in the morning?" I felt the hot potatoes sticking in my throat. Did he think I did it?

"No, I woke up early today and decided to go down and see her."

"For some of her famous coffee, I imagine." As he spoke he kept his eyes riveted on me while swirling a large chunk of chicken fried steak in gravy with his fork. He popped it right in his mouth without losing a drop of that gravy. From the looks of him, he'd had lots of practice. I hesitated again. Would he understand if I explained about the ring? Or would he think I was a nutcase?

"Her coffee is legendary," I said. "But I really went to look at her silver ring again."

"One that was stolen?" he raised his eyebrows.

"Yes."

"Um hum," he said. "Were you gonna buy the ring off her?"

"No, I just wanted to see it. It's very unusual. It's got petroglyphs etched in the face. You know~"

"I know. Pictures. You were getting a real early start there, weren't you?" He'd finished the steak and was working on the green beans, making sure he speared little bits of ham with each bite.

"It was early. And I couldn't sleep." I didn't tell him about the dream. It sounded strange, even to me. I quickly moved into a recital of my arrival at the store, the open door, my search for Xylia, my discovery of her on the floor and calling 911. He listened intently, tearing off small pieces of biscuits and carefully buttering each bite before taking them in his mouth like a communicant tasting a host.

"Did you notice anything missing, other than the ring?" he asked.

"Well, the cash register was open. And a flashlight was on the floor, next to her. At first I thought maybe they, I mean, the robber, tried to take a flashlight, but later I realized this was probably what they hit her with." He maintained a poker face while letting the final bite of flaky biscuit melt in his mouth. "Did they get any money?"

"I can't say right now. Did you touch anything when you were there this morning?"

"Only her, and the phone, when I called the ambulance."

"Know of anyone who might have a reason to hurt her?" he asked. I thought of Xylia's big smiling face, the warm homey feeling that she created when she entered a room.

"As far as I can see, she's the glue that holds the community together. And her store? It's a pit stop that can turn a miserable day into a good one. She's like a built-in Dear Abby. And of course there's the chalkboard with the sayings. Gives people something to think about, other than their own problems." Sometime a person had to almost die before you realized just how much they meant to you. I felt tears starting to rise up as I thought of the cold steel rod sticking out of her head.

"I've seen the sayings board when I stopped to get coffee myself," he said. "Xylia's a good one, alright. Do you think she'll make it?"

"The doctors don't know yet. I hope so," I said. He gazed at the rows of peach cobbler laid out on the counter behind us.

"Can I buy you some dessert?"

"No thanks. I really need to get back up there." He stood up as I did and shook my hand.

"Thanks, Miss Avie. Sorry to have kept you. If she comes to, let me hear." I nodded and he made a beeline for those cobblers. With his eating habits, it was amazing he hadn't ballooned up to 300.

Back up in intensive care, I found there had been no change. I sat with Xylia another few hours, talking to her every now and then, about the sheriff, what I'd eaten, how we would make another batch of apple dumplings. If she was somewhere inside that bandaged head, I wanted to give her a reason to wake up.

Around eight that evening, a hard, rail of a woman, about 35, entered the cubicle and introduced herself as Sue Lynn, Xylia's niece. She was dressed too neatly in matching powder blue pants, blouse and sweater that looked almost like a uniform and her lipstick had worn off, leaving the faint traces of lipstick pencil framing the edges of her thin lips. She had driven up from Jackson after Earl had called her to tell her the news.

"Something like this was bound to happen," she said, motioning to the steel rod. "I've been telling her to sell that store and come on down and live with me. I'd let her buy into my motel with the money. And that Ernie, if he was my son, I'd put a broom in his hand and tell him to get to work or get out. Make him toe the line." I knew there was a state prison in Jackson, and it occurred to me that she might have worked as a guard there at some point.

"Ernie actually does very well, for his intellectual level and his mild autism," I said. "And Xylia loves running the store, and her place in the community."

"Aw bullshit," she said. "Ain't nothing wrong with him some strong discipline wouldn't fix. And that store, hell, it's a nuisance," she said. "She doesn't break even, most days. When she gets out of the hospital, I'll get Ed to drive up the Mack truck and we'll move them down ourselves." If Xylia could hear, I was sure she was boiling somewhere down in her brain.

"Perhaps we should focus on one thing at a time, Sue Lynn," I said. She gave me a sour look but didn't respond. "How long can you stay?"

She plopped her large, vinyl handbag on the floor and took a seat.

"I'm staying here till she wakes up. And if she don't, I'll need to stay on and tend to her affairs." She pulled out a dozen or more old issues of The National Enquirer from the cheap vinyl bag and placed them in her lap.

"I've got to catch up on my reading. I left Ed in charge and there's no rush for me to get back. Things have been slow." She crossed her legs and flipped to an article on a 250 pound baby. "Ain't no point in you stickin' around. Besides, not to sound rude, or anything, you look like shit." I brushed my hair back, and felt my dry, tired skin. She was probably right. I'd been up since before dawn. It was a tough decision, leaving her there, but I felt

I needed to get back to the valley, check on Joseph. I gave her my number and made her promise to call me if there was a change.

"I will," she said, and added, "You know, if anything happens to her, I'm in charge of Ernie." I shuddered and said a silent prayer for Xylia's recovery.

On the way out of the hospital, I called Jolene to check on Joseph. She had already tucked the children in, both were exhausted after helping out all day at the store. She said she'd managed the store just fine, and the sheriff was investigating the robbery. Ernie had been difficult and didn't understand what was going on, and had started butting his head against the wall when he heard his mama had been taken away, but Uncle Earl had taken him home for the night. The community was in an uproar about the crime, and Ardelia had stopped by Jolene's to warn her about the Taylor's Crossing crime wave. She had given Jolene a spare shotgun and a round of ammunition before leaving to barricade herself in the house with her binoculars and police scanner. We both laughed.

"I'm not afraid," Jolene said. "Of course it was some stranger passing through."

"Most likely," I said. "At least they didn't kill her." She remembered to tell me Will had called.

"The only good news in an otherwise horrible day," I said.

"Better call him back tomorrow," she said. "It's late and he's probably asleep." She urged me to go on home and get some rest. She was about to turn in herself since she was waking up early the following morning to open the store, although the ladies of the church were going to take over after lunch. While I would have liked to stop by to see Joseph, I knew she was right.

Once I left the insular world of the hospital, I realized I was starving. It had been a long time since Sheriff Young's free lunch and inquisition. A steaming bowl of buttery grits at the Waffle House, the chanting back and forth of the waitresses and cook and the clang of the spatula against the grill brought a small degree of comfort. But when I got back in my car, gripped the chilly steering wheel in my hands, I felt empty and frightened. I drove along in the black night, alone with thoughts of death. I felt much the same as I had when Joseph and I'd arrived four weeks before to settle the estate. It was too late to go to Jolene's, and I knew I couldn't face Dad's empty house. I needed to talk to someone.

There was no moon that night and the ridge was difficult to navigate. Although I drove slowly, I almost missed his driveway and made the turn at the last minute. Through the forest, I could see the lights of the cabin, the thick curl of smoke coming from its chimney. He was still awake, even though it was late.

He must have heard me, because when I walked up to the front porch, he was standing there, waiting.

"I heard," he said. He opened his arms and pulled me into his chest. His body was hot, full of life and I breathed in his smell: leather mixed with a clean soap scent. It was a warm, safe place and I never wanted to leave. He pulled away, and said, "Let's go inside before we freeze." He kept hold of my hand, led me in to stand by the hot fireplace and helped me pull my arms out of the sleeves of my thick, wool coat. "Can I get you something to drink?" he asked.

It was an easy question, requiring a simple yes or no, but as I stood staring at him I realized what I wanted, and it wasn't coffee or liquor. He slightly cocked his head as he waited expectantly for my answer. I moved toward him and wrapped my arms around his strong back. My chest pressed against his flannel shirt and I could feel his heart thumping. I leaned in and pressed my lips onto his, felt a warm curl start down low. He wrapped his long fingers against the small of my back and pulled me close, then whispered in my ear.

"Are you sure?" he asked. I responded by running my hand down his chest, below his navel, under the denim's stiff edge. His hands moved under my sweater, tugged down the waist of my jeans. Then suddenly, I felt him scoop me up and carry me into his bedroom where he lay me down on a thick Indian blanket. As he took me in his arms, I thought of the thick curl of smoke and the way it rose up high in the sky, dissipating until smoke and sky were one.

Laughter followed after we were done, spilling out between us like a balm. And as I lay there in his arms, I felt life in every cell of my body and soul, and I remembered what Xylia had said about sex after death. And although death had not yet claimed her, it hovered at her bedside even as I lay in Will's arms.

"We're alive," I said to Will.

"Um," he growled into my ear.

Xylia would have been proud of me that night. Will and I retaliated against death another two times before dawn came up over on the east side of Taylor's Ridge. Sometime during that long and satisfying night, it occurred to me that I'd just had the best sex of my life with a cousin. I was glad Will used protection, but when I asked if he thought what we were doing was wrong, in fact, against the law, he got a big grin on his face.

Yesterday, he explained, he had visited his uncle in Asheville to look at the family Bible containing the birth, marriage and death records. He had confirmed that his grandfather was married to my grandfather's first wife, but briefly. She had died in childbirth and his grandfather quickly remarried another Cherokee woman who had the same first name, Catherine, as the first wife. This Catherine gave birth to Will's father. We weren't related at all.

"Yes," I said, and wrapped my arms around his wide shoulders, feeling like a girl who's just received the Christmas present she always wanted. He tenderly pulled a lock of my auburn hair out of my face, brushed his index finger along the side of my neck, traced over my collarbone and moved his hand directly over my heart.

"We're both part Cherokee," he said, "in our blood and in here." He pulled me into the crook of his arm. I lay my head on his chest and listened to the sound of his heartbeat and thought how right it felt being with him. It had been a long time since I was close enough to appreciate a man's heartbeat. I felt so soothed by the sound, and then I heard a low hooting noise coming from somewhere out in the forest. Will and I listened together and it came again, an eerie screech.

"An owl. He visits every night. The Cherokees believed birds calling in the night were witches in disguise, or even ghosts," he said. I shivered and buried myself deeper in his chest and thought of Xylia. Would she soon be a ghost? Reluctantly, I pulled myself away from Will and telephoned the hospital.

"There's been no change," her nurse told me. I gave her Will's number and made her promise to call if Xylia took a turn for the worse.

Back in bed, we talked off and on for several hours, about life and death and how fate had brought us together.

"Tyler's the one we should thank, really," I said. "For digging in Daddy's pasture that day."

"Or," Will said, "going farther back, you could thank the collective imaginations of the white settlers. They wanted another Dahlonega, but would have settled for a silver mine." He referred to the gold rush down in Dahlonega, Georgia, which was one of the primary reasons the government decided to remove the Cherokees and take the land for themselves. He continued. "No wonder they shot the Cherokee friend of your blacksmith ancestor. They knew greed would bring their demise."

"Do you believe there ever was a silver mine?" I asked him, weaving my fingers up through the thick, dark hair on his chest.

"I know there was," he said. "Grandpa spoke of it often, along with the other tales of our history."

I told him about my dream, about my theory that Xylia's ring might be a map of my land. He propped up on his elbow next to me and listened as I described the realistic images that made up my dream: the Cherokee woman, the opaque pond, the log house, the blue heron and the talking trees.

"What did they say?" he asked.

"I'm not sure, I didn't understand." I sounded out the words for him. "A-de-lv-u-ne-gv." His eyes widened.

"A-de-lv-u-ne-gv, is that what you heard?" he asked.

"I think so. Why?"

"That's Cherokee for silver," he said. A quiver spread through me and he must have felt it. He squeezed my shoulder.

"Don't be afraid," he said. "It was your ancestor speaking to you through your dreams. It's the rare person who listens. But I don't think I'd tell anyone about this dream."

"I won't," I said. "They'd think I was crazy."

"You're not," he said. "You're simply open."

"I want to see the land again, the way it was in my dream. Would you walk the ridges with me?" I said.

"Of course," he said. "But we'll have to wait till sometime next week." He glanced at his alarm clock on his bedside table. "In fact, in just a few hours I've got to drive up to the Ocoee and guide a boatload of Baptists down the river." It was still dark out, but dawn was only an hour or so away. I wanted to get back to Dad's house before my sister dropped off Joseph. I snuggled back down in the warm crook of Will's arm and ran my hand low across his abdomen.

"We've still got a few minutes, don't we?" I asked, and he answered by taking me, once again, in his arms.

I slipped down the mountain just as the sun was rising over the crest behind Will's cabin and guilt started to dance at the edge of my consciousness. Although Michael and I were separated, I couldn't help feeling I had betrayed him on some level. Yet guilt was tinged with joy. I shoved the guilt away and put it over in the revenge department where it seemed to fit perfectly. Despite a lack of sleep, I felt renewed from my night with Will.

Back at Dad's house, I got a hot shower, changed and put on some coffee. I had a long day ahead. The phone rang. It was Xylia's niece.

"Avie? They're taking her to surgery. The pressure got too high in her brain."

"Let me get my son squared away and I'll be right there," I said.

"No point in it," she said. "She won't be out for another three hours. I tell you when she'll need you is when she wakes up, if she does. Nurse says she needs folks to talk to her. I run outta things to say a few hours back." I thought of all I'd tell Xylia when I saw her, of Will and me and our night together. She would laugh when she heard we'd told off that whore, death. And she would be truly happy for us.

"Do you need anything?" I asked Sue Lynn.

"Matter of fact, I do," she said. "The hospital food sucks. Could you stop off at the Waffle House and get me some waffles and a side of bacon?"

"Okay, I'll be there at 10." I hung up the phone and silently asked God to let Xylia live. It was a selfish request. She had become part of the fabric of my daily life, an irreplaceable best friend and confidant. I couldn't imagine the valley without her.

I heard the garage door open and Joseph rushed in and flew into my arms. He clung to me, as I had clung to Will. He mumbled into my shoulder, "I love you, Mom." I squeezed him back hard and told him I loved him, too. "Is Xylia going to be okay?" he asked.

"She's in surgery at this very moment," I said, and explained all that I knew.

"I hope she doesn't die," he said. "'Cause I've got a surprise for her." With Jolene's help, he had reorganized the stock so Xylia wouldn't have to use her stepstool any longer.

"There was plenty of room," he said. "I just put out the stock deeper into the lower shelves. Now she won't fall again."

"That's great," I said. "I know she'll be thrilled." I didn't want to tell him it wasn't a fall, that a robber had knocked her out.

"And after breakfast, I'm going right back down, if that's okay with you. Aunt Jo needs me to watch Sammie Jo while she works. Tyler's at school."

"That's fine," I said. I was proud of him for pitching in. "Did you take your meds this morning?" He laughed.

"Of course, Mom." I looked at him through new eyes and realized not only was he the picture of health, but he had matured so much in the last few weeks. The clean air and space of the valley had been good for him, and me too.

CHAPTER 25

Elmwood's was a beehive of activity. Three women from the church had stopped by to offer their help. They clustered around Jolene, who filled out the calendar for the next week's worth of shifts for those volunteering to mind the store. Two regulars, men wearing bibbed overalls and chewing tobacco, were over by the coffee pot theorizing on the robbery, and Ernie was back in the front window with his notebook counting. I went over and spoke to him.

"Ernie, your mama's in the hospital. She'll come home as soon as she's able," I said. He ignored me, but I know he heard because I saw his knuckles squeeze tight around his pencil. "I'm going in to see her in a little while and when I do, I'll tell her you are keeping an eye on the store." I reached out and patted his hand but he continued staring out at the highway.

I went over to Jolene and the group of women and updated them on Xylia's condition. Mrs. Lee, a stout woman whom I recognized from my potluck dinner dream, stood up and held out her hands. The others held hands and formed a circle and motioned for Jolene and me to join in. Sammie Jo, Joseph and the men stepped over and joined us. She spoke in reverent tones.

"Heavenly Father, please we lift up our prayers to you for sister Xylia. Please guide the hands of her doctors as they work on her, and bring her your loving, healing light. Be with her, Father, comfort her. And if it is your will, bring her back to us, in your own time. We praise thy name, oh Jesus. Amen."

"Amen," everyone echoed back. The silence was interrupted by the slam of a car door outside. As if on cue, everyone broke away from the circle; the ladies sat back down at the desks to finalize their shifts, the men went to pour more coffee, Joseph handed Sammie Jo some crayons to draw a get well sign for Xylia before ducking behind a display. Ernie didn't even look up when Ardelia stormed into the store, leaning hard into her cane. She tapped it hard against the concrete floor to get attention, her meaty hand wrapped tightly around the silver handle.

"You can pray all you want to," she said, "but I'm gettin' more ammunition. Bullets is the only way to protect yourselves against the robbers and thieves." She caught my eye. "And outsiders." Jolene reached for a box of shotgun shells.

"I've ordered more, Aunt Ardelia," she said. "They should be in by tomorrow."

"Better stock up," said Aunt Ardelia. "They'll be back." Mrs. Lee stood up, stepped towards Ardelia, who towered above all the other women.

"Best not to get folks alarmed, if you know what I mean," she said, nodding towards Ernie. Aunt Ardelia snorted.

"Any plain fool knows he don't hear nothin'," she pulled out a few dollars and paid Jolene. Mrs. Lee inclined her head towards Sammie Jo.

"There's little ones to consider," she said. She thumped her cane again and Sammie Jo looked up. Ardelia leaned against the counter, held the cane by the bottom tip end, so Sammie Jo could see the gleaming handle. Being unaccustomed to doing so, and with great effort, Ardelia forced her wrinkled lips into her version of a smile.

"See the birdie?" she asked my niece, her grand niece. But Ardelia's feral grin was too much for Sammie Jo. She shrank back and pulled away. Aunt Ardelia laughed too loudly, a cruel cackle that caused everyone, even Ernie, to stare. She shook the cane in the air, into the path of the sunbeams that washed through the lace-curtained window behind the counter. Light reflected off the handle as she twirled it around. Flashes of light moved around the ceiling and even Ernie noticed, turning his full, dark head up to stare at the kaleidoscope effect. For a few seconds, everyone was hypnotized by the display. Then Sammie Jo ran away, hiding behind a rack of videos. Joseph scrambled after her.

"You ought to teach that young'un some manners, Jolene," she said. She snatched the paper bag of shells away from Jolene and huffed out, her cane tapping along as she left. Her departure left the room quiet, empty. Her brief visit had sucked out all the life in the store.

Joseph peeked his head around the video rack and looked out towards the door.

"Is she gone?" he asked.

"Boy, is she ever," said Jolene, and the room broke out in a nervous laughter. A few minutes later, when the church ladies had left and the tobacco chewers had gone to patrol the back roads looking for more gossip, I pulled Jolene over behind the candy counter and whispered that I'd fallen hard for Will.

"What's he like?" she asked. "On a scale of one to 10?"

"Jolene!" I said, and then, "Eleven. But that's all I'm saying. You might get ideas."

"Ha," she said, in a classic show of sibling rivalry. "Trent is a solid 14, and besides he's richer." I couldn't argue with that, but I'd had already had rich. Instead, I told her I was proud of the way she was running things for Xylia. She beamed. As I looked at her standing in her tight pants with her size 36 D breasts encased in a hot pink sweater, I realized the only compliments she usually heard came from the lips of men trying to woo her to bed.

Xylia would be out of surgery in an hour. I said my goodbyes and started for the door. As I passed by Ernie, I felt something graze my sleeve. He had his arm fully extended and was holding a wrapped Moon Pie like a priest offering a communion chalice. He stared off into space, not making eye contact. I took the

Moon Pie.

"I'll give it to your mama," I said. "She'll like it, Ernie. That's very sweet of you." He didn't answer. I left, climbed into the car and drove towards Ringgold.

The air was clear and crisp and the sun was brilliant and the day was so beautiful it was hard to believe anyone anywhere was fighting for his or her life, particularly Xylia. As I drove the back way to Ringgold, away from the familiarity of the valley, my mood grew darker as I thought about my friend, and the absurdity of someone hurting her. Why had she been the victim? And for so little a prize? A ring and a hundred dollars, or so. "Passing through," the sheriff had said. The faces of the other drivers loomed in the windshields of their trucks and cars. Was her assailant passing me just now? Morning dew and sunlight enhanced taut silver lines strung across low branches that hung down over the highway. Spider webs, I thought, or razor-thin piano wire.

The head of Xylia's attacker could be easily severed by an unyielding piano wire strung between these trees. He'd pass through on a motorcycle rushing towards his next crime. His mangy head would roll off and bounce along the old pavement of the road leading to Ringgold, where it would be left until it had been thumped over a million times by the tires of the locals. Or perhaps the road crew who cleaned up the occasional dead cat or possum would simply scoop up the assailant's lifeless body, dispose of it like so much trash.

It was with these murderous thoughts on my mind that I swung into the driveway of the Waffle House to pick up Sue Lynn's order. The bright sun blinded me as I climbed out. There, some 15 feet away coming through the swinging glass door, was the familiar soiled pant legs of Uncle Earl's yard sale overalls. He shuffled towards his old white truck with Cottie alongside him, pulling the sleeves of her windbreaker over her jangling charm bracelets. I observed from behind another parked car, squinting against the harshness of the sun as Cottie turned towards me. The sun reflected off something shiny, like a compact mirror. I stared hard to see where the light was coming from. For a brief moment, a flash of silver seemed to bounce off her throat area, but then she finished zipping her jacket up against a brisk wind. Seeing me, Earl tugged her along towards their truck. The brilliant sun seemed to be playing tricks with my eyes. Spider webs, piano wires and flashes of silver. The pressure of Xylia's illness was getting to me; my imagination was working overtime. I shoved down the thought that threatened to emerge and went in to order takeout.

Back at the hospital waiting area, Sue Lynn pounced on the waffle and gobbled down the bacon. The food disappeared in under two minutes, and she stood there with greasy, savage lips and eager eyes, scanning the brown bag I'd brought.

"Got anything else?" she asked. I opened up the bag to show her the contents: Xylia's clean flannel nightgown. Thankfully, the Moon Pie Ernie had meant for Xylia was hidden at the bottom.

"Not unless you're a boll weevil," I answered. She puckered up her hungry lips, then whipped out her wallet and moved towards the vending machines down the hall like a wolf searching for prey. The doctor came in to report that the surgery was successful and Xylia was in recovery. We would be able to see her soon.

Over the next hour, Sue Lynn devoured three chocolate bars and two bags of chips and four Little Debbies. She gulped down cups of coffee and paced the room, waiting for the pay phone, which was occupied. When she finally called her Ed, she found out a tour bus had broken down while passing through Jackson. Ed was going crazy trying to fit 95 Japanese tourists into their 40 motel rooms. She sure hoped Xylia would get her ass better soon, because she had to get on back down to the motel before the toilets plugged up. The sewer pipe to the main was filled with roots but they couldn't afford to fix it until they got some cash. When the nurse came out and announced Xylia could have a visitor, just one, I let her go in first. She moved a little too eagerly towards the recovery room, her thin shoulder blades protruding through the powder blue sweater. As she passed by, I felt a chill. I was glad Xylia was surrounded by watchful nurses.

A few minutes later, she returned with a scowl on her face.

"She's still out cold," she said. "No telling how long it will be. I've got to get back to Jackson. Will you call me if there's a turn for the worse?"

"Absolutely," I said, silently vowing to make Xlyia see the lawyer to change her will as soon as she was able. She scribbled down her number, grabbed up her bag of old tabloids, and left. As I walked towards the recovery room, and Xylia, I turned to look back at her, to make sure she was leaving. The last time I saw her, she was plugging quarters into a vending machine.

Xylia didn't look quite as pale. When I went in and took her hand, I spoke to her in a soft voice.

"I brought you a Moon Pie, from Ernie," I said. "Had to hide it from Sue Lynn." I looked at her lying there and saw a slight twitch cross over her dry lips. I went over to the sink to get some drops of water to place on her lips to wet them a bit.

"Real piece a work," Xylia muttered. I turned around and saw her lips form into a smile and I knew she was going to be fine. Just fine.

Except for those words, she didn't come around until an hour or so later. In an effort to bring her back, I talked to her nonstop and told her about Sue Lynn's plans and had just moved into a full-scale narration of my night with Will, G-rated, of course. I was explaining about how she was absolutely right about sex and death, or near-death, in this case, when I was startled by her voice.

"Sorry I didn't die," she said. I moved up close to her and watched as her eyes fluttered open.

"Xylia?"

"Sex would have been even better," she said. I laughed and squeezed her hand. She was too weak to laugh out loud, but I saw her stomach move up and down with the ripple of a chuckle. I kept talking to her, as the nurse had told me to, although she drifted in and out of sleep. She didn't talk much, except when I told her she definitely needed to get into town and change her will, she spoke up and said, "Get the buzzard off my back," I knew she referred to Sue Lynn. She slept off and on until a few hours later, when some ladies from the church arrived, carrying old-time paper fans, the kind used at revivals during the summer. I remembered my stepmother explaining to me once that a person on his deathbed will gasp for air. Thus, it was a local custom for the ladies to show up and fan the air. Before I could stop them, the two ladies moved to either side of Xylia and waved the fans over her face. Xylia opened her eyes, shooed them away.

"Lordy girls, put those fans away before I get pneumonia," Xylia said, then told me to leave and go home to the valley. "Avie, you get back at that whore death some more for me."

"Yes, 'Ma'am," I answered, and noting Miss Hunnicutt's red face, added, "Xylia's on some heavy-duty pain medication. Don't pay her any mind."

On the road back home, the bright harshness of the day had mellowed into a warm afternoon. Bathed in the late afternoon sun, the entire landscape appeared changed from earlier. Xylia was going to be all right, and Will would be home soon. A twinge of excitement moved down my core as I thought of seeing him later that night. I stared at the sun, perched well above the tree line that ran across the rolling ridges. I wanted to reach out and shove it down, to force the dark to come to the valley, but the sun had a mind of its own. Now it was softer, letting its tawny light gently spill over the earth. Earlier, its harsh, midday self seemed foreboding as it played tricks wherever it shone. Spider webs looked like piano wire; a flash of silver coming from Aunt Cottie's wrinkled throat looked strangely familiar. I replayed the parking lot scene over and over in my mind. The annoying flash of light, Aunt Cottie's sudden retreat. I had to find out what I suspected: could Cottie have been wearing Xylia's ring on a chain around her neck?

CHAPTER 26

When I pulled into Uncle Earl's driveway, I sat frozen in my car, unable to get out. Cottie might have the ring, but I felt shame when I thought of facing her. She and Uncle Earl were my elders and my kin. What if I were wrong? Were they capable of committing the crime that had almost killed Xylia? Earl had a mean streak but maybe Griffin was right: my uncle was all talk. Then I saw a faded red Bulldogs cap hanging from the rearview mirror of Earl's old white truck. Was it another of Dad's caps, purloined by Earl? I walked over to the truck, reached through the window and took the cap. After firmly placing it on my head, I returned to my car and retrieved the riding crop from the trunk and headed out toward my uncle's front door.

Their porch was cluttered. Empty clay pots were stacked up along the wall alongside a spade and potting soil. Several trash cans were filled to the brim with aluminum Coke cans. Five or six pairs of old loafers and muddied boots sat next to a snuff pot containing a brown, tobacco-stained newspaper. A note had been taped to the screen door.

"Duane, leave feed in barn. Me and Cottie gone for Buttermilk in ridges," was scrawled in Earl's uneven handwriting. So neither one was home. Realizing a confrontation wasn't necessary, I was relieved and considered my options.

Dusk was near. I could wait until I saw them tomorrow on some pretense or another and take a closer look. This, however, might give him time to hide the ring. If I caught them by surprise in the pasture, I could find out tonight. My curiosity propelled me forward. I returned to my car to grab a flashlight and headed to the gate.

That evening I walked farther back on the ridges than I'd ever been, up the hill, past the grazing cattle, but my uncle and aunt were nowhere in sight. I went beyond the stream to where my brother wanted to lay down asphalt paths for his new housing development. As I approached the ribbon of muddy water, I found a narrow spot, gathered myself up, ran and jumped over, landing in the soft red clay before climbing up the other side. I passed the sycamore where I'd first seen Will, and traveled higher up, from the grassy areas to the woods.

My eyes searched the forest, but all I saw were the trees: maple, oak, redbud, dogwood, sweet gum trees and of course, pine. I walked beyond the meteor crater where Griffin and I had talked, past the small, opaque waters where I had spotted the blue heron.

I moved deeper into the forest, under a myriad of tree branches, through fading shafts of light that fell between the trees, listening all the while. I stopped for a sip of water, looked up through arcing branches at the pale crescent moon and remembered the old German saying I'd drawn from the sayings jar down at the store, "never look at the moon through trees." I quickly looked away.

I ran into what appeared to be a cow trail, or perhaps an old Indian path, and followed it deeper into the woods searching for my uncle. He had to be out here somewhere. After five minutes or so climbing up another ridge, I spotted a pile of rocks about 20 feet off the path. Perhaps the cow had somehow gotten a leg caught in the rocks and I would see the back of Earl's thick, ruddy neck hunched over, trying to free it. I tightened my grip on the riding crop and headed over.

Instead I found what appeared to be a house foundation. There were four corners stacked with piles of heavy rocks. Three stairs led up to nowhere at what once might have been the front entrance. I climbed up the stairs, stared at the ground below, at what once might have been a living room. I jumped down, imagined I was walking through the rooms of the house. There were no visible old boards, and I had a distant memory of my dad telling me people often gleaned vacant, older structures in search of oak with wormholes to use in constructing furniture. As I stood in the overgrown living room by a pile of old bricks, I thought about the family who'd once warmed their hands by the fire.

A bubbling noise emanated from somewhere to the rear of the house. Perhaps a stream where I would find Earl with his cow. I moved about 20 yards to the rear of the house, inhaled the dampness. A small spring gurgled out of a ledge. I wet my fingers in the spring and tasted it. Sulphur. As I squatted by the water, I found myself looking up, into the large limbs of an old oak tree, and I remembered what Will had told me.

The oak tree is to the Cherokees a symbol of strength and eternal life. This tree looked like it had been around since before the Cherokees. The trunk was massive and I went over to see if I could get my arms around it. I leaned in to touch the bark, noted an indentation on the bark where someone had carved something a long time ago. I pointed my flashlight at the area.

The carving was in the distinctive shape of a feather, tilted to the right. I looked towards the direction the feather pointed, and turned to walk that way. The leaves crunched under my feet as I moved along in a straight path, wondering where it would lead me. I thought I heard a rustle of leaves somewhere in the distance behind me, and turned to look. Could I have passed Earl up, and could he possibly be following me? I quickened my pace, crackled over brown leaves and thorny gumballs.

Suddenly the ground gave way beneath me and I shot down through the earth, into the dark. My screams were muffled by the earth as I fell into a damp, dim space. I landed on my back, alongside a couple of rotten planks that seemed to have fallen with me. The riding crop and Bulldogs cap were nowhere in sight.

Uncle Earl had been right after all. It seemed I had fallen into an abandoned well.

About six feet above, lingering light filtered through a tiny hole into the dark space I occupied. The rotten boards that had covered the opening had given way under my feet. I patted myself to make sure nothing was broken or bleeding, crawled around to see if there was an exit other than the one out of my reach. The earth smelled musty and rich and I knew no one had been here for years. My hands groped the hard ground that formed the floor of the well. Then I remembered my flashlight. Thankfully, it was still in my pocket. I switched it on, pointed it at the walls, where I saw two by fours driven into the walls. It was comforting to know someone else had been here before, even if it might have been long ago.

As I explored, I began to think it was not a well after all. The walls were not as nature had made them. They'd been chopped away, or excavated, by someone, exposing the layers of stone. They were light gray, streaked with milky quartz. A dark gray-bluish layer ran through the quartz, like a layer of frosting through a cake. My heartbeat quickened as I remembered Joseph's description of native silver. When exposed to air, it would appear the color of tarnished silver. I ran my finger along the black layer, or vein, and followed it deeper into the shaft. As I crawled along, the jagged edges of something pressed into my knees, and I felt as though my jeans might rip. I reached down to move away the rock in my way, and found six or seven more. I picked one up, held it to the light.

About the size of a walnut, it was completely clear quartz, almost. Locked inside its middle was a tiny treasure: a silver whitish nugget about the size of a peanut in a shell. I stuffed it in my pocket, switched off the flashlight to conserve the battery and sat down to contemplate the irony of my situation.

I had stumbled into the silver mine, proved my skeptical husband wrong. Joseph would have been delighted with my discovery. Would I ever surface to tell him? Would I stay buried in this dark space with the treasure for another 100 years or so? I was as trapped in this place as the silver nugget was in the quartz. Worst of all, I had ended up all alone, abandoned, not by my Uncle Earl, my father, Michael or anyone else, but as a result of my curiosity about whether or not my aunt was wearing Xylia's ring. Would my life end because of my overwhelming curiosity? Surely the gods were laughing somewhere. I joined them, laughing hysterically till I almost choked.

Laughter turned to tears and I found myself there, in the growing darkness, alone and weeping. Then I thought of Uncle Earl and his search for his cow. I stood up, tilted my head towards the shaft and repeatedly screamed out his name until my voice grew hoarse. Nothing but my own echo answered me. I imagined the afternoon turning into night, the night into morning, the morning into afternoon, the afternoon into night, the cycle repeating itself, draining me, until I died alone from lack of water. All because of a lousy six feet of rock wall that I could not scale. I would come up with a plan.

I stood up, pointed the flashlight at the hole, or airshaft I'd fallen through and saw its ragged edges above. If I could somehow build a platform and climb up, I could escape. My first step would be to inventory the cave, or mine, for materials.

There was wood, five or six rotten boards that had fallen through the hole with me. Apparently wood had covered the opening to the mine but finally time and the elements had weakened them. I tested the boards and found some parts still sturdy. Then there were the two by fours I'd noticed driven into the walls. Even if I could pry them off, what would be the point if their removal weakened the walls causing them to cave in? I would simply have to go deeper into the cavern for an answer.

I crawled away from the light, down the shaft, which seemed to slope. Along the sides, I began to find rocks or pieces of ore which had been removed by the miners. A few were the size of oranges, one the size of a grapefruit. Every time I found one, I'd roll it back up the shaft, towards the hole where the light came in. This was a difficult and tedious process and I worked slowly. Although I paced myself, I was soon sweating with the effort. I had moved deeper into the mine, perhaps 30 to 40 feet, and was concentrating on moving back along the walls to the small pile I had gathered underneath the hole. I looked up to find the pale beacon of light from the airshaft, but it was no longer there. It had grown dark while I'd been gathering the last rock. I sat down beside the small pile and measured it with my hands. It was, at its greatest height, only about half a foot tall. A good start but not anywhere close. I reached into my pocket, pulled out a partially empty bottle of water and rewarded myself with a tiny sip. I was exhausted. Fearing I might need it later, I switched off the flashlight, buttoned my jacket up tight and lay my head down on the pile of rocks to rest a bit. I shut my eyes against the bleak reality around me, and slept.

A clear blue body of water. A small school of shimmering fish skims just under the smooth surface of the lake. A Cherokee woman steps out from a glade and wades into the water, plunges her arms through the mirrored surface and scoops under for the fish. They dart away. A loud swooshing noise in the air. She looks up to see the six-foot wingspan of the blue heron pass over. She watches as it lands on the distant shoreline, opposite her. It slowly wades into the water, stands patiently, waiting. Suddenly, the heron drops its head, breaks the smooth surface of the water with its long bill, snaps up a glittering fish.

Later I awoke to a white sliver of moonlight coming through the opening in the top of the mine. I stood up and moved around until I could see a crescent moon. Like the heron, I would be patient. I would work with the rocks nature had provided. Using my flashlight sparingly, I crawled back to gather more rocks.

In the dark and musty depths of the earth, your mind will play tricks on you. A dark shape on the ceiling looks like a bat, your breathing echoes back to you, sounding like another person, although you know you're alone. Time passed slowly as I worked through my fear, found another large rock, this one the size of a honeydew melon. I had almost rolled it to my escape pile when I noticed the moon had moved away, was no longer visible through the opening. I did not want to drain the flashlight battery, and decided my escape plan would have to wait until morning. Laying my head against the growing pile of rocks, I wondered if Joseph would be worried about me. I wavered on the edge of sleep until

I noticed the dark begin to be replaced by feeble light.

A pale dawn filtered through the shaft above. I sat up, rubbed my eyes and saw that the mine continued farther back than I had initially believed. I thought of Joseph, and something he'd explained about reading one of the books Will had given him. Older mines had not necessarily been laid out in an organized fashion, but often were a maze-like series of tunnels and paths of varying depths. "Almost like one of those ant farms," he'd explained to me. I stared at my pitiful pile of rocks, the impossible high ragged hole I'd fallen through. There had to be an entrance somewhere and the only way to find it was to explore the maze-like tunnels.

I gathered up small pieces of ore and put them in my pockets. Every 15 feet or so I'd mark the way I'd come from. At the very least, I'd be able to return to the spot beneath the airshaft where I'd fallen through, and although I would still be stuck in the mine, it was a known quantity.

I began my wanderings cautiously, following the beam of the light along the darkened passages, walking slowly and counting out 15 steps at a time. I kept my right hand on the closest wall except when I bent down to place a piece of ore on the path at the 15th step. The process was slow as I twisted and turned along the walls, and I had no idea how much time had passed until I reached into my pockets and found two pieces of ore remaining. The beam of the flashlight was growing pale. With hope, I moved forward another 15 steps and found myself with a fading flashlight and one piece of ore, its tiny nugget encased in quartz crystal.

I sat down on the hard ground, took a tiny sip from my almost empty water bottle and pondered my choices. The thought of the ragged hole was comforting. I could return there and yell some more. Perhaps Will or Jolene or even Earl was looking for me at this very moment. I would go back and wait under the ragged hole of light for someone to rescue me. It was the only wise and sensible thing to do. I stood up, turned around and headed back picking up the ore pieces as I found my way back.

As I retraced my steps, I thought of my marriage. How safe it had been to remain in a familiar, though stale, relationship. For many years it had been so easy to let Michael fight my battles, to let him set the pace for our cautious, orderly and mostly predictable life. But with the death of my father, an unraveling had begun, and then a soft unfolding from inside me. With no parent around to disapprove of my actions, I had finally begun blossoming into a more mature version of myself, one who needed neither father's nor husband's approval. I thought of this and stopped. I reached into my pocket and my hand fell upon the silver quartz nugget. I thought of Will.

He didn't operate in fear but rather with a sense of adventure. I knew if he were here, he wouldn't necessarily take the safe way out. He'd try to find an exit. I put the nugget into my pocket and zipped it up. I turned back towards the unknown. I'd take my chances.

My hands became calloused as I groped along the dark passages, my eyes grew wearier, the beam of my flashlight dimmer. I arrived at the juncture of two tunnels and couldn't decide which way to go until I thought I heard the faint call of a bird in the distance. I chose the passage I thought it had come from.

Several minutes later I saw a tiny speck of light ahead, although I considered it could be a hallucination. I halted, turned off the flashlight, closed my eyes and prayed that it wasn't. I reopened my eyes. The light was still there.

I moved quickly toward the growing light, finally arriving at what appeared to be a small opening. Surrounded by rocks, the opening was big enough for a small child but not for me. I thrust both arms through and felt a light mist on my arm and screamed with joy. I tugged at the rocks around the entrance and working quickly, soon had made a space large enough to crawl through. Like one of Uncle Earl's legendary rattlesnakes, I emerged from the mine on my belly. I lay on the damp ground and inhaled the fresh mist. A heron called in the distance. I stood up and stretched and looked up at the cloudy sky. It was impossible to tell what time it was, but what did it matter? Looking back at the mine entrance one final time, I turned and ran back down the ridges, through the woods, where I knew Taylor's Ridge stood.

CHAPTER 27

The ground thudded under me as I jogged my way through the trees, towards the distant sound of a ringing bell. The emergency bell! My pace quickened but the land was rough in places and I stumbled, twisting my foot in a gopher hole. I threw my hands out in front but still landed hard on the ground, thankfully covered with long grass. I was still for a moment, until I felt a gust of raw wind smart my cheeks. I collected myself, stood up and began moving once again towards the ringing bell, keeping the long, hard shadow of Taylor's Ridge always in front of me like a beacon.

I needed to slow down. I took a few deep breaths, inhaling the morning air. It was good to be free. I'd put death back in its place, at least for the present. A sharp whistle pierced the darkness; it didn't sound like a bird. Thinking it might be someone looking for me, I whistled back.

"Avie ?" Will called out. His hardy voice came from a distance, but I was sure it was he.

"I'm here. I'm okay," I called back. We called back and forth until we spotted each other. He folded his warm arms around me and held on tight. His chest heaved up slightly against mine in a sigh of relief. We didn't speak; we didn't have to. Calmness overtook us as we stood there wrapped in each other's arms. A minute or so later I heard his husky voice next to my chilled ear lobe.

"You're freezing. Better get moving." He handed me a bottle of water and we continued walking back, holding hands and talking as we journeyed towards the gate. I told him how I'd been trapped underground and thought I'd never escape.

"I was in the silver mine, Will," I said, expecting him to be thrilled about my discovery but he wasn't.

"I can't wait to tell Joseph," I said. He squeezed my hand.

"I wouldn't," he said.

"Why not?" I asked.

"Some secrets should remain secrets." I felt my cheeks began to flush. It wasn't like Will to tell me what I could and could not say, and I didn't want us to get started down this path. This relationship would be different; we would be equals.

"Look Will, the silver mine is on my land. I own it. What could possibly be wrong with telling Joseph?"

"You know you can do whatever you want, but here's how I see it, I mean the Cherokee me." He stepped back but kept his hands on my shoulders. His face grew serious, his chestnut eyes full of determination. "The last time folks found out about mining opportunities they ran us out."

"You mean Dahlonega? And the Trail of Tears? That was eons ago, Will. And besides, this is silver, not gold."

"Yes, but don't you see? It always comes down to one thing: greed. It's timeless and universal. No good will come from sharing the mine with the world. Trust me on this one, Avie. Let's keep it a secret for now, okay?" I didn't have a chance to answer. We heard men's voices and soon after, saw Trent and Joseph approach.

"Mom?" Joseph spoke. "You heard the bell! I rang it for you." He ran to me, grabbed me in a hug. I wanted to tell him about the mine, but glancing up at Will, I hesitated. Instead, I skirted around the truth by explaining I'd lost my way and waited to come back once there was light. There would be plenty of time later to tell him about the silver mine.

"Well, I'm glad you got back okay," Joseph said, "I missed you." He glanced back to make sure no one was listening, but Trent and Will were trying to dial up Jolene on Trent's cell phone. "I was scared."

"Me too," I said. "Hey, Xylia woke up. She's going to be fine."

"Good. I like working at the store, but it's not as much fun without Xylia, you know?"

"I know," I said. He whipped out his inhaler and took a quick puff.

"Are you having trouble with your asthma, son?" He shrugged.

"A little bit, but I'm fine, Mom. I hit 525 this morning."

"You're kidding!"

"Nope," he beamed as he said it. Will and Trent came over and all of us started down the slope towards home. Joseph and I looped our elbows together and followed.

Back at Dad's house, Jolene celebrated my return with a big batch of biscuits and tomato gravy. Trent, Jolene, Tyler, Sammie, Joseph, Will and I sat around the kitchen table talking and eating.

"Any word from Xylia?" I asked.

"I called her and she's doing fine. I told her you had been lost, and found. She was worried about you. Michael also called and I told him you were out, which is all I figured he needed to know. What I can't understand is how you got lost, as much as you walk up there."

"Nighttime navigating is a bit more difficult," Will offered, coming to my defense.

"Well, shoot, why were you out there after dark, anyway?" Jolene asked as she spooned another ladle of gravy onto Trent's second serving of biscuits.

"I had this hunch about Xylia's missing ring," I said. Jolene laughed.

"Bet you thought one of the cows took it, huh?" she asked. Everyone laughed except me. I still wondered if Cottie had Xylia's ring.

"Seriously, mom, what were you thinking?" Joseph asked.

"Well, I thought maybe Cottie and Earl had some information I didn't."

"Did he find it?" Tyler asked. Remembering that Taylor's Crossing really was a fish bowl of a community, and that I had no real evidence, I hesitated.

"No, just had a hunch he could be helpful," I said, deciding in this instance, discretion was in order. I reached out and touched Joseph's hand.

"I'm so tired I'm about to nod right off," I said.

"Well shoot, I guess so," said Jolene as she took my arm. "You better go get yourself a nap, girl."

"She's right. Thanks everyone for helping get me back home. And Jolene, thanks for that delicious tomato gravy," I said.

"It's mater," she said.

"Mater. And Will, we'll talk later." He winked at me and I knew talk wasn't all he had in mind. I rose and headed towards the bedroom, suddenly feeling completely spent, as though someone had pulled the plug and drained out all my energy.

"It'll be real quiet so you can rest," Jolene called out. "The boys and I'll lock up before we head on back to mind the store."

"Sleep tight, Mom," Joseph said.

While undressing in my bedroom, I cleaned out my jacket pockets and found the quartz rock and set it on the table by the bed. I thought of the Cherokee mine, and Xylia's missing ring. I picked up the receiver and dialed Sheriff Young's office. I got through to him right away and shared my hunch about Cottie and the ring. Although he sounded skeptical, he promised to follow up, probably to appease me.

I put my head down on the fluffy pillow, thankful it wasn't a hard pile of rocks. I looked over at the objects on the night bedside table, the buffalo nickel and the quartz rock with the silver embedded in the middle. Feeling safe and warm, I drifted off into a deep sleep.

I awoke to a light tapping noise from behind the curtained French doors. It was dark already, and glancing at the clock, I saw it was 11 p.m. I'd slept the day away. The tapping against the glass persisted and I heard a voice speak in low tones.

"Avie?" It was Will. I jumped up, pulled back the curtain and let him in, shutting the door behind him against the cold. Although he was wearing his buckskin jacket, his cheeks were ruddy. He placed his cold hands in my warm ones.

"Feeling better?" he asked.

"Um," I answered, stifling a yawn. "Much."

"Joseph tried to wake you up for dinner but Jolene wouldn't let him. He's already gone to bed," he said, stepping over to lock the door leading to the hallway. "We don't want him to get the wrong idea." He pulled off his jacket and took a seat in the chair by the window. "I could tell you wanted to talk earlier, so I thought I'd see if you were awake."

"Well, I am now," I said. He smiled.

"Okay, the truth is I wanted to apologize for telling you what to say to Joseph about the mine. I was out of line, wasn't I?"

"I thought so."

"So you can do whatever you think is right. It's not my mine, after all."

"I planned to," I said. "I'm going to have to think it through." He reached for the quartz nugget on the bedside table.

"A souvenir?" he asked.

"Yes. It reminds me of you."

"Because?" he asked.

"Because when I had to make a choice on how to get out of the mine, I thought of you, what you would do. I decided you'd risk getting lost in the tunnels to try and find an exit."

"I'm glad you did," he said. He came over and sat down on the bed next to me.

"Me too," I said, and leaned in to burrow against his chest. He brushed his finger along the lace edge of nightgown that ran along below my collarbone. My skin prickled under his touch. He slipped off his shirt, pulled me close. I snuggled up next to him and lay my head in the crook of his arm and inhaled him. He was buckskin and something else: the fresh, familiar smell of pine trees up on Taylor's Ridge, a scent I'd grown to love.

The rim of the sun was peeping over the top of the ridge when Will got up to leave. We didn't speak of our future before he left. We didn't have to. Ours was an evolving love and seemed to demand no promises. But I knew the bond between us was a growing one. This was what had come to matter.

It was almost light as he slipped out the French doors, but I didn't care if anyone saw him leaving. Trapped in the mine, thinking I might die, had given me time to figure out what was important. In the grand scheme of things, idle gossip ranked low.

But not for everyone. The phone rang about 10 minutes after Will left. I picked it up after the first ring, hoping it hadn't woken Joseph. It was Aunt Ardelia.

"Fornication is a sin, plain and simple," her alto voice informed me.

"Since when did you develop x-ray vision?" I asked.

"Don't get smart with me, young lady. I saw him come and I saw him go. You're an embarrassment to the family."

"Behind closed doors, Ardelia, behind closed doors, no one else knows what goes on. Not even you. Mind your own business." I slammed down the receiver.

I thought of calling Michael back to find out what he wanted. But looking at the clock, I realized it was much too early. Instead, I showered and slipped into my clothes and went to wake Joseph.

After breakfast, we set off to see Xylia. Driving past Uncle Earl's, we saw the back of their two thick necks as the sheriff and Earl stood in a tête-à-tête by the patrol car parked in front of Earl's house. When I passed by, I could see Earl's fast moving mouth trying to explain something. His chubby index finger pointed towards the porch as we passed. Joseph asked me why the police were there.

"Probably still investigating the robbery," I answered.

Xylia had moved out of intensive care and was sitting up in bed watching a news program when we entered her room. Thankfully, the steel rod had been removed from her skull, and she looked almost normal, except for the bandage on the side of her head. Joseph ran to hug her, not unlike a grandson hugging a grandma. He babbled away about the store and told her he'd restocked the shelves so things wouldn't fall on her anymore.

"I appreciate that, son. I'm getting too old to be climbing up and down step stools." She ran her fingers through her silvery hair.

"You're not that old," I scolded her. I laid a stack of magazines on her table and handed her a crayon drawing Ernie had made for her. She studied it.

The page was full with a green expanse of grass dotted with 50 or so simple squares with triangles on top. Houses. Brown roads and black cars snaked all over the page. A turquoise lake was over to the right and two people stood there, fishing.

"I don't know where it is, but they all look happy," she said.

"Especially the two guys fishing," Joseph said.

"How do you know they're guys?" I asked. Joseph pointed.

"That one's Ernie. See the mustache?" I leaned in to look. A tiny black line was drawn over a thin pink lip.

"I think you're right," I said.

"And the one next to him? I'll bet it's Uncle Earl. See, he's wearing overalls."

A nurse bustled in.

"I hate to make all you art critics scoot, but I have to change Mrs. Elmwood's bandages," the nurse said, placing a tray of supplies on the bedside table. Xylia persuaded her to let us stay and the nurse compromised by swooshing the curtain shut around the bed.

"But you have to keep still, Mrs. Elmwood, for the next five minutes," said the nurse. "And quiet, so I can concentrate." Xylia chuckled, and I smiled to myself. Obviously this nurse had recently started her shift and had never met this patient. I sent Joseph off to the vending machines with some change and flipped through a People magazine, and eavesdropped. The nurse talked to Xylia as she worked.

"Looks good, real good," she said. "That's interesting."

"What?" Xylia grunted in reply.

"Your wound is deeper at one end, almost like whatever hit you had a little point protruding on the end," she said.

"Could be," said Xylia. "I don't remember a thing." Paper crackled as the nurse opened a bandage. I thought about the shape of flashlights. Slender barrels and round circles at the top. No protruding points, at least in the ones I'd seen down at the store.

"Ow!" Xylia said.

"I'm almost finished," said the nurse. A minute or so later she snapped the curtain open and left the room. We visited for an hour or so, chatting and laughing, until it was time for Xylia's sponge bath.

On the way home, we stopped at the bank where I picked up the loan papers for the money that would allow me to buy out my siblings' share of the estate. Then, after a quick lunch at Aunt Christie's Cafe, we drove back to the valley to help Jolene out at the store.

CHAPTER 28

Elmwood's parking lot, if you could call it that, rarely had more than a couple of cars. So I was surprised to see four vehicles jammed into the narrow gravel area in front. I recognized Earl's pickup and the truck Trent had loaned Jolene. The sheriff's cruiser was parked alongside a silver Lexus. Joseph and I hurried in to see what was going on.

School was in session, or so it seemed. All the desks were pulled around in a circle and Jolene was passing out icy cans of soda. At the desks sat Earl, Cottie and a man in a suit who looked vaguely familiar. Sammie Jo watched Ernie coloring a picture on a large sketch pad. Uncle Earl looked up when we entered.

"Good," he said, pointing at me. "I want her to hear this too, so she'll stop spreadin' her vicious gossip around." I stared at his full, sagging jaw, a Bulldogs cap and wanted to tell him he looked like the bulldog's ugly brother, but I held my tongue. Joseph ran to the stock room and brought in a couple of extra chairs. Sheriff Young ripped the cellophane off a Moon Pie and took small bites while he opened up his notebook. The man knew how to eat with style. Joseph came back with the chairs and we took our place in the circle.

Sheriff Young lay down a half Moon Pie and went over to lock the front door.

"May I?" he asked. Jolene nodded and he turned the "Open" sign around to read "Closed." "This should take only a few minutes." He took his place back in the circle and began.

"Miss Jolene, thanks for letting us meet here. I wanted all of you all to hear what Mr. Blevins here had to say because that's what Earl wanted. And since it was easy for Mr. Blevins to locate the store, and since he's squeezing us in between appointments, I agreed to let him meet us here." Mr. Blevins nodded amicably but I could see his fingers in his pocket, fiddling with his cell phone. In his business suit, he looked out of place. The sheriff continued. "Mr. Blevins, could you tell us when you last saw Mr. Earl here?"

"He met me early Saturday morning, around 6:15 in the morning, up at the Waffle House."

"Was he alone?"

"No. Mrs. Williams was with him."

"Six fifteen's awful early. What was the purpose of the meeting?"

"Well, I was on the way to Chattanooga and I met him to give him the architect's proposal."

"For what?" said Sheriff Young.

"The proposed development, of course." We all looked dumbly into one another's faces, except Earl and Cottie, who grinned like a pair of chimpanzees high on bananas.

"Development?" the sheriff broke the silence.

"Earl and Cottie are acquiring a huge parcel of land. The property is beautiful. Up on those ridges there across the road, behind their house. It's going to be an upscale development with custom homes built on two-acre lots. I was hesitant to build out this far from town, until Earl proved to me how much traffic passes through here. On an average day, it's between a thousand and eleven hundred cars, not counting big rigs."

"Nine hundred ninety-eight," Ernie's voice spoke up from over by the window. Jolene and I stared at him. No wonder he'd been so attached to his green, spiral-bound notebook, the one, I realized, I'd seen Earl carrying at the Waffle House that rainy day. He'd shown it to this man, Mr. Blevins.

"I paid him for countin' them cars," said Uncle Earl. "Fair and square."

"A real equal opportunity employer, I'm sure," I said. Jolene laughed. Uncle Earl glared at me while Cottie's hooded eyes provided reinforcement. Sheriff Young cleared his throat.

"Mr. Blevins, if it comes to down to it, would you be willing to testify that you were with them that morning?" the sheriff asked.

"I don't see why not," he said. "I'll be coming up here quite a bit once we break ground over there, probably in the spring." A scalding surge of anger rose in my throat. I stood up.

"I don't think so, Mr. Blevins. You're talking about my land, not theirs. They're acquiring nothing, as far as I know. I'm not selling. You've been duped Mr. Blevins." He looked confusedly at Earl.

"She'll come around, Phil. I'll talk to her husband," Earl said, ignoring the fact I was in the room. Mr. Blevins rose from the desk as if to leave.

"You've got a week, Earl. If I can't get it in writing by then, the deal's off." He buttoned up the jacket on his gray tweed blazer and turned to Sheriff Young. "Can I go now? I've got firm deals to attend to."

"Yes sir," he said. "I'll call you if I need to see you again." Earl got up and followed Blevins out the door, trying to reassure him things would work out. Aunt Cottie turned to me, rattling her wrist full of charm bracelets close to my face. I stared at her chest and saw she was wearing a silver chain, but not Xylia's ring.

"You done blown it now, gal," she said. "Big time." Jolene and I looked at one another and burst out laughing. Sheriff Young took another bite from his Moon Pie. We all looked up when we heard the gravel crunch under the Lexus' tires as the developer pulled away. Earl slammed the door as he came back in.

"You'll change your mind," he said, narrowing his dark eyes into slants, glowering at me. I thought of the cow brains and how he'd tried to make me eat them, how he'd left me alone that night long ago. I looked at him and smiled.

"Pony brains," I said. His eyes squinted up and he scowled at me.

"Ma'am?" he asked.

"You can't scare me anymore, Uncle Earl," I said, and I meant it. At that point, Sheriff Young stuck his hand on the butt of his pistol.

"Earl, Avie, settle down now," said the sheriff. Earl sat back down at the desk, his tobacco-stained lips twisted into a pout. I eased into another desk, folded my hands together and looked at the sheriff, who continued.

"Earl, I know you may be disappointed, but I want you to keep a cool head. You know as well as I do, folks 'round here can do what they want to with their property." The sheriff looked at me, pulled Xylia's ring out of his pocket. You could hear the collective gasp in the room.

"Now where did you say you got this from?" he looked at Earl.

"I told you, I found it on my porch when I got back from the Waffle House that morning." Brought by the Tooth Fairy, no doubt. Sheriff Young looked down at the ring.

An awkward quietness filled the room. The big hand on the wall clock clicked as it passed over the short one; the motor on the old Coke cooler whirred in the background. No one was ready to make the next move. Gravel crunched as another car pulled up. Through the plate glass window, I saw the red hood of Ardelia's Le Sabre pull into view.

"Oh great," Jolene said. Sheriff Tate stood up and tipped his hat as Ardelia, leaning heavily against her cane, swung through the door. The afternoon sun spilled in after her and Jolene told her to leave the door open.

"I think we could all use some fresh air about now," Jolene said. Ardelia limped over to the desk vacated by Blevins and sat down. She laid her cane on top and began speaking.

"Sheriff Young, I came down here to speak up for my baby brother. Avie's been spreading rumors but they're not true. Earl's done nothing wrong." She played with the cane, slowly turning the wooden end around like she was checking the rubber stob for manure.

"Settle down, Miss Ardelia, it's routine questioning, that's all," he said. "Routine." She droned on about how things had been fine until the rotten egg had rolled into town, nodding her head in my direction. She turned the cane around by its end, rotating the rubber tip like a handle or knob, causing the entire cane to rotate slowly. Its silver bird head reflected the afternoon sun.

Then I saw it: a pointy ear on one side of the cane's head that protruded out in a sharp angle. It looked dangerous, although it was simply the ear on what I now realized was an owl. I closed my eyes as her voice droned on. I thought of the owl I had heard up in Will's woods the night we spent together. I saw how it looked: its small pointed ears, like Ardelia's cane. But not so sharp. Ardelia's cane tip looked like it could do some damage. Had done some damage. Aunt Ardelia's cane was the weapon that almost killed Xylia!

I jumped up, and before she could resist, snatched the cane away from my aunt, grabbing it on the wooden shaft just below the steel owl's head. She stared incredulously at her empty hands, now clutching only thin air.

"You give it back, Missy," she growled. I ignored her.

"See this, Sheriff? This cane is what hit Xylia last Thursday morning. This cane nearly killed her!" I said. Ardelia snorted.

"Everyone knows I'm crippled. Besides, what would I want with her dumb ring?" she asked. "I've got better things to do than wear costume jewelry." But the sheriff didn't like something he'd seen or heard, and he went over and leaned down by Ardelia. He said something in a real low voice. She hollered back at him.

"No, I will not go in with you for questioning. Give me my cane back, you whore!" she shouted and we all watched as she unfolded her long body from the desk and walked surely, steadily and cane-free, across the concrete floor like a woman suddenly healed in a Bible story. She charged at me and grabbed for the cane but I held on tight as we tugged back and forth.

It might have been her height or her anger, but I had never felt a woman with such physical strength. I thought I'd lose my balance, but I planted my feet into the floor and held on tight, blocking out everything around us. It was her against me and I wasn't letting go.

Suddenly I felt no resistance and I lost balance and fell over backwards, into Jolene's arms. The sheriff had his thick hands clasped around my aunt's strong biceps and had pulled her back. She let out a low roar like a mother cow as he wrestled her hands around behind her. I heard the comforting metal snap of handcuffs locked into place. A cacophony of voices filled the room as he read Ardelia her rights, Earl pleaded with him and Ardelia spewed out a string of curses. Cottie muttered repeatedly in my general direction, "Ought to be ashamed of yourself."

Joseph stood protectively by Sammie Jo in the front window while Ernie scribbled furiously on his pad, trying to shut out the madness. Jolene opened the door. She stood there, waving her hands in the air, trying to encourage their departure, like a picnicker shooing away an annoying platoon of insects.

"I'm closin' up for the day," Jolene said, "so you all have to leave. "Goodbye." Everyone filed out and Jolene locked the door behind her and made sure the "closed" sign was positioned correctly. Then, we all peeked past the "today's specials" sign in the window to see the sheriff load my aunt into his patrol car. Her curses died away as he locked her in the back seat. Earl and Cottie started back towards the store entrance, but the sheriff intercepted and told them to head on home. He came back to the front door and Jolene let him in.

"Miss Avie, I have to take that cane as evidence," he said. Reluctantly, I handed it over. Then he stepped behind the counter and opened up a drawer, the one where Xylia kept the little slips of paper after she'd posted the quotes on the chalkboard. He asked Jolene for a paper bag, and then dumped in the contents of the drawer. "Evidence," he said. He moved to the front door and was about to leave, when he said to me, "Earl drove your aunt's car back and parked it behind her house. I think he'll stay out of your hair, but if he bothers you, call me." He gave me one of his business cards. I took it and thanked him. He was almost out the door when he turned back to me and spoke again. "I need you to promise me one thing," he said. "You stay out of his hair, too."

Jolene put her arm around me and answered for me.

"You can count on it, Sheriff. She's not leaving my sight."

As soon as they'd all pulled away, Jolene closed and locked the door and we dialed up Xylia to tell her the news about Ardelia. She was elated and disappointed at the same time.

"If Ardelia's convicted and sent to prison, what will the valley do for entertainment?" she asked. "Things might get pretty dull without her."

"Don't worry," I assured her. "You'll be back soon to liven things up." We hung up with her and Jolene rounded everyone up to leave.

"Let's go celebrate the end of the Taylor's Crossing crime wave," she said. We headed back to Dad's house where she cooked us dinner while the kids taught Ernie to play video games. After work, Will and Trent showed up and we all sat down to eat and tell them the story of Ardelia's arrest, and about the cane that she used as a weapon.

"Her cane?" Will said. "Well that certainly makes sense. Joseph, Tyler, remember what I said about the Cherokees' beliefs about certain animals?"

"The rabbit is the mischief maker," Tyler said.

"And owls? Remember?" Will asked. He was a natural teacher, even when he was "off duty." I admired his silhouette as he spoke, the strong, aquiline nose and deep-set eyes. Joseph tilted his head for a moment and thought.

"I've got it. They thought owls were witches in disguise," he said.

"I'd say the shoe fits," Jolene said, and we all laughed.

After everyone had left, and Joseph had gone to bed, Will helped me clean up in the kitchen. When we had loaded the final plate into the washer, I stood with my hands on the edge of the sink, looking out the window. He came up behind me and stroked my hair. He put his arms around me and we stood together, peering through the darkness at the pale orb over Taylor's Ridge.

The moon had gone through all its phases since I'd first arrived in the valley, since I first saw it suspended over the ridge's firm back. That first chilly night I'd sought out the source of the smoke. Standing there in Will's embrace, together admiring the moon over Taylor's Ridge, I felt at that moment I had found all the warmth I needed.

CHAPTER 29

Monday morning was a cold, hard slap in the face. Joseph and I had slept in until I heard the phone ring. I answered and immediately regretted it.

"I've decided to seek custody of Joseph," Michael said in clipped, harsh tones. I sat up in bed, tried to pull my thoughts together.

"Good morning to you, too," I said.

"I'm serious, Avie. If you're not back here by next week, I'm filing papers. Now I'd like to speak with my son." Speechless, I walked the phone into Joseph, handed him the receiver and returned to the kitchen table to collect my thoughts on the whole sorry mess.

I found myself shivering as I drank a cup of hot tea. Michael wasn't the type of person to make idle threats. His bullying angered me, but I realized returning to California might be my only option despite the fact I had not completed my fiduciary duties. All the commotion with Xylia, the silver mine and the sheriff's investigation, not to mention Will, had been a temporary distraction from the estate. If I pushed the lawyer, and Jolene and Griffin, I could probably get the settlement agreement signed by the end of the week.

Rubbing the sleep from his eyes, Joseph sauntered into the kitchen. He came up and hugged me from behind.

"Are we really going home next week?" he asked, a smile on his face. So Michael had done his dirty work, assumed he'd get his way. I hated him for controlling me, and I hated myself for being controlled.

"If I can finish a few more things on the estate," I said.

"Good," he said. "I miss Dad. And he said when we get back he's going to take me to buy a new laptop." He walked over and peered into the refrigerator looking for food. He didn't see me grimace.

"That's nice," I said. How easy it would have been to tell Joseph about the silver mine at that point. To make him want to stay on longer. But I would not stoop to toying with his emotions, as Michael had so artfully done.

I felt sick with the possibility that he might take Joseph away from me. Fear is a great motivator. I got to work immediately, scheduled the lawyer for the signing of the settlement agreement for Friday and contacted Jolene. Predictably, Griffin balked, then launched into a full-scale lecture. He told me I would regret not letting him develop the land and I was being foolish. I admitted he might be right, but that I needed closure and this was the simplest way to achieve it. Furthermore, I explained Michael had threatened to take away Joseph unless I wrapped up the estate and came home. This triggered his brotherly soft spot, the one he seldom used. Like most big brothers, he had to feel downright sorry for his sister before easing up. He backed down and asked what time he should show up at the lawyer's.

After breakfast, and perhaps contemplating the journey home, Joseph seemed restless. He announced he was walking to the store to help Jolene out. As I watched him tuck his inhaler in his pocket, I once again found myself amazed at how he'd grown in so many ways since we'd arrived that cold night more than a month before.

All that remained to do was sort through a few more of Dad's things in the back closet. There were two huge cardboard boxes, unlabeled. I put the first one on the bed and opened the lid to find hundreds of photographs. I wanted Jolene there, but she was busy minding the store. Besides, it was my fiduciary duty. So I sat down and made three piles: one for each sibling.

It was painful, slow work, sorting those frozen moments of time, jumbled together in a single box. Dad and his new bride, Mama, smiling into the camera, oblivious to the future. Daddy standing by Mama's graveside with a worn-out expression on his face. The baby me, wide-cheeked and wide-smiled, aiming to please. My emotions zigzagged as I made my way through the snapshots to the bottom, where I encountered the 5 x 7's and the 8 x 10's. The main events.

Michael and I stood in the center of the bridal party in the beachside gazebo. His arm was wrapped around my waist, and he looked down at my face with concern. Just before the shot was taken, when we'd climbed up the gazebo steps, I'd tripped over the long hem of my wedding gown. Michael reached out to catch me before I fell and whispered, "You should have taken my hand," referring to his earlier offer to assist. He smiled when he said it and offered his hand once again, then steered me to the top. At the time I appreciated his cautiousness. As I had felt with my father the night lightning struck our house, with Michael, I also felt safe and protected. I began to cry as I put the photo aside and moved to the next picture.

We were at our 10th anniversary party. A decade of Michael calling the shots, no longer smiling when he second-guessed my decisions. His tender look of concern had been replaced with one of annoyance. The anniversary photographer had asked us to feed each other a forkful of cake. At first Michael flatly refused. He'd found out about his high cholesterol and cake was off his list, even one forkful, even for the millisecond of a shutter opening. Finally, after I pulled him aside, gave him a napkin and told him he could spit it out right after, he cooperated. He wore a long-suffering, tortured expression. It pained him to do anyone's bidding but his own.

I held the wedding photo next to the anniversary photo and

saw the stark contrast. It was clear that the man I had married had changed. To be fair, I had changed too. Fifteen years earlier I had sought someone to be my protector, lead me along through the daily battles of life, to serve as my shield, if necessary. With my husband at my side, I had been safe from the Uncle Earl's of the world, safe from being abandoned. I had followed in Mama's footsteps, compromised part of myself to stay in a relationship for the safety it provided.

Michael's wariness had killed the spontaneity that life offers, its randomness that can bring joy to routine. He needed to control his environment and everything in it, including me. Why had I not noticed sooner?

I placed the three piles of pictures into smaller boxes, put the old versions of us aside. I no longer needed Michael to direct me. In fact after we signed the settlement agreement, I would have settled the estate on my own, without his help. My escape from the silver mine had unearthed something that had been buried inside me all along. Confidence. I was perfectly capable of finding my own way.

I picked up the empty cardboard box that had held the pictures, saw a slender stick-type object wedged in between the flap below. I reached in the box, pulled out a paintbrush. One of Mama's. It was then that I was certain what I would do once I returned to California. I called my broker in Los Angeles and arranged for the sale of some of my separately held stock. Remembering what my mother had told me about keeping a little "mad money" to myself, I had wisely set aside savings in my own name. The investing courses I'd taken in the early years of our marriage had paid off and I had accumulated enough "mad money" to see me through.

Before I left, I tied up loose ends. On Friday, Griffin came by to pick up the antique dresser, washbasin and tools he'd requested from the estate. I split the guns, giving my brother the rifle and Jolene the pistol. Just for fun, I gift wrapped the toilet plunger and left it in Griffin's back seat when he wasn't looking. Later, we all met in Ringgold to sign the settlement agreement. Griffin actually hugged me and told me it was all right. He'd find another parcel for now but to call him when I changed my mind. Jolene rushed back to Elmwood's to relieve some of the church ladies.

Our goodbyes were difficult. I hated leaving Xylia in the hospital, but when I told her about Michael's threats to take Joseph away, she wanted to know why I wasn't already on the plane back. Tyler promised Joseph he'd keep up the search for the mine until we came back and call us if he had any news. Jolene said I'd better get back in time for the spring wedding, I was to be her matron of honor. Will came over and gave Joseph a short blowgun he'd made himself. Joseph thanked him, shook his hand and said he'd come back as soon as he could. I walked Will to his truck so we could say our goodbyes alone.

"I'll be here when you get back," he said as he held me in his arms. "You know where to find me." Together, we looked up at Taylor's Ridge. I took a long, deep breath, inhaled his pine scent. I exhaled the air but the memory of him I did not.

We departed early Saturday morning wearing Dad's Bulldogs caps. I left the house the same way I'd come that first September evening that seemed so long ago, through the garage door. Joseph ran ahead to say goodbye to Sammie Jo and Jolene. I hesitated for a moment to stare at the empty space where Dad's wheelchair he'd used after the surgery had been parked. I'd let the auctioneer take it away. Along with the things in the barn, it would be sold in a few weeks at auction as Dad had specified in his will. I knew my father would have been proud of the way I handled my fiduciary duties, a task that at first seemed overwhelming. As I locked the garage door, I murmured thanks to my father, in case he was listening, for the bittersweet gift he'd given me by making me executrix of his estate.

Dressed in a hot pink lacy creation and holding Sammie Jo, Jolene waved us off as we drove away from Taylor's Crossing. I turned onto the Old Alabama Highway, slowed the car down and looked east. Through the morning fog that clung tightly to its sides, the ridge was barely visible. Although I couldn't see it clearly, I could feel the strength of it beckoning, even as I drove away.

We arrived back in California and took a taxi home. Predictably, Michael was tied up at the office and couldn't come to the airport. Welcoming us upon our arrival at our townhouse were my pots of geraniums, returned to their rightful place on our front porch. It was a good sign, or so I thought. A peace offering, perhaps.

I would like to say the night went easily, but it did not. I was settling into the guest room when Michael arrived home. When I saw him embrace Joseph, I knew that coming home, at least for now, had been the right decision. Their bond was a strong one. Michael was cordial to me, but I'd seen him act friendlier to well-heeled clients. His remoteness would make my job easier.

After a dinner where he and Joseph chatted and I mainly listened, Joseph went to his room to unpack his things. Michael and I sat down to talk. I was about to tell him the truth, how I'd discovered we'd both changed and that it simply wasn't working anymore. I wanted to share with him how I felt about the land, the soft rolling hills that gave me peace when I walked, the strong ridge that gave me strength. I wanted to explain how I needed to end our marriage once and for all. I wanted a divorce.

Before the words ever made it out of my mouth, he slapped some papers into my hands. While I was on the plane back, he had filed the papers in court to prevent me from taking Joseph out of state. In the clipped, cold voice he reserved for cross-examinations he explained his lawyer had advised him to do it and he did not twist his blonde hair, not even once.

I pretended to study the papers as I felt the curl of pain assault me down low in my stomach. His swift initial parry was something I should have, but didn't, anticipate. I had been down south so long I had let down my guard, allowed myself to be lulled by the gentle, rolling rhythms of the valley.

"I won't let you take him away from me, Avie," he said. "No matter what you decide to do." Clutching the papers in my hand, I rose and said I was really tired and that I preferred to talk when the jet lag wore off.

The cheerful primary colors of our guest bedroom contrasted sharply with my dark mood as I settled down on the double bed. I studied the papers carefully. The lawyer who had drawn them up was noted for his viciousness. I was up against two of the sharpest legal minds in L.A. Legally speaking, I didn't stand a chance. I had to come up with my own strategy, and it would not be a legal one.

The next morning before Joseph woke up, we drank coffee on our deck overlooking the neighbor's postage stamp garden. My bags were packed and sitting in our guest room.

"I don't feel comfortable staying here, Michael. Not since you've started legal proceedings against me." He looked genuinely surprised.

"Don't be ridiculous, Avie. I had to protect my interests."

"And I've got to protect mine. I'm going to interview family lawyers next week and hire one."

"You can use Gould and O'Day. I'll call Roger up." His need to control me was a strong one.

"I'm perfectly capable of finding my own lawyer and it's not going to be one of your buddies. After breakfast, I'm going over to stay at Rebecca's."

"Fine. Be that way. You can come back after I leave for work."

"No, I've got a lot of business to take care of, now we've moved into this phase of our separation. Besides, Joseph needs you to spend some time with him. He's really missed you, Michael."

"And I've missed him."

"His asthma's under control and now that smog season is over, I'm sure he'll do fine. He's handling all his own meds and taking his air levels himself."

"You think he can manage all that?"

"If you give him a chance. He's matured a lot, but he still needs you."

"And you? What do you need?" he asked. I shrugged.

"I'm still figuring it out," I answered, not so truthfully. Strategy is strategy. He softened a bit.

"Would you mind tackling some of those bills? You can take them with you," he said. I nodded. "Things have really backed up in your absence."

Over breakfast, I explained to Joseph that I would be staying at Rebecca's and he didn't seem bothered in the least. In fact, he asked if that meant he and his dad would get to eat takeout every night. Michael smiled and tapped him lightly on the arm.

"Whatever you want, Bud." I knew they would get along just fine without me.

Before I left, I went up to Joseph's room to put away some of his clean clothes. Lying on top of his desk, next to his computer mouse, was the blowgun Will gave him. I picked it up, ran my hand over its smooth wood and thought of Will. His soft drawl that melted in my ears, was a balm to my soul.

The next week I focused on taking care of business. My cell phone was on at all times, in case Joseph needed me. I interviewed, and hired, an acquaintance of Rebecca's who had handled her share of messy child custody cases. I met with our broker who showed me the latest figures. Our joint portfolios all had high balances. And in my own name, there was the "mad money," half of which I instructed the broker to liquidate. He would call me when the check was ready.

The rough draft of the loan papers arrived from Georgia on Wednesday and I looked them over. The total loan I was taking out in my own name was for $800,000. Michael would have been furious had he known.

Every night or so I called Will, Xylia or Jolene to simply hear their friendly voices and find out what was going on. Xylia was back at home and almost ready to return to the store, which was a good thing, Jolene had said. She needed more time to work on her music for her Barn performances and to prepare for the wedding. Will's voice sounded low and sexy when he said he missed me and I found myself closing my eyes and breathing in his scent as I listened. It was a hard time for me because I couldn't honestly say when I would be back to Georgia. I had to give my design time to work.

By Thursday, Michael was wearing down. All the carpooling, take-out Chinese and 8th grade algebra were taking their toll. He called to ask if I was available to pick up Joseph from school, it was an early dismissal day. I said I was sorry, I couldn't, but did he want to have dinner on Friday night, we needed to talk? He said he'd arrange to have the housekeeper stay late.

While reading about the Cherokees, I had learned about their belief in the circle of life. The sun comes up, moves across the sky, goes down. The moon takes its place, journeys across the heavens, and goes back down again. Life flows in a circle.

It seemed appropriate for our marriage to end where it had started 16 years ago when he had proposed to me. I arrived early amidst the Friday night margarita drinking tourists and singles munching on tortilla chips. I ordered a glass of zinfandel and waited. As usual, predictably, Michael was running late. During our marriage, his tardiness had been a sore point between us. Waiting for him, which could run from 20 minutes up to an hour, had made me at first angry, and then lonely. I had felt abandoned by him. But my night alone in the silver mine had changed all that. I had been as alone as possible and survived.

When he finally arrived, we were seated at a table overlooking the Pacific. Reflecting the navy blue of his suit were his blue-gray chameleon eyes, the same eyes that had once lured me to bed in an instant.

"Nice pick," he said, referring to the restaurant, but his voice dripped with sarcasm.

"Thanks," I answered, treating it as a compliment. He ordered himself an iced tea and for me, another glass of wine. I knew I could use the warm rush it gave me, the calmness to carry out my task.

"You've made your point, Avie," he said. I cocked my head to the side.

"Meaning?"

"You know I can't give Joseph the time he needs. My work is too demanding."

"You could cut back."

"Cut the crap, Avie. You of all people know how the law is." The volume of his harsh voice blended in with the laughter of the margarita drinkers, and I was glad.

"What do you suggest then?"

"I'm suggesting we get things back the way they were." I didn't say a word. He shifted in his seat, edged his hand up to his hair, slowly and methodically twisted a blond tendril around his finger. We both knew 'the way things were' was never going to happen.

"Temporary joint custody would be a start," I said. He nodded.

"I think so." I took a deep breath.

"Until the divorce is finalized," I said. His expression changed. He looked like he'd bitten into a bitter nut.

"Because of your new boyfriend?"

"No, because of us. We've both changed too much, Michael. It won't work." He swallowed hard.

"You've made up your mind, haven't you?" he asked.

"I have," I said. A deep flush of anger washed over his face and his beautiful eyes narrowed. I was glad we were surrounded by the margarita people. He excused himself, left the table and walked out the door. He stood at the pier's edge, looking at the ocean. I was relieved he'd left to deal with his anger out of my presence. His eyes would have changed by now, reflecting the teal of the water. I looked past him there on the end of the pier, towards the blue-green waves that rolled in, never-ending liquid wheels.

CHAPTER 30

In the South, spring announces herself in early March with the blossoming of the redbuds and the Bradford pears. Although called redbud, the tree blossoms are actually pink-purple. And the Bradford pear tree, prolific in white blossoms, never bears fruit. But these facts are easily forgotten when journeying down country roads bordered with an abundance of pink and white blossoms.

It was a warm April day and almost dusk. Will, Joseph and I passed under the redbud trees by Daddy's house, the ones the Baptists planted almost 200 years ago. We were on horses Will had borrowed from a friend. Pollen was in the air and Joseph had donned a mask: he looked a little like the Lone Ranger, sitting tall on a roan mare. But the mask was really not necessary; he hadn't had an asthma attack in months. And when I had the occasional remorseful thought about the break-up of my marriage, I also considered Joseph's newfound robustness.

We rode in single file past the old gate we had used to enter the estate lands, now my ridge lands. After some heated debates between the lawyers, Michael signed the divorce papers and my land purchase was finalized. He had agreed to let Joseph leave the state to accompany me on the trip back at spring vacation. He was busy on a big case and I suspect also seeing a new friend, a 50-year-old attorney, also a workaholic. Joseph told me they got along famously.

An electronic glow emanated from Earl and Cottie's living room window and I saw them in silhouette, watching TV. I waved my riding crop high in the air, just in case Earl was looking. We passed by Aunt Ardelia's windows. Instead of spying, she was in a psychiatric facility undergoing mental competency evaluations. In the mean time, criminal proceedings against her were stalled although I had heard the sheriff had strong evidence to convict her. The silver-headed owl's cane had left a muddy, distinctive star pattern track on the cement floor down at Elmwood's that damp morning of the robbery. Furthermore, the "rotten egg" saying slip had never been found, leading the sheriff to believe Ardelia had written it herself on the board after she attacked Xylia. The handwriting on the chalkboard was also matched up to Ardelia's distinctive style. The sheriff had pieced together a motive. Aunt Ardelia hadn't meant to kill Xylia, only to get the silver ring for Earl after he'd told her he thought it might have something to do with the silver mine. Apparently he'd eavesdropped more than I thought. My aunt had simply been trying to help her baby brother.

Will rode in front of me. I looked at his broad shoulders and remembered what Xylia had whispered to me when we stopped by Elmwood's earlier. "I heard men with wide shoulders make good lovers," she'd teased.

"Don't I know it?" I said and winked. She shot me a victory sign and turned around to supervise the cutting of the old dead tree. She'd finally saved enough money to hire a professional. "It's not right to keep something around that's dead," she'd reasoned. "And besides, it's just plain ugly." Old man Powell and Ernie helped her supervise the cutting and I was surprised to see Ernie give a little wave of his hand as we rode off.

We passed by the skeleton of Jolene and Trent's new house that was being built behind Trent's old trailer, to the east. Two days later, I was to be her matron of honor and I was staying on for another week after the wedding to watch Tyler and Sammie Jo while my sister honeymooned.

At last we reached the wooden gate Will had built a month ago when he received word his grant had tentatively been approved. The sign there at the gate said it all: "Future Home of Cherokee Park" and in smaller letters, "In memory of the original inhabitants and caretakers of this land." On either side of the gate, the geraniums we had planted would blossom in a month or so. Dad would have been pleased to see his cuttings had made it back home to settle their roots in Georgia soil once again.

Will and I would have a lot of work ahead of us the next year or so, until we built the Folklore Center and prepared the interactive exhibits and programs to teach visitors about Cherokee customs. Joseph was especially excited about the Anesta program where visitors would be able to play a milder version of the Cherokee ball game similar to lacrosse. Will and I had been busy researching the seven festivals of the Cherokee year, including the Green Corn Ceremony, my favorite. In the olden days, the Cherokees had recited their history at the annual Green Corn Ceremony. At our Folklore Center, Cherokee descendants would reenact the ceremony once a month and perform the Green Corn Dance. Pulling it all together would be more than a full-time job.

Will closed the gate after we passed through, and we rode the horses up over the first gentle crest of the 240 acres. The sky darkened as we continued towards the black, lacy branches set against a redbud-colored sky. The pearly crescent moon was already rising and would provide some light, enough for us to follow the trail through the hardwoods and pines, up towards the spring, towards the silver mine tucked under one of the ridges.

The discovery of the silver mine was a secret Will and I shared, and perhaps one day I would tell Joseph and the others. Yet I would never forget the time I had been lost there, and all that I had discovered about myself down in the deep, damp red earth below the gentle, rolling ridges of the valley.

About the Author

Born in Chattanooga and with strong family roots in Georgia, Janie Dempsey Watts left the South to study journalism at the University of California, Berkeley (B.A.) and at the University of Southern California (M.A.). After many years in California, she returned to Georgia and now lives near the family farm in Woodstation with her husband, son, and American bulldog, Bella.

She enjoys writing fiction and non-fiction. Her short stories have been published in "Southern Women's Review," in "Blue Crow Magazine" and in "A Tapestry of Voices," a Knoxville Writers' Guild anthology. Another story was honored by the Pirate's Alley William Faulkner Creative Writing Competition as finalist. Her non-fiction stories have been published in the "Ultimate Gardener," the "Chicken Soup for the Soul" books and in a "Guideposts" anthology, "Stories to Warm a Grandma's Heart." Her stories have also been published in "Georgia Backroads Magazine" and her column, "Boomerang," is a regular feature of "Catoosa Life Magazine."

She has twice been asked to present her short stories at the Southern Women's Writers Conference at Berry College in Rome, Georgia, and also was a guest speaker at the Dalton-Whitfield Public Library as part of the Davison Lecture Series. She is a member of the Chattanooga Writers Guild, and is also active in the Chattarosa Writing Group.

She spends most days writing and tending to her family and horses. Her current project is a collection of short stories, "Mothers, Sons, Lovers and Other Strangers." She also is working on a second novel set in the South, "Tarnished Moon."

Please visit her Facebook author page, www.facebook.com/pages/Janie-Dempsey-Watts/307003082668494 or her website at www.janiewatts.com.

Book Club Questions

1. What is the first clue that something is amiss in Avie's and Michael's marriage?

2. How does the relationship with Xylia help Joseph grow?

3. What is your favorite quotation found in Xylia's jar or on the board?

4. The author has described the land with evocative images. Compare and contrast Taylor's Ridge versus the rolling ridges.

5. Why did Avie decide not to share the secret of the silver mine?

6. Who is your favorite character and why?

Coming Soon:

"Mothers, Sons, Lovers, and Other Strangers"
A collection of short stories by Janie Dempsey Watts

**Jan-Carol
Publishing, Inc**

Mountain Girl Press

LITTLE CREEK BOOKS

*Fiction that celebrates the wit, humor, and
strength of Appalachian women*

Books for discerning readers

www.jancarolpublishing.com

www.facebook.com/MountainGirlPress
www.facebook.com/LittleCreekBooks

CPSIA information can be obtained at www.ICGtesting.com
Printed in the USA
LVOW102320080513

332960LV00007B/191/P